TECH HUNTER

LEGEND OF IRONHEART
BOOK 3

ALLAN BOROUGHS

FASTER
THAN
LIGHT

And I will cause it to rain upon the earth for forty days and forty nights; and every living thing that I have made will I destroy from off the face of the earth – **GENESIS 7:4**

1

HOME

Homecomings are dangerous affairs.

The old motorcycle and sidecar crested the top of the hill and stopped. The engine clattered to a standstill and the headlights snapped off as the rider dismounted. She wore a leather jacket with a satchel over one shoulder and canvas trousers with heavy boots caked with mud from the road. Her long brown hair was scraped into a tight ponytail. She might have been considered beautiful, save for two things: her curiously mismatched eyes, one the colour of sky, the other as brown as the earth, and a long scar that carved a pale line from cheek to chin.

She pulled up her collar against the rain and scanned the area with calm watchfulness. At the bottom of the hill, a swollen lake stretched into the foggy distance, grey and oily as a sheet of lead. About a mile offshore, the ruined towers of the old city looked just the way she remembered them. Rotten spires of broken glass and steel sticking out of the lake like clusters of diseased teeth: a broken reminder of everything they'd lost in the Great Rains.

Close to the water's edge, a collection of stone houses

The man snorted. 'Yeah, but you've been away ten years. What makes you so sure?'

'I'm sure.' She patted the satchel at her side. 'He's going to need what I've got in here.'

She stopped as she saw movement in the distance. Two figures had emerged from one of the stone cottages and were walking away from the village, bent low against the rain. She reached into her satchel and pulled out a small pair of binoculars with one cracked lens. 'They're just kids,' she said, adjusting the focus. 'They won't cause us a problem.'

'Kids have parents,' he said. 'If they see us and start shouting, then plenty might come running.'

'Then we'll just have to make sure they don't see us. It'll be dark soon and we'll keep out of sight, close to the tree-line. We'd better hide the bike before we go too.'

They rolled the motorcycle back across the path and pushed it behind some low bushes. She pulled a hunting knife from her boot and hacked down several branches, then arranged them over the bike. When she was finished, she inspected her work and sucked her teeth. It might fool a casual observer, she thought, but if anyone was looking in earnest they'd find it soon enough. They couldn't afford to wait here for too long.

They descended the hill, sticking close to a line of trees that shielded them from the village until they reached a stretch of muddy ground bordered by drystone walls. The sodden ground was pockmarked with mounds of freshly turned earth and dozens of crude wooden crosses, sprouted from the mud like strange flowers.

'The graveyard's got a lot fuller since the last time I was here,' she said, half to herself. 'I guess life is cheap on the

Northside these days.' He didn't answer but she noticed he kept a hand resting on the butt of the gun.

She studied the names on the wooden crosses. Some carried carved inscriptions, a solitary name or a date, but many were blank. Simple markers of an unremembered life. When she reached the end of the row, she stopped.

The man looked around and fingered the pistol impatiently. It didn't do to be standing out in the open like this, he thought. She might think the locals weren't dangerous, but he didn't share her faith. He walked across to where she stood and looked over her shoulder.

The grave marker at the end of the row was larger than most of the others and painted with crude letters in red paint that had run down the wood. *Here lies Rose Bentley*, it read. *Mother and wise woman.* And beneath that, in a different colour: *Also Constable John Bentley. A good man who never saw it coming.*

'Relatives of yours?'

'My parents.' There was a long silence in which only the thick splattering of the rain could be heard. 'Mum died when we were little. Dad got killed in a Southsider raid about five years ago. I wasn't here at the time. The bastards shot him in the back.'

He looked at her curiously. 'Is that why you're here? To get some revenge?'

She snorted. 'That won't bring him back.'

She glanced quickly at the gravestones on either side of her parents and then up and down the adjoining rows. When she had finished, she sighed and stood deep in thought.

'Missing someone?'

She shook her head. 'No. There's no more of my family buried here.'

'But there are more of your family somewhere, right?' The cold eyes drilled into her so that she shifted uncomfortably.

'Maybe. I had a sister. But she's not here. I reckon she must have moved on by now.'

He looked around again. 'OK, so why are we still standing out here?'

'I told you: I'm here to meet a friend.' She sighed. 'But I don't think he's coming or he'd be here by now.' She turned away from the gravestone. 'He might have moved on too, I guess. I need to talk to someone who might have seen him.'

The man hawked a gob of spit onto the ground, not seeming to care that he stood in a graveyard. 'Thought you said you wasn't welcome here any more.'

'Maybe not. But if I can find someone who didn't know me from before...' She paused and squinted through the trees.

A way off through the thin branches, she saw the same two figures picking their way along the shoreline, a boy and a girl. She judged the boy to be about eleven and the girl a little younger. They were scanning the mud intently, bending down occasionally to pick up some small piece of driftwood or scrap metal. The boy seemed to be the one in charge. He would rinse each find in the water and then scrutinise it closely under the grey light. If it met with his approval, he would hand it to the girl, who tucked it away safely in a cloth bag.

He saw the half smile form on her face as she watched the children and thought she might be pretty if she did that more often. 'Something funny?'

'Mudlarkers,' she said, indicating the children. 'Me and my sister used to do that along here when we were that age. On a good day we might find a decent bit of nylon rope or a tyre they could use in the furnace. One time we even found an old TV set. Dad said that before the Great Rains, they used to pick up pictures beamed through the air and you could watch them right there in your house. Can you imagine that?' She laughed. 'We knocked the glass out of the front and used it as a puppet theatre. Kept us amused for a whole winter.'

The man took off his hat and ran his hand through long, lanky hair the colour of coal. He turned his face up to the sky and opened his mouth to drink down some rainwater. Then he replaced his hat and turned to her with a frown. 'Much as it's fascinating to listen to tales of your happy childhood, you said you came to find your friend you'd pay me an ounce of gold to watch your back. But if all you're gonna do is stand here and talk about the old days then I got better places to be.'

Her smile shut off immediately. 'You've got nowhere better to be, Sid,' she said. 'You're a hired gun and I hired you, so you just do what I say when I say it. Now stop griping and let's see if we can find someone to talk to.'

Sid narrowed his eyes at her and scowled. 'I shot people for talking to me like that,' he said. 'And if you and me didn't go back as far as we did, I reckon I'd have shot you too.'

'That's your solution to everything, isn't it? If you can't argue the point, then you just resort to your gun.'

'Settles the argument every time.'

'Yeah, well, not this time. I'm starting to regret bringing you along. First chance I get I'm going to—'

She broke off mid-sentence as a shrill scream carried across the mudflats. Sid dropped to a low crouch and both guns were out of his belt as quick as blinking. 'What was that?' he hissed.

'It came from over that way.' She pointed back along the waterline. 'I think it was one of those kids.'

He shot her a quick glance. 'Then it's nothing to do with us.'

'They're just kids,' she snapped. 'If we can help, then we should.'

'And end up in the plot next to your folks? No thanks.'

'Sid, I—' She was cut short as a second scream rang out, high-pitched and terrified.

Sid saw the indecision in her eyes. 'Let it be,' he said forcefully. 'It ain't our business.'

'Screw you, Sid,' she snapped. 'I just made it my business.' She reached down and pulled the hunting knife from her boot and, before he could stop her, she took off at a run through the trees.

He watched her go and then let out an exasperated sigh. 'A pox on you, India Bentley,' he growled. 'It ain't worth getting killed for an ounce of gold. I oughta leave you here to rot, I reckon.' And with that, he started to run after her through the trees.

2

DOG SOLDIERS

They found the children on top of a sand dune close to the water's edge. The boy was holding a long branch, swinging it wildly around his head. The girl cowered close behind, clinging to his jacket, her screams loud enough to split glass.

Around the base of the dune, a dozen wolfish dogs circled the children with hungry yellow eyes. Every few seconds one would rush up the low dune and attempt a slavering lunge at one of the children. Each time the boy would swipe at the animal, cracking the branch hard across a mangy back.

But it was a losing battle; each time a dog was beaten back, two more would attack from different sides. As India and Sid emerged from the trees, a grizzled animal with a blind eye caught the girl's sleeve and began dragging her down the dune as the boy tried to pull her back.

'Help us, *please!*' he cried when he saw them.

Sid held back, surveying the scene, a hand resting on one of his pistols. But India moved instinctively. She rushed towards the dogs, waving her arms to drive them off. When that didn't work, she plucked a heavy nugget of concrete from the mud and hurled it, striking the flank of the grey dog. The animal let go of the girl's coat and turned on India, teeth bared in a furious snarl.

India stayed still as the dog dropped on its stringy haunches and lowered his head, its good eye fixed on her as it crept forwards with slow, deliberate steps. The other dogs took their lead from the older animal. They broke off their attack on the children and spread out behind their leader, trying to outflank India on both sides. She looked quickly left and right, trying to keep track of the two outlying dogs as she gripped the knife tighter in her hand. The attack was quick and merciless.

The dog on the left came first. A heavy, broad-chested creature, it charged with teeth bared in a death snarl. India's reactions were fast. As the furious animal lunged, she stepped to one side and plunged the blade deep into the animal's broad chest. The creature yelped and rolled over, pumping its lifeblood into the mud. The second dog was on her immediately. Before she had time to turn, the animal clamped its heavy jaws around her arm, knocking the knife into the shallows.

The pressure exerted by the beast's massive jaws felt strong enough to crack her bones. She struggled to pull free as the razor teeth tore through her leather sleeve and pierced her flesh.

A gunshot shattered the stillness of the mudflats and sent a flock of small birds into the sky. The bullet exited through the top of the dog's skull, scattering brain matter and bone shrapnel across the mud and immediately releasing India's arm from its vice-like grip.

Ten yards away, Sid kept his pistols trained on the pack, waiting for the next attack. But the noise of the gunshot had broken the pack's will. Most ran away immediately while others stood their ground and barked furiously at their attackers, before turning and following.

Finally, only the grizzled old leader was left. With its good eye, the old dog glared first at India then at Sid. Then, with a last longing look at the children on top of the dune, it turned and walked away, padding slowly across the mud as though challenging them to do their worst.

When the dogs had gone, Sid returned the pistols to his belt. 'How's the arm?'

India cradled her injured limb and winced. It felt as though her entire arm had been crushed in a vice and she could feel the warmth of the blood soaking her shirt. 'It's fine, no thanks to you. What took you so long to shoot?'

'Bullets are hard to come by,' he said with a shrug. 'And I don't have that many to waste.'

She frowned and glanced at the guns in his hand. 'How many bullets *do* you have?'

'Three.' He paused. 'Including the one I just fired.'

Her eyes widened in surprise. 'You only brought *three bullets?* And this is what I hired for a bodyguard?'

'Just saved your ass, didn't I? You're welcome, by the way.'

India glared at Sid. She had known him since he was a gangly youth with an infuriating manner and a predilection for mindless violence. These days the violence came in slightly more measured bursts, but he was no less irritating. Still, she thought, at least if she found what she was looking for, she wouldn't have to rely on Sidney Stone for much longer.

'Please, miss. May we come down?'

It was the boy who had spoken, still cowering on the

dune, with his sister clinging tightly to him. They looked pale and terrified.

'Sure. Come on down. The dogs are gone. It's safe now.'

They came down slowly, looking around warily as though they didn't fully trust India's assurance. When they saw the two dead dogs lying in a mess of blood and fur, the girl let out another scream.

'It's OK,' said India. 'They can't hurt you now.' She looked at the two children more closely. They looked like a hundred others she had grown up with on the shores of North London. Half-wild and undernourished and with a feral look in their eyes that was always searching for something they could eat or steal. The boy seemed to have got over his fright now and stared at her brazenly.

'Who are you? I never seen you round here before. Are you a Southsider? My pa says Southsiders should be shot on sight. He says Southsiders is just vermin that preys on decent people like us. Is that what you are, a Southsider?'

India kept herself from smiling as the boy's words came tumbling out in a rush, curiosity overcoming caution. 'No, I'm not a Southsider,' she said. 'And you're welcome, by the way. For saving your scrawny backsides.'

The boy looked back in the direction of the dogs, then turned to her again with a shrug. 'That weren't nothing special.' He pointed to the branch he had been holding, which now lay on the ground. 'I had it covered.'

He crouched down to inspect the two dead dogs that lay stretched out on the mud. He was particularly interested in the large exit wound in the skull of the dog that had been shot, and let out a low whistle. 'Took his brains clean out of his skull,' he said in an awestruck voice. Then his face resumed its previous scepticism. 'That was a lucky shot, I reckon.'

'Luck didn't come into it,' said Sid. 'I hit what I aim at. Always.'

The boy regarded Sid cautiously as though he hadn't yet decided what to make of him. By now the girl had stopped her snivelling and peered out at India from behind the boy's back.

'So what are you if you ain't Southsiders?' she said timidly.

'Visitors,' said India. 'I used to live here.'

'I never seen you 'afore.' The boy again.

'It was before you were born. How long have your people lived here?'

'We came here about five years ago when I was younger than her.' He jerked his head towards the girl. 'The village was empty when we arrived, but Pa said there was good tyre-burnin' to be done here so we stayed. He's the village leader now,' he added proudly. The eyes turned suspicious again. 'So why did you come back?'

Don't worry, I don't want anything from your village. I'm just looking for an old friend of mine. Perhaps you know him?'

'We know everyone in these parts.' The boy puffed out his chest, reasserting his seniority. 'What's he look like?'

'Tall,' said India. '*Very* tall. And probably dressed in robes and a hood, like a monk.'

'What's a monk?'

India frowned. 'It's... like a holy man. A shaman.'

'You mean like a witch?'

India nodded.

'We gotta witch,' he continued. 'She leaves out in yonder tower.' He threw an arm carelessly towards the tallest tower in the lake. A hollow spike of glass and steel that looked like a knife.

India glanced at the tower. 'She?'

'Yeah, she's a woman witch. We ain't got no man witches living here. I'd have known it if there was.'

'Tell me about the woman witch.'

A sly look came across the boy's face as though he was remembering an important principle. 'Whassitworth?' He rubbed his thumb and forefinger together in a universal sign whose origins had long been forgotten.

India shrugged. 'I don't have much. But... wait...' She reached into the satchel and pulled out a square slab wrapped in foil. 'How about a piece of chocolate?'

The word cast a magic spell on the faces of the two youngsters. Their eyes widened and the girl's mouth dropped open. 'Horse dung,' said the boy, eying the slab. 'That ain't choclit. No one round here's got real choclit.'

'Like I said, I'm visiting.' She tapped the bar with a fingernail so that it made a cold clicking sound.

The boy licked his lips. 'Her name's Cromerty. My pa says she was here before the village. Before the towers, even. Some folks say she's a thousand years old.'

India's eyebrows went up in surprise. 'Cromerty? Are you sure?' Surely there couldn't be two people with that name? It had to be the same woman. But she had been ancient when India had last seen her, a decade previously. 'Have you actually seen her?'

The boy wiped his nose on his sleeve and held out his hand. 'How 'bout some of that choclit first?'

India dutifully broke two squares from the cold brown slab and pressed them into two grubby palms. The boy immediately stuffed his piece into his mouth and rolled it around his tongue, savouring the thick sweetness as it melted. The girl nibbled at the edges of her portion, then closed her eyes as if she had been transported to another place.

India allowed them a decent interval to savour the rare piece of sweetness before asking her question again. 'Have you ever seen this Cromerty? You ever met her?'

The boy rolled his tongue around his teeth, then licked the silver paper to retrieve every last crumb of sweetness. When it was obvious India wasn't going to produce any more, he shook his head.

'There ain't hardly no one that's seen her. She never comes ashore. My pa takes her out some supplies every two weeks or so, but he just leaves them at the bottom of the stairs. If they've gone when he goes back, that's how he knows she's still alive.'

India's mind raced. If Cromerty really was still alive, then the old woman would almost certainly be able to answer her questions. 'Can I talk to your pa? I need to ask if he can take me out there.'

Sid tugged at her arm. 'What are you playin' at, India? I thought we were meant to find your friend and get out of here without no one else seein' us.'

'If Cromerty's still alive, then I need to talk to her. Most likely she's the only one who knows where he is. I just want to talk to the head man on his own, that's all. No one else needs to see us.'

As she was speaking, Sid stiffened and looked past her shoulder. 'It's too late to be hoping for that. Somebody already has.'

She turned to follow his gaze. Three squat figures were approaching through the gloom from the direction of the village. They were dressed in baggy canvas clothes, rendered the same colour by the mud. They wore tangled beards and carried shotguns and one of them held on to a large black and brown dog that strained at the leash. All of them had meanness and suspicion in their eyes and although she had never seen any of them before, India knew them all instantly.

'Village security,' she whispered as they approached. 'Don't do anything to provoke them. They generally shoot quicker than they can sneeze.'

The three men spread out as they came towards them, much as the dogs had done. One man kept a shotgun trained on India and Sid, while one of his companions darted forwards and grabbed the children, pulling them both out of reach.

The man with the shotgun jerked the barrel in Sid's direction. 'The guns. On the ground. Nice and slow.'

Sid obeyed, pulling the pistols from his belt with a thumb and forefinger and laying them both down on the ground before him. The man approached slowly, as though he was stalking a wild animal. He took short, nervous steps forwards, his eyes locked on Sid. He looked so twitchy that India was afraid he might shoot accidentally simply because he was so tensed up.

Sid kept perfectly still while the man retrieved the guns and slipped them both into a large gunny sack he carried over one shoulder. Then he turned the shotgun in his hands and clubbed Sid viciously around the head. There was a thick sound of wood striking bone and Sid hit the ground like a sack of wet cement. He tried to raise his body on one elbow and clutched at his head as a thin trickle of crimson ran through his fingers. The man with the shotgun stood over him and took aim at his head.

'Don't shoot 'em, Cyrus,' pleaded the boy. 'I don't think they're Southsiders.'

He did not look at the boy. 'They're Southsiders all

right,' he growled as he looked down the barrel at Sid. 'I can smell Southsiders anywhere, and these is Southsiders.'

'She said they was just visiting, Cyrus,' insisted the boy. 'She's got choclit and we had some.'

'Chocolate?' Cyrus glanced at the boy and then nodded to one of his men. 'Digby, take a look.'

Digby snatched the satchel from India's shoulder and searched through the contents. He retrieved the chocolate and the three men gathered close to gawp at it. The dog began slaver and whine.

'It looks real,' said Digby. 'I ain't never heard of Southsiders having chocolate before. Maybe we should—'

'Maybe you should shut your mouth.' Cyrus snatched the slab out of his hand and shoved it into his pocket, his eyes daring them to stop him.

'Hey,' said Digby after a moment. 'There's something else in here. Look at this.'

He laid the satchel down on the ground and then reached in with both hands to lift out something heavy, wrapped in a piece of towelling.

India stiffened. 'Be careful with that. It's...' She tailed off as Cyrus shot her a glare.

Digby unwrapped the cloth carefully and his eyes widened. 'Well, hit me with a shovel, get a load of this!'

The others drew close to inspect the object. Lying in the cloth was a sleek metal tube about a foot in length with a black plastic handle in one end. The object had a smoothness and precision that clearly belonged to a different time.

Digby turned the object over to reveal an oval glass window. Behind the glass, thick blue liquid moved like syrup, glowing a spectral blue like the light from a jellyfish.

'Never seen nothin' like it,' said Digby.

'What is it?' demanded Cyrus.

'It's nothing important. It's just...' India bit her lip. 'It's something I need, that's all.'

Digby held the object to his ear and shook it vigorously, like a cocktail shaker. India started forwards. 'I *strongly* suggest you don't do that.'

Cyrus looked at her suspiciously, then jerked his head towards the device. 'Digby, bring that thing with us. Vincent will know what it is.'

Digby shoved the tube roughly into the long pocket of his coat, his eyes shining. 'D'you think it's valuable?'

Cyrus shrugged. 'I dunno. Is it heavy?'

'Yes, very.'

'Then it's valuable. Now stop asking dumb questions and get these Southsiders tied up so. We'll take 'em to the village and torture the truth out of 'em if we have to.' Then he grinned with a mouth full of gaps. 'After that we'll string 'em up on the shoreline as a warning to their friends.'

3

VINCENT

Once their hands were tied, the men marched them back towards the village. Cyrus walked up front like a man leading a parade while his two companions marshalled India and Sid, and the two children brought up the rear.

India felt the slack in the inexpertly tied rope and knew she could free herself if she needed to. She glanced sideways at Sid. A line of dried of blood ran down one side of his face and his head hung low so she couldn't see his eyes. But she could see his body was tense and that he was working the loose knots. When the time came, she knew she could count on Sid.

The village was surrounded by low earthworks, not high enough to keep out a serious attack but enough to offer a tactical advantage to those inside. A gap in the wall was bridged by a crude gate made of sodden wood, which swung open as they approached.

Inside the village, the stone cottages were scattered randomly, looking more like growths that had erupted from the ground than buildings. In the central square, a tyre furnace exhaled oil-thick smoke and two men paused in the task of feeding chunks of rubber into the flames to stare at the newcomers. More children began to gather and soon they found themselves part of a ragged carnival with Cyrus at its head, his chest puffed out with self-importance.

At the far end of the village, the parade came to a halt before the last cottage. The cottage was more broken-down than India remembered but she recognised it as the house that had always belonged to the village leader: the same one she had grown up in when her father had done the job.

The crowd hung back at a respectful distance while Cyrus marched his prisoners up the muddy path and rapped on the door. The man who answered was tall enough that he had to stoop to step outside. He was bull-necked, with broad shoulders and a face that betrayed no sense of what its owner was thinking.

He considered the strange parade with simple curiosity, his gaze lingering on India and Sid. 'Why have you inter-rupted me at supper, Cyrus?' He spoke in barely a whisper but was heard clearly by them all.

Cyrus pulled off his greasy cap and wrung it in his hands. 'Begging your pardon, Vincent. But we found these two Southsiders on the mudflats outside the village.'

The big man's expression did not change. He examined first Sid and then India as if studying an ancient manuscript, looking for clues to its origins.

'You're Southsiders?' His voice had weight and depth that demanded to be listened to.

India cleared her throat. 'We're not Southsiders. We're just visitors.'

'That sounds like something a Southsider would say.'

'Or something a visitor would say.' India met his eyes

and had to fight the urge to look away from his gaze. 'I used to live here in the village,' she added. 'About ten years ago.'

'Where have you been living since?'

India frowned. 'A lot of bad places. Look, I'm telling you the truth. My father was the village leader here; his name was John Bentley.'

The gaze was impassive. 'You could have read that name off his gravestone.'

'Don't let them fool you, Vincent; they're Southsiders all right,' piped up Digby. 'They were trying to steal the children. It's a good job we came along when we did.'

'That's not true, Pa.' The boy pushed his way through the crowd and went to Vincent's side. The big man extended a large hand around the boy's shoulders like a protective cloak. 'They weren't trying to take us away. Me and Gilly got caught by a pack of wild dogs down on the mudflats and they saved us.'

Vincent looked down at his son and frowned. 'You took Gilly to the mudflats at sunset? How many times have I told you, that's when the packs are at their most dangerous.' He did not raise his voice and his tone remained even, but the boy still hung his head.

'I-I'm sorry, Pa. I just didn't think.'

Vincent crouched down to the boy's level and looked him directly in the eyes. 'We can't afford not to think, Tom,' he said softly. 'Not when we live here on the edge of the lake. I expect better of you in future.'

Tom nodded and bit his lip. 'Yes, sir.'

'Now, take your sister inside and get some supper. There's fried fish and potatoes.'

'Oh boy, fried fish.' The boy was instantly all smiles. He gathered his sister's hand and they disappeared into the house. Vincent returned to India and Sid.

'You're both hurt,' he said.

India's arm was now bleeding through the bite wounds in her jacket her while Sid's face was clotted with dried blood. Vincent examined Sid's face, then threw a disapproving look at Cyrus. 'What happened, Cyrus?'

Cyrus stiffened and stuck out his jaw. 'They were armed. They had two pistols and a knife, look.' He held out the open mouth of the gunny sack so Vincent could see inside. 'They needed a bit of ... encouragement to hand 'em over.'

'The woman was carrying this too,' said Digby. He took the long metal tube from his pocket and held it up. He hooked his fingers through the handle and swung the device back and forth carelessly. 'Cyrus said you'd know what it was.'

Vincent's eyes widened and for the first time he raised his voice. 'Give me that, you fool!' he barked.

Digby flinched and nearly dropped the tube but managed to catch it and hand it over to Vincent.

The big man turned the machined metal gently in his hands. 'Items like this are very hard to come by,' he said after a while. 'Where did you get it?'

'Not from around here, that's for sure,' replied India. 'I've brought it a long way and it cost me a *lot* of money. So, if you don't mind?' She held out her hand.

Vincent shook his head and tucked the device under one arm. 'I think I'll keep hold of this until I have some better answers as to why you're here.'

'It belongs to me.'

'So you say.'

Cyrus had been following the conversation with increasing confusion. 'So, do you want me to lock them both up, Vincent? Maybe have a couple of the boys work 'em over for answers?'

Vincent stroked his bristled chin, his dry palm rasping across the stubble. 'I don't think that's necessary just yet,' he said. 'Untie their hands and then fetch the medic to attend to their wounds. You two, come inside and tell me your stories. Then I'll decide what to do with you.'

It took Cyrus a few moments to realise he was being dismissed. 'Untie 'em? But, Vincent, they're strangers. They could be dangerous.'

Vincent nodded. 'Well, you have their weapons now. So, I guess there's not much more harm they can do. Now, the medic if you please, Cyrus.'

He moved aside to let Sid and India pass and then followed them through the low doorway, leaving Cyrus gawping after them with a face the colour of beetroot.

As they stepped inside the little cottage, India gave an involuntary gasp at the sudden immersion back into her past life. The kitchen was smaller than she remembered, but it carried the same damp gloominess it had always had. An iron pot bubbled on the age-blackened stove, banked with burning logs. A large wooden table occupied the centre of the room where Tom and Gilly were shovelling potatoes into their mouths. The children didn't look up when they came in.

Vincent placed the metal tube carefully on the table, then beckoned them to sit down and poured two glasses of water from an earthenware jug. 'The water's good to drink here,' he said. 'There's a well up on the hillside that's not been polluted by the groundwaters.'

Sid gulped the water greedily while India took a tentative sip. It tasted cold and sweet and clear, just the way she remembered. 'I helped my dad to dig that well,' she said, placing her glass back on the table. 'I'm glad to see the water's still good.'

'We didn't do anything to your people,' said Vincent suddenly. 'When we arrived here eight years ago, the village was almost deserted.'

'Do you know why they left?'

Vincent shrugged. 'From what I could gather, it was a succession of poor harvests and Southsider raiding parties. I guess when your father got shot, folks finally decided they'd had enough.'

India nodded. Even when she had lived there, the Southsider raids had been a problem and she could easily imagine how they could have got worse. When food was scarce, then even the best people would kill to feed their families.

'Almost deserted?' she said.

'What?'

'You said the village was almost deserted. Who else was here?'

Vincent shrugged. 'A few that were too old or sick or beyond caring.'

India opened her mouth to speak again but Vincent held up a solitary finger to silence her. 'I've answered enough of your questions. Time for you to give me some answers.' He patted the metal tube gently. 'Like, for example, what you're doing with this?'

India shrugged. 'It's just a piece of old junk. I was hoping to sell it in one of the tech markets down south but it's probably not worth much.'

A frown creased Vincent's forehead. 'It's a military-grade plasma charger,' he said softly. He rotated the tube enough to see the glowing blue gel within. 'And it's got a full charge. A device like this carries enough energy to power a small town.' He paused. 'Or blow a crater in the ground the size of this village.'

He levelled his gaze on India so that she felt like an ant, caught under a magnifying glass in the sun. 'That's the first time you've lied to me,' he said. 'If there is a second time then I will assume that Cyrus was right about you and hand you over to his goons.'

'I'm sorry,' said India. 'I didn't mean to lie to you. I just didn't think you'd know what a plasma charger was. They're very rare.'

'I'm not quite the yokel you take me for,' said Vincent. 'What are you doing with it?'

'I... can't tell you,' she said. 'Other than I need it for a friend of mine. But it's nothing to do with the village. I'm not with the Southsiders and I wouldn't do anything to hurt your people; I just can't tell you about this. Please trust me.'

Vincent stroked his chin thoughtfully, the bristles making a rasping sound in the quiet of the kitchen. 'I've got no reason to trust you,' he said eventually. 'But my children seem to like you so I will give you the benefit of the doubt for now.' He patted the charger. 'But this stays with me. At least until you feel able to give me some better answers.'

'Does that mean I can get my gun back?' said Sid. He had been silent up to now but India could see he was becoming restless. Meeting new people had never been one of Sid's strong points.

Vincent gave him a cool look. 'Your friend may be from here originally. But that doesn't mean she's not a Southsider now. And I know nothing about you at all. So, I guess you can wait for that gun too.'

'Sid's OK,' said India quickly. 'I'll vouch for him. I hired him as my security for this trip.'

'He's a crack shot too, Pa,' said Tom, through a mouthful of fried fish. 'He shot that dog right through the eye at twenty-five paces, clean as a pipe.'

'Get on with your meal, son.' Vincent looked at Sid with renewed interest. 'Is that true?'

Sid shrugged. 'I hit what I aim at.'

'Then I suppose I ought to thank you for saving my children.' He sat back in his seat and India could almost see the thoughts running behind his eyes.

He's looking for soldiers, she thought. Cyrus and his men were thugs but they would be no good in a real stand-off against the Southside. *He's going to try and convince us to stay.*

'I still need to be sure you're not Southside,' he said. 'Can you prove your story? Is there anyone who could vouch for you?'

India shrugged. 'Your son said the old witch, Cromerty, was still alive. She'd know who I was.'

Vincent shook his head. 'Cromerty lives alone in one of the dead towers. She's over a hundred if she's a day and blind as a stone and she doesn't welcome visitors either. Is there anyone else who knows who you are?'

'I do,' said a voice from the doorway.

They turned to the silhouetted figure in the doorway and India narrowed her eyes. The woman was slight, with long blonde hair scraped back behind her ears and she carried a heavy bag over one shoulder. It was difficult to see her clearly, but something in the set of her shoulders triggered a recognition in India. It was as though someone had struck a bell deep inside her.

India stood up as the woman came into the room. Her face was older than India remembered and there were lines around her eyes that had not been there when she had seen them last. But the firm set of the mouth and the determination in her gaze was something that could not be disguised by the years.

'Bella?' she breathed. 'Is that really you?'

The woman dumped her bag on the floor unceremoni-ously. 'Yeah, it's me,' she said. 'How are you doing, sis?'

'Bella!' The word came out as a half sob. She took a step forwards, then stopped as Bella stiffened and stepped out of her reach.

'Let's skip the big reunion, if you don't mind,' she said. 'I've got work to do right now.' She turned to Sid and lifted his hat to look his head wound. When he flinched, she punched him hard on the shoulder. 'Sit still, dammit! I need to see what I'm dealing with.'

While India looked on, open-mouthed, Bella retrieved a bottle of iodine solution and a clean rag from her bag and proceeded to dab it onto Sid's forehead. 'Crap, that stuff stings worse that getting hit,' he snapped.

'Yeah, well, it's either that or lose half your face to gangrene,' she shot back. 'I don't much care either way so let me know which you'd prefer.' Sid fell into a startled silence and stared at the woman.

'Bella,' said India. 'How are you here? I thought you'd moved away from the village after Dad got shot.'

'You thought wrong.' She put away the iodine and pulled a small packet of needles from the bag, then threaded one with a length of fishing line.

'You stayed here alone?' said India.

Bella bent close to Sid's forehead and he winced as she proceeded to sew up the wound with an expert touch. 'Dad took a bullet in the back in that Southsider raid,' she said as she worked. 'But it didn't kill him straight away. When everyone else left to get away from the Southsiders, I stayed behind to nurse him.'

'Bella is our medic,' said Vincent. 'When we arrived, she'd been living here by herself for six months. She had some skills at healing, so we asked her to stay. She's one of us now.'

'I sent someone to look for you,' said India. 'But when I didn't hear anything, I assumed the worst. I thought you were...'

'Well, you needn't have worried,' said Bella. 'As you can see, I'm alive and kicking.' She clipped the end of the fishing line with a small pair of scissors and placed a clean piece of cloth over the suture.

Sid touched his fingers to the wound lightly. 'Not bad,' he said grudgingly. 'I guess having your own medic is pretty useful in a place like this?'

'Bella's saved plenty of lives around here,' said Vincent. 'She sets bones, cures fevers and cleans gunshot wounds. We'd be lost without her.'

Bella seemed embarrassed by the praise. She busied herself putting her medical kit away. 'Did you need anything else, Vincent?' she said.

'Take a look at her arm,' said Vincent, indicating India. 'Dog bite.'

Bella looked at the blood seeping from India's sleeve and made her remove her jacket. When she saw the injured flesh beneath, she made a face. 'That needs irrigating before I do anything else,' she said. 'Come outside to the pump so I can get some clean water on it.'

Before India could respond, Bella had picked up her bag and headed out of the room. Vincent nodded to India. 'Go and get your arm fixed,' he said. 'Then we'll talk about what happens next.'

India followed her sister out into the muddy yard where Bella was already working the pump handle to produce a stream of clear, icy water. 'Put your arm under here,' she instructed.

India did as she was told, wincing at the stinging cold on the raw flesh as she watched her sister work the handle. Bella had been only eleven the last time she had seen her. Now she was a fully grown woman and a respected medic with a tough attitude. India was finding it hard to make the adjustment.

'I'm sorry, Bella,' she began. 'If I'd known you were here, I'd have come back for you sooner.'

Bella dabbed at the wound with a piece of cloth but did not look up from her work. 'Like I said, you don't have to worry about me.'

'You're my younger sister. It's my job to protect you.'

'Well, you left it a bit late to start, didn't you!'

India was startled by the sudden ferocity in her sister's voice. 'What do you m—'

'I mean where were you while I was spending my childhood living in this miserable shithole and hiding from the Southsider raids. I could have used a big sister in those days but you were off enjoying yourself.'

'That's not fair, Bel,' cried India. 'I had a job to do.'

'Oh yeah, how could I forget. You were a *tech-hunter*. Running all over the world digging up old-world crap and calling it "treasure".'

'I was making money. Enough to send back to you and Dad to keep you from starving, or had you forgotten about that?'

'It would have been more to the point if you'd been here when we needed you,' said Bella. 'Do you have any idea how many people got taken by Southsiders while you were gone, India? Dad did his best to fight them off and keep everyone safe. Perhaps if he'd had someone with your skills, he might still be alive. Had you thought of that?'

India stared at her sister in disbelief. India had always

put family first, hadn't she? She had always worked to support Bella and her dad and make sure they didn't starve. But was that really all there was to it? She had always enjoyed being a tech-hunter, the adventure, the risk, the excitement. But perhaps if she'd stayed at home instead of seeking adventure then John Bentley might still be alive.

India's shoulders slumped. She felt like she had found her sister then lost her again in the space of half an hour. 'I'm sorry, Bel,' she said. 'I thought I was doing the right thing. I didn't know you saw it that way.'

'I guess truth hurts, huh?' Bella splashed some of the bright orange iodine solution onto India's arm and then laid a clean dressing over the top, wrapping it tightly with bandages. 'Fortunately, Vincent and his people found me before the Southsiders did. They're good people. They took me in and treated me like one of their own. They'd just lost their healer so I sort of took on the job. I remembered some of the healing potions that Mum used to make and I learned quite a bit from looking after Dad.'

The mention of their mother brought a bittersweet smile to India's face. This place brought back so many memories but even the good ones had a way of hurting you.

Bella finished dressing the wound and tied off the bandage. 'With a bite like that, there's a fifty-fifty chance of getting some sort of infection,' she said in a business-like way. 'If that happens, we might need to take off the arm. There's also the possibility of rabies. But if you get that then all I can do is shoot you.'

'Your bedside manner needs a bit of work, Bel.'

'Just giving you the facts, India.' Then her face relaxed into a half smile. 'I don't really expect any of that stuff to happen. Believe it or not, I *am* glad to see you.'

'I'm glad to see you, too, Bel.' She smiled back.

'Don't think this means I'm not still mad at you.'

'I know.'

'Living here while you were off enjoying yourself was pretty rough and you weren't here when I needed you.'

'I know.'

Bella paused and frowned, as though she was seeing India for the first time. 'And what the hell happened to your face?'

India flinched. She flushed as her hand instinctively went to her cheek. Most of the time she didn't think about her scar and most of the people she associated with had so many of their own that it didn't seem unusual. 'Something that happened while I was off enjoying myself,' she said. 'It gets pretty rough out there too.'

For a long time, neither of them spoke. Then Bella broke the silence. 'So, how long are you staying?'

'I'm not sure. I came to look for a friend.'

'Anyone I know?'

India shook her head. 'It was someone I sent to look for you.'

'You sent someone to look for me?' Bella raised an eyebrow. 'I don't know whether to be grateful or even more pissed off.'

'It was after I heard about Dad. No one knew what had happened to you so I asked him to come and find you.'

'Why didn't you come yourself?'

'I couldn't, Bel, trust me on that.'

'Uh-huh. So you sent some random guy instead.'

'He wasn't some random guy. He was someone I trusted with my life.'

'Oh, I see. So, you and he were an item?'

'No! Shit, Bella, it wasn't like that. He's... sort of like a monk or a holy man.'

Bella frowned. 'Wow, you sent me a monk, I'm flattered. Anyway, he never showed up here, so what happened?'

India sighed. Conversations with her younger sister were still as tiresome as she remembered them. 'That's what I came to find out. He was meant to find you and offer you protection but I never heard back from him.'

'Well, he can't have tried too hard because I've been right here where you left me. Maybe he skipped out on you.'

India shook her head. 'He wouldn't have done that. Once he agreed to do something I know he'd never have let me down unless something happened to him.'

She looked out over the great lake which was now sunk in gloom. The dead towers were like blackened spikes sticking out of the water but there was a solitary light burning in the tallest of the towers. A jagged shard of glass standing alone near the centre of the lake.

'One of the kids told me Cromerty was still alive,' she said. 'Is that true?'

Bella shrugged and began putting her medical kit away. 'The crazy old witch bitch? Yeah, I guess it's true. At least, Vincent keeps taking her supplies out there and somebody keeps eating 'em. But nobody ever sees her. She lives at the top of that old tower and never comes down.'

'Could I get out there to see her?'

'You'd be wasting your time. She never speaks to anyone.'

'She might speak to me,' said India confidently. 'I have a feeling she might know what happened to my friend.'

Bella shrugged. 'Suit yourself. Vincent's got a small sail-boat you could use. He could get one of the kids to take you out there if you asked him nicely.'

India smiled. 'Yeah, well, asking nicely was never my

strong point. But Vincent would be short of a couple of kids by now if it weren't for me and Sid so I reckon he owes us.'

'I guess so,' said Bella. 'But if you ask me, you'll stay away from that crazy old bitch. I heard some strange tales about that old woman.'

'You might be right,' said India. 'It's a long time since I spoke to her and she may not be too pleased to see me. But I owe it to my friend to try and find out. I only hope the old woman doesn't want to kill me on sight.'

4

THE TOWERS OF LONDON

They spent an uncomfortable night on Vincent's floor in front of the kitchen stove, curled under threadbare blankets. Sid had immediately pulled his hat down over his face and was snoring within two minutes. She looked at his sleeping form and, not for the first time, envied his ability to sleep anywhere. She had known him get a full night's sleep in a muddy ditch.

But for India, sleep refused to come. It wasn't the hard floor or the damp stone; she was also used to discomfort from her years on the road. It was the ghosts that haunted the old house that kept her awake.

She lay in the dark of the kitchen, thinking of family meals shared around the table: roasted fish and potatoes in the good times and cabbage soup in the hard ones. She remembered mudlarking on the tidal flats, cheeking the nightwatchman and going to lessons with old Mrs Crumney. She smiled to herself as she remembered how the old woman could never quite remember the kings and queens of England and how she would always fall asleep in the afternoon classes.

Then her smile faded and she lay, stone-faced, in the darkness. They were all gone now: Mrs Crumney, her mother, her father. Gone with nothing to remember them except for a painted headstone.

That was the thing about life since the Great Rains. People did their best to survive but in the end they died anyway with nothing to mark their lives. It was as if they'd been wiped from the face of the Earth. People should count for more than that. *She* would count for more than that.

She woke to the greasy light of dawn filtering through the kitchen window and Vincent standing over them holding two tin plates. 'Thought you could use some food,' he said, putting the plates down on the table.

Most mornings, India pushed away thoughts of food, preferring to eat sparingly when she was living off her own supplies. But if you were offered food from someone else's stores then it was wise to make the most of it. She climbed out of the blanket and sat down at the table.

On each plate, Vincent had placed a chunk of black bread, some blood sausage and some slices of apple, preserved in vinegar and honey. India knew it was probably more than Vincent's family would eat most mornings. Vincent was trying to impress them, and she had a suspicion she knew why. The previous evening, she had found Sid, deep in conversation with Vincent. Vincent had returned Sid's gun and had even given him enough ammunition to fully load both of his pistols.

Sid took the seat opposite her and examined his plate before starting to chew on a piece of blood sausage. She waited until Vincent was out of hearing and then leaned across the table. 'My, my, someone is a teacher's pet, aren't they.'

Sid's face adopted its default expression of hostile suspicion. 'What d'you mean?'

'I mean none of this is just kindness. This breakfast, giving you back your gun, fresh ammunition. He's trying to buy you.'

Sid looked away. 'I don't know what you're talking about.' India smiled to herself. Sid had many qualities but being a good liar wasn't one of them.

'I mean he's trying to bribe you to stay here, in the village,' she said. 'He knows he needs good people to fight off the Southsiders and you're probably about the bad-assest thing that ever drifted into town.' She sat back in her seat and took a bite of sausage. 'So, are you going to do it?'

Sid shrugged. 'Maybe, maybe not. I ain't decided.'

India stuffed the last piece of sliced apple into her mouth and pushed her plate away. 'Well, just watch your step. It might be all apples and honey now but dealing with Southside raiding parties is no joke. Those bastards killed nearly everyone I cared about, and you could be next.'

Sid grinned. 'That mean you care about me, India?'

'I care about my bodyguard doing his job. Before you go accepting any new contracts, just remember you've got this one to finish first.'

They were interrupted by Vincent, coming back into the kitchen with Tom. 'Bella said you wanted to visit the old witch, Cromerty,' he said. 'So I've asked Tom to take you over there in the sailboat.' The boy looked puffed-up with the importance of the job he had been given.

'That's good of you,' said India.

'We look out for each other in these parts. This can be a good place to live as long as we all stick together.' Vincent glanced at Sid as he said this and India had to hide her grin behind her hand.

'So, does this mean you believe we're not Southsiders?' she asked.

Vincent shrugged. 'I reckon if you were here for trouble you'd have done it by now. Just be careful out there on the water. Tom knows how to keep out of sight of the Southside patrols but don't you go attracting any unwanted attention. If I thought you were trying to send a signal to a raiding party from the top of them towers, I wouldn't hesitate to have you both strung up in the trees.'

'Don't worry,' said India, getting up from the table. 'I lived on these shores for a long time before you even got here. I know how to stay out of the way of Southsiders.'

They prepared to leave while Tom collected a burlap sack stuffed with vegetables for Cromerty. Then they said their goodbyes to Vincent and followed the boy down to the water's edge with Gilly trailing along behind, complaining that they were walking too fast for her.

The day was overcast; a fine haze blurred the line of the horizon and shrouded the top of the towers in a cloak of grey. Tom led them along the shoreline, checking the horizon for skim boats, just the way India had been taught when she was his age.

At one point, he and Gilly paused to crouch down over the water's edge. Tom sank his hand up to the elbow in the thick mud, and pulled out a wriggling mass of flesh that wrapped itself around his wrist. 'Fang worm!' he said delightedly as he placed it in his pocket. 'They're good eating if you put plenty of salt on 'em.'

He led them to a place where scrubby bushes grew close to the water's edge. Hauled up on the mud among the branches was a sodden sailboat with the name 'Rose' painted on the side in flaky red letters.

'This is my boat,' said the boy proudly. 'Well, it's Pa's boat really but he's usually too busy to take her out.'

India eyed the dead towers in the lake as they dragged the boat across the mud. 'Do you always take the supplies out to Cromerty?'

'I'm the only one Pa trusts to do it right.' He glowed with pride.

'Have you ever spoken to her?'

The boy shook his head. 'She don't talk to no one. I saw her once, though. I was leaving the food at the bottom of the tower, like usual, and she came out of the shadows and grabbed me by the wrist.'

'What happened?'

A shudder seemed to pass through the boy's frame. 'Nothin' much. She just held on and stared into my eyes. It felt weird.'

'Weird in what way?'

'It was like I was nothing but an empty box and she was looking inside me.' His eyes became distant as he remembered the scene. 'It felt like she was *reaching* into me to take something out.' He shook his head to rid himself of the memory. 'I remember I didn't feel warm for days after that. The strange thing was, she had eyes just like yours.' He threw a glance in her direction. 'You know, two different colours, like they belonged to different people.'

India and the boy clambered into the boat and Gilly attempted to follow. 'Not you, Gilly,' said Tom at once. 'Pa said it was too dangerous for you.'

'That ain't fair!' foghorned the little girl. 'You always get to go and I don't get to do nothin' 'cept hang around the village waitin' for you to get back. There ain't nothin' to do here.'

'There's plenty to do. Why don't you see if you can find

some more fang worms for supper.'

'Crap on fang worms – I want to come with you.'

'Well, you ain't coming so get used to the idea.'

The little girl scowled at her brother and her lip trembled before she turned and stormed away up the beach. 'Well, a pox on you and a pox on going to the towers too. I never wanted to do that anyhow.' India smiled, remembering the many similar arguments she had had with her own sister on these very shores.

When Gilly had gone, Sid pushed the boat out into the shallows. India helped Tom to pull the mainsheet tight until the throat of the sail caught the wind and the boat began to pick up speed through the water. Tom pointed them towards the sharp-edged building in the middle of the lake and then settled back onto the bench at the rear of the boat.

He looked longingly at the guns stuffed into Sid's belt. 'You sure are a good shot with them pistols,' he said. 'I never saw anyone take out a dog with a single shot before. Cyrus shoots 'em all the time but he uses buckshot and you can't miss with that.' He licked his lips and leaned forwards in his seat. 'Can you teach me how to shoot like that?'

Sid didn't take his eyes off the horizon. 'No.'

'Oh. Well can I shoot one of 'em? Just once?'

'No.'

'Well, can I hold one? Just fer a bit?'

'No.'

Tom sank back in his seat, looking dejected, and adjusted their course. India shivered and pulled her jacket tighter. Even though it was morning, the sun was just a watery disc behind the clouds, its feeble light failing completely to shed any warmth. She had forgotten just how dismal this place could be.

A stiff breeze carried them across the water as though

the surface was made of glass. In less than an hour, the immense dead towers loomed in front of them, breaching the heaving waters like granite cliffs streaked with bird-slime. They fell silent as Tom steered them through great watery canyons where the gulls wheeled in the narrow spaces and the oily water slapped thickly against glass and stone.

India shivered. The city felt as cold and dead as a mausoleum, fit for no one but the birds. When she was young, they had taken boats out on the water many times but had never dared to venture this close to the towers. She helped Tom to wind in the mainsheet, then took the oars, working hard to keep the boat steady in a swell that threatened to dash them against the tower walls.

One tower rose higher than the rest, like a broken glass spike. India stared up at its soaring mass and the cold waves slapping against its impregnable sides. Now that she was here, a sort of supernatural terror took hold of her soul. Every fibre of her being wanted to tell Tom to turn the boat around and leave this this monstrous building behind.

On the far side of the building, Tom guided them towards one of the huge glass windows that was broken and gaping. The sucking waters swirled around the window like a treacherous reef. Tom laid the mast flat and took over the oars to manoeuvre them through the narrow space.

The sides of the boat grated against broken glass as Tom hauled them into the building. They found themselves drifting through a giant hallway, made permanent twilight by slime-blackened windows. The waters heaved and sucked like the lungs of a giant sea creature and the air smelled of river mud and dank rot.

Sid moved to the front of the boat and tied the mooring rope to a steel handrail. A marble staircase ascended from the murky waters and continued up into the gloom. A faded sign told them they were on the sixteenth floor.

'Holy mother of all riggers,' said Sid, climbing out of the boat. 'There's a whole fifteen floors under the water.' He peered up the staircase. 'How many more d'you reckon are up there?'

'Pa said he went to the top once and there were more'n seventy floors,' said Tom. 'But, like I said, I usually just leave the witch's supplies here and she comes down to fetch 'em. '

'Seventy floors!' India blew out a sigh. 'I guess there's nothing else for it – we're just going to have to hike it. Tom, give me the sack. Stay here and watch the boat; we'll be back in an hour or two.' She didn't think the boat would take much watching, but she had no idea what kind of reception she might get from Cromerty and she didn't necessarily want the boy around to witness it.

If Tom was disappointed at being left behind, he didn't show it. He handed over the sack and then rummaged beneath the seat. 'Here. You'll need the torch if you're going up them stairs.'

He passed India a clunky device, with home-made batteries and bare copper wires. She clicked it on hopefully and it squeezed out a thin, yellow light. *Better than nothing, I suppose*, she thought.

She stepped out of the boat next to Sid and shone the heavy torch up the darkened stairwell. She immediately let out an involuntary cry and took a step back so that Sid had to catch her arm.

Every crack and crevice in the broken staircase walls was occupied by nesting gulls. The air was filled with their mewling and wheezing and a thousand pairs of yellow eyes gleamed in the torchlight, like little drops of bile in the darkness.

Sid grimaced. 'Why did it have to be birds?' he muttered. 'I hate birds.'

'Birds are nothing to be afraid of,' said India. 'Just follow me and don't make any sudden noises.'

A frenzy of outraged screeching and wing-flapping began as they started up the staircase under the greedy gaze of the creatures. The going was tough as the stairs were thickly coated in green-black bird-slime, and the stench of ammonia burned their nostrils.

'Why the hell would anyone want to live in a dump like this?' gasped Sid after they had spent half an hour negotiating the slippery steps. He held a ragged cloth over his face to keep the stink at bay and looked like a man who was ready for death. 'How much further is it?'

India shone the torch upwards again but its thin light barely penetrated the gloom. 'I can't tell, but I don't think we're anywhere near the top yet. Come on, keep moving.'

For Sid's sake, India was doing her best to make light of the gulls, but even she felt the urge to turn and run when she looked up into their pitiless yellow eyes. She had to agree that this was the most dreadful place that anyone could choose to live in.

They spent nearly another hour climbing endless flights of slimy stone steps. As they climbed higher, they left the gulls behind and were relieved to find the staircases quieter and less filthy. On every floor, rain poured through rotten ceilings, spreading dampness and decay throughout the building, but there was no sign of Cromerty.

Towards the very top of the building, the stairs became narrower and more utilitarian until, finally, they terminated in a fire escape door. Sid wiped the bird slime from a sign on the wall. 'Floor seventy,' he read. 'Well, I don't care how important this weird woman is – if she ain't here, I ain't going no further.'

India snapped off the torch and stepped through the stairwell door, then immediately screamed and pressed herself back against the wall, shaking in terror.

'What the hell—' Sid burst through the doorway behind her, his guns already in his hand. Then he stopped and stared at the scene around them.

The place where they stood might once have been a public viewing gallery running right around the building, where people could look out over the city in comfort. Except that now the glass had been smashed out and a high wind shrieked through the shattered windows. Sid braced against the force of the wind and stepped up to the nearest window. 'Damn!' He let out a low whistle. 'Would you look at that.'

They were standing at the highest point of the old city with the grey expanse of Lake London stretching beneath them in all directions. India took a deep breath and stepped closer to the edge.

She looked down on the broken, stunted fingers of smaller towers with gulls wheeling slowly between them. On either side of the lake, she could make out the small settlements scattered along the shoreline and the fires of the tyre-burners sending filthy black plumes into the air.

She found that looking down made her feel wobbly and clutched at a handrail, suddenly afraid that her legs might not hold her up. Sid seemed unconcerned, stepping right to the edge and leaning over to look down the side of the building.

'Damn, if you fell out of here there wouldn't be much left to find when you hit the bottom.' He turned to look back at India standing behind him and grinned. 'What's with you? Not afraid of heights, are you?'

India bristled. 'Being afraid of heights is pretty sensible, Sid. It makes a whole lot more sense than being afraid of birds, anyhow.' She let go of the handrail and stepped right to the edge, determined not to show fear in front of Sid.

'I can see the village from here,' she said, pointing. 'And over there I can see settlements on the Southside. They look just the same from here.'

Sid seemed to have lost interest in the view and was exploring the rest of the viewing gallery. 'Hey, look at this.' He beckoned India to the centre of the room where a peculiar assortment of items had been arranged in a circle on the floor. India crouched down next to Sid to examine the strange collection: a bird's feather, a rat's skull, some painted stones and a tied bunch of herbs, all spattered with what looked like blood.

'I've seen these before,' she said. 'They're dream relics. The shamans of the north use them to cast influence on people.'

Sid frowned. 'Influence 'em how?'

'They can make people do things and think it was their own idea.'

Sid glanced sideways at her. 'Is that the kind of thing you learned from the witch woman in Krasnoyarsk?'

India shrugged. 'That, and some other things besides.'

'What kind of things?' The sudden sharpness in his voice made her look up.

'It's not something I like to talk about. And it's none of your business.'

'It's totally my business, India.' His pale face looked even more bloodless than usual and his eyes burned. 'I know you spent time living with a shaman woman and I've seen how your eyes changed colour; that ain't natural. You forget I grew up in Siberia and I heard plenty of tales about shamans and their weirding ways. And now you've brought us up here to meet some old crone that everyone says is a witch and we find... *this.*' He swept a hand over the relics. 'I know when someone ain't telling me the truth, and you definitely ain't. So tell me what's going on here or you can just find yourself a new bodyguard.'

India could see he was serious. Usually, there was very little that got Sid rattled but she could see in his eyes that he was scared now. Perhaps she did owe him an explanation for what they were doing here. Perhaps she needed one herself.

She took a deep breath and let it out slowly. 'I remember when I was a kid, just after Mum died. If I listened really hard to the sound of the wind or the rain, I used to imagine I could hear voices, carrying on the breeze. Cromerty told me it was a special gift and that I should learn to use it properly. She said all the women in my mum's family had it and that I could use it to unlock the world's secrets.'

'Voices?'

'Not exactly voices. It was more like... whispering. Telling me things that were going to happen, like how well the crops would do, or who was going to have a baby, that sort of thing. The funny thing was they always seemed to come true. I never thought much about it as a kid, but when I was older and went to Siberia, I met a shaman called Nentu. She was the one who taught me about weirding magic.'

Sid frowned. 'What sort of magic?'

'Nentu could... do things. Extraordinary things. She knew how to travel places in her dreams, extend her lifespan with spells or even see into a man's soul. She called it being a "soul voyager".'

'And she taught you to do that stuff?'

'Some of it.' She grimaced. 'But it came at a cost, Sid.

Weirding magic always costs you something and it's not always a price you want to pay. The first thing that happened was that my eyes changed colour. After that, I felt that every time I used the magic, it was trying to take something from me, to turn me into something... *dark*. I hated it and I hated myself for what I was doing.'

'What did you do?'

India shrugged. 'I did what any teenager in my position would have done; I ran away. But things weren't much better when I got home. Everybody here hated me for being a witch and Cromerty was furious because I hadn't finished my training. So I ran away again, and this time I kept running for ten years.'

Sid nodded slowly. 'And now you're back and you need Cromerty's help?'

India shivered. 'I don't know how she's going to take it when she finds out I'm here. People think Cromerty is just a mad old crone but she's much more than that. People like Cromerty and Nentu can be really dangerous if you cross them.'

She stood up and stirred the relics on the floor idly with her foot. A brief gleam caught her eye and looked closer at the bundle of herbs, then reached down and plucked up something small and bright. When she held it up to the light, her eyes widened in surprise. It was a ring, small and thin with a cheap stone in the centre.

'What's that?' said Sid.

'A ring.' She stared at it in amazement. 'I think... it used to belong to me.'

'When?'

She shook her head. 'It was years ago. I was just a child. It was a gift from my mother and I wore it everywhere until one day I lost it in the lake. I was heartbroken; I must have dived into that lake a dozen times to try and get it back.' She turned it curiously in her fingers. 'And now it's here.'

'You say a witch can use this sort of magic to make you do things?' said Sid. 'Does that include bringing you here and making you think it was your idea?'

India frowned and shook her head. 'I don't see how,' she said quickly. 'Cromerty couldn't possibly have known I was in London. It has to be just a coincidence.'

'Some coincidence.'

India gazed at the ring. It was crazy to suggest that Cromerty had somehow brought her here. It was she who had sought out the old woman, not the other way around. And yet, she was in absolutely no doubt the ring in her hand was the one she had lost as a child. She knew the feel of its weight in her hand and every scratch on its surface and she remembered vividly just how anguished she had been when she lost it in the lake. So, what was it doing here?

Some coincidence, she thought.

On the other side of the gallery, they found a short flight of wooden stairs that led up to a mezzanine level. A faint light flickered from the top of the stairs, like a candle or a small fire. India pressed a finger to her lips and jerked her head towards the stairs.

Together, they ascended slowly to a flat roof, open to the elements. The rooftop was ringed with rusted metal girders that poked up from the skin of the building like an iron crown. In the centre of the roof, a rough shelter had been built from broken furniture. There was a damp mattress inside and a small lamp spilled a faint light over a bundle of dirty blankets. Rain pattered softly on stretched tarpaulin. As they took in the scene, there was a movement from beneath the blankets.

India dropped the sack she was carrying and crossed the

roof in three strides, stooping to kneel beside the makeshift bed. 'Hell's teeth, it's Cromerty,' she cried. 'What's she *doing* out here? She'll freeze to death.' She took one of the old woman's hands, and rubbed it gently. She was cold to the touch and her skin was pale and stretched thinly over her bones.

'She dead?'

Cromerty's eyes fluttered like pale butterflies and the thin-lipped mouth moved. 'You came. The dream relics never fail.' Her voice was as faint as a breath of air.

'Lie back, Cromerty,' said India. 'We have to light a fire before you catch your death of cold.'

The old woman managed the weakest of smiles. 'Too late, deary. I already caught it.' She struggled to sit up and caught the collar of India's jacket, to look into her eyes. 'I have stretched my life energy waiting for you to return and now my hours run short.'

The old woman's eyes were weak and milky but India could see clearly that they were two different colours. The mismatched stare of a shaman. 'I have seen dark things, India,' she croaked. 'The god of rain comes and he will destroy the world of men.' She seemed agitated, her bony fingers grasping at India as she spoke.

'Cracked,' said Sid. 'She's lived on her own for too long.'

She clutched desperately at India. 'I know of what I speak,' she hissed. 'I have brought you here for a reason. Ignore me at your peril.'

'Cromerty, stop talking. We're going to try and move you now.'

'No!' The old woman's cry was suddenly strong and there were dark undertones in her voice. 'You have a job to do, India Bentley, and world may depend on how well you do it.'

'I... I don't unders—'

'Be quiet and listen to what I say. The god of rain *is* coming. My sisters and I have seen it but we are all too old and too weak to deal with him. This is why I have brought you here.'

'Brought me? I came here to find *you*.'

'So you believe. But you are here for a purpose, India. You are the only one with the power to fight the god of rain.'

India sighed and rolled her eyes. 'This again? It's like I told Nentu. I don't have any special powers. The only reason I'm here is because I'm trying to find a friend.'

Cromerty regarded her critically. 'After everything, you still doubt your gifts,' she said. 'Well, like it or not, you *will* use that power, and sooner than you think.'

'Cromerty, I don't have much time. I need to know about my friend. He was dressed as a sort of monk or holy man. I thought you might know what had happened to him.'

The old woman sank back onto the mattress and she closed her eyes. 'I met the one you speak of,' she said contemptuously. 'But he was no holy man. He was something without a soul. A *demon*.'

'So he was definitely here?' India leaned closer. 'Where is he now? '

Cromerty closed her eyes and breathed deeply. 'Your demon is dead,' she said. 'He would have brought destruction on your village. I buried him where no one would find him. Take my word, you should have nothing to do with him.'

'Cromerty, listen. It's important that I find him. Please tell me where he's buried.'

The old woman waved an irritated hand. 'Not important. Not important at all. Right now you have work to do. You must prepare for the god of rain.'

India rolled her eyes. She was beginning to think that Sid was right. The old woman had lived alone too long and had lost her grip on reality. She looked up and saw thick storm clouds gathering overhead and wondered if they would be able to get Cromerty down the stairs and into the boat before the storm broke.

As she thought this, fat pellets of rain began to spatter onto the tarpaulin. Within moments, the rain had become a torrential downpour that formed lakes on the uneven roof and made waterfalls down the steps. A sudden flash of lightning was accompanied by an almost simultaneous clap of thunder that shook the bones of the old skyscraper.

'Dang, that storm came out of nowhere,' yelled Sid. 'It's pretty much directly overhead.'

'He is here,' cried Cromerty, throwing her arms up towards the sky. 'He has come to deliver death to us. I can *smell* him.'

The next moment, the sky was split with a noise like the gates of hell being cracked open. A searing bolt of white lightning lanced into the exposed steelwork and sparks cascaded around them as the rain redoubled.

'We're too exposed out here,' cried Sid. 'We've got to get off this roof.'

India pointed with a trembling finger. Sid, look at the steelwork!'

As the flare of the lightning faded, a blue-violet light remained clinging to the steel girders like the ghost of a flame. The air crackled and hissed and the smell of electrical burning filled their nostrils.

Cromerty grabbed India's collar again and pulled herself up with all her strength. India thought she could see terror in the old woman's eyes. 'My time is nearly up,' she hissed. 'The god of rain is in the East. He eats the souls of the innocent to make himself strong. Promise you will stop him before he kills us all. *Promise.*'

The old woman was dying, she could see that now. But India had known Cromerty all her life and she deserved to find some peace in death. 'I promise,' she said softly.

'Then we have a chance.' Cromerty closed her eyes again and lay back on the filthy mattress.

India swallowed. She felt wretched about what she was about to do but she had no choice. 'But there's something I need from you first, Cromerty,' she said.

The old woman opened her eyes and the suspicion and fear had returned. 'What is that?'

'Tell me where you buried my friend. It's important. Please.'

Cromerty sighed. 'If that's what it takes,' she said. She reached a papery hand beneath the covers and brought out a small wooden box, which she slid across to India. 'The answers are in here,' she said. 'But if you are friends with demons then I fear you have lost your way, India Bentley.'

India opened the wooden box and found a scrap of paper with Cromerty's bird-like scrawl scratched into the paper. It looked like a map drawn in incomplete, spidery lines; a large cross was marked near the edge of the map with the word 'demon' scored into the page.

'Is this where you buried him?' When there was no reply, she looked up to ask again but the words stalled in her throat. All the pain and anxiety had gone from the old woman's face. Her eyes were closed and her papery skin was drawn tight across the fine bones of her face.

'Cromerty?' She placed a finger against the old woman's arm but the skin was already growing cold.

The old witch was dead.

At that moment, the purple glow that had lingered

around the tips of the steelwork faded and went out and they were alone in the darkness and the rain. Sid examined the hot girders.

'St Elmo's fire,' he said. 'Sometimes it'll attach itself to the mast of a ship. I heard about it from the old sailors but I ain't never seen it before. It's meant to be a bad omen.' He turned to look at India. 'So what was all that stuff about "the god of rain"?'

India looked Cromerty's peaceful face and then carefully pulled the blanket up over her head. 'I don't know what it meant. But she went to a lot of trouble to bring me here and tell me about it. She obviously thought it was important.'

Sid shrugged. 'Don't sweat it too much. The old woman was alone and half crazy. You can't take it seriously.'

India shook her head. 'Women like Cromerty know things about the old world, Sid. Things that can hurt us if we don't pay attention to them.' She glanced back at the body. 'I don't know what this 'god of rain' is, but it was something that scared Cromerty and so that scares me too.'

Sid looked up at the sky. 'Well, the rain's letting up, anyhow,' he said. 'I guess the god of rain ain't coming this afternoon.'

India looked at the scrap of paper that Cromerty had given her. There was a wavy line that looked like the shoreline of the lake and a small cluster of circles that might represent the village. To the north of that was the cross and the word 'demon' in spidery scrawl. It wasn't much to go on. She scoured the rest of the page for more clues.

Close to the cross was a small red circle that seemed to have been drawn in blood with a blue line through the middle of it. The words 'Cam'en Town' were written next to it.

India frowned. Cam'en Town... it sounded familiar, like

a name she remembered from somewhere in the old town, but surely she couldn't have buried him there?

The old town lay about a mile from the village, a collection of broken and blackened buildings too ruined and dangerous to be of any use and which had been deserted for nearly a hundred years. When India and Bella were children, their father had warned them about straying into the old town on pain of a horrible death. 'It's where the dead go to die, India,' he would say, though he never explained what he meant.

On summer evenings, the kids in the village would build campfires down by the lake and tell each other stories about people who'd been unwise enough to stray into the old town. '*I heard old man Purkiss went there looking for his dog and they found his head on a spike and nothin' else.*'

She smiled at the memory and ran a finger over the map. 'It's where the dead go to die,' she murmured. 'But if it's where she left you, then it's where I need to go.'

'India?'

Sid's voice broke into her thoughts. She looked up and saw he was standing at the edge of the roof, looking out across the lake. 'I think you should come look at this.'

She walked to the edge of the roof and saw at once what he was looking at. Far across the lake, a dozen tiny skim boats were approaching the northern shore, leaving foaming wakes in the grey water. There were more boats already pulled up on the mudflats and shadowy figures could be seen darting up the beach towards the village.

Fear blossomed in India's chest and her heart beat faster. 'It's a Southsider raid,' she said quietly. 'We have to go, Sid. We have to get back to the village right away.'

And at that moment, the first cottage began to burn.

5

SOUTHSIDERS

They hurtled down endless flights of stairs, struggling to keep their footing in the bird slime as mewling gulls exploded into a furious, squawking frenzy around them. Sid took off his coat and used it to beat back the angry creatures as a hundred sharp yellow beaks pecked at their exposed skin.

They found Tom where they had left him, terrified by storms and the wild birds that now poured out of the building around them. But for all his terror, the boy had remained at his post and waited from them to return, for which India was hugely grateful.

With frozen fingers, she fumbled with the wet mooring rope until Sid pulled out his hunting knife and slashed through it in one swipe. Then, taking an oar each, they scraped the boat through the gap in the glass and back into the open air. As soon as they were clear of the building, Tom hauled the mast upright and pulled the sail taut. The wind filled the canvas, the ropes tightened and creaked and the boy set about coaxing every ounce of speed from the little boat until they were skimming the water through the canyons of the old city.

Once clear of the old skyscrapers, they had a good view of the shoreline. It seemed that the whole village was ablaze now. Flames licked the walls of the cottages and raced across reed roofs, sending orange sparks spiralling skywards. They could hear the sounds of gunfire carrying across the lake now, like corn popping in a pan.

'They got a Southsider problem for sure,' murmured Sid.

'My sister and the rest of Tom's family are over there, Sid,' snapped India. 'So stop being a smart-mouth and get ready to help.'

'D'you think they'll be all right, India?' The boy had said little since they had left. He understood the urgency of the situation and had put all of his energies into helping them get underway. But now that they saw the burning buildings, he couldn't help but let the fear show in his face.

India gave him a reassuring smile. 'Don't worry, Tom. Your house is well back from the water; I'm sure your family will be fine. As soon as we get there, you need to stay low in the boat while me and Sid go and investigate. We'll find them, don't you worry.'

But when she looked towards the village, she did not feel so sure of her words. The shoreline was now a continuous line of fire and smoke and it was impossible to tell whether any of the houses would be left untouched.

Sid sat in the bows, checking his pistols. 'When we get there, stay close behind me. We'll get to the house and try and hold them off from there.'

By the time they reached the shore, it was almost dark even though it was only late afternoon. They pulled up in the shallows alongside half a dozen Southside skim boats, leaking oily slicks into the water.

While Tom lay low in the bottom of the boat as instructed, India jumped out and began to splash ashore. There was a sharp *pop* to her left and an angry bee zipped past her ear. Before she could react, Sid's pistols fired twice and a dark shadow tumbled into the water with a splash.

'Don't stand there gawping, git moving.' Sid grabbed her arm and ran her up the beach until they reached the edge of the village. More buildings were burning now, and the air was filled with woodsmoke, gunfire and screaming. Panicked figures ran in every direction, silhouetted against the flames so that it was impossible to tell Northsider from Southsider.

India led them into the rat lanes that ran behind the cottages where the smoke was less thick. At the end of the lane, she breathed a sigh of relief when she saw Vincent's cottage, untouched by the flames. The back door was splintered and smashed from its hinges and the kitchen was in darkness; the sounds of fighting faded as they stepped cautiously through the doorway.

'Vincent? It's India – are you in here?' There was no reply.

A figure lurched suddenly from behind the doorway, swinging something heavy. There was a dull crack of wood on bone and Sid fell groaning to the floor. India turned as the sawn-off ends of a shotgun were jabbed into her chest.

'Who's this, then?' said a ferrety voice. 'Let's 'ave a butcher's at you.' She flinched as a light snapped on in her face. The man had meaty breath and smelled of stale sweat. 'My my, you are a pretty one,' he cackled. 'We'll get a good price for you in the flesh markets.' He turned towards the kitchen doorway. 'Marko,' he yelled. 'Get in here; I've found a juicy one.'

As he called out, the man made the mistake of taking his eyes from her for an instant. It was only momentary but it was enough for India. She grabbed an iron skillet from the stove and swung it. The man turned back, just in time to meet the skillet full in his face. The pan gonged loudly and he hit the floor like a piece of cold meat.

Sid sat up and groaned. He blinked first at the unconscious man and then at the pan in India's hand. 'Damn!' he gasped. 'Maybe I need to get me one of those.'

They were startled by a groan from the other corner of the room and a crumpled shape shifted in the darkness. India recognised the bulky figure. 'It's Vincent,' she said.

She crossed the room and crouched over the slumped figure while Sid lit the oil lamp. Vincent's nose and mouth were streaked with scarlet and his right eye was beginning to swell shut.

'Lie still,' said India. 'Looks like they roughed you up pretty bad.'

'I'll live,' he grunted. He tried to sit up but his face twisted in agony. 'Dammit, I think they broke my leg.'

There was a commotion in the doorway and a second man burst into the room, blinking in the light. 'Snitch? Where are you, mate?' As his eyes adjusted to the light, he gasped at the sight of his unconscious friend. When he saw India and Sid, he immediately turned and fled.

'Get after him, Sid!' yelled India. 'Stop him before he tells anyone we're here.'

Sid drew his pistols and sprinted after the man. Vincent reached up and grasped India's collar. 'I never saw a Southsider raid this big before.' He spoke with difficulty, his words coming in pained gasps. 'Get out of here until it's all over.'

'I won't leave you behind. They'll kill you if they find you here.'

'I'll be fine. Just pass me my shotgun then take the kids and hide in the woods. Do it now!'

India nodded. 'All right. As soon as Sid gets back, we'll fetch Tom from the boat. Where's Gilly?'

Vincent's eyes widened. 'She's not with you? I saw you all leave to go to the towers this morning.'

India shook her head. 'Tom told her it was too dangerous and she went off on her own. I assumed she'd come back home.'

'No. I haven't seen her all day.' A look of fear crossed Vincent's face then, almost at once, the leader took control. 'All right, let's stay calm. Gilly's a sensible girl. She'll lie low somewhere until the trouble stops. I need you to go down to the shore and find her before the Southsiders do and then get out of sight.'

Sid returned, carrying the smell of gunsmoke with him. 'That's one Southsider that won't be going home.' He slid the pistols back into his belt and looked down at the still unconscious man on the floor. 'We'll see what this one can tell us when he wakes up.'

'There's no time for that, Sid,' snapped India. 'The kids are outside somewhere. We need to find them before someone else does.'

They left Vincent on the floor of his kitchen with his shotgun and crept down to the water, sticking close to the reeds to avoid the light from the still-burning cottages. 'If Gilly went looking for fang worms, she'd probably have gone to the sand flats on the far side of the village,' said India. 'It's where we used to go when we were kids.'

The fighting had died down a little by now, although there was still some gunfire from the main street. Several of the skim boats were now heading back across the lake and only a few were left bobbing in the shallows.

'They'll be back for these boats anytime,' whispered Sid. 'We shouldn't hang around.' He cursed as he stumbled over something heavy. 'Damn! What's that?'

India clicked on the torch to reveal a man's body lying face upwards in the shallows. He was heavyset and bearded. One eye was wide open and the other was a ragged and bloody crater where the bullet had entered. A thin line of blood trailed into the water like silk ribbon.

'It's Cyrus, the village constable,' she said. India felt oddly calm and detached as she looked at the body. 'Come on,' she said after a few moments. 'There's nothing we can do for him.'

She started to move but Sid pulled her back sharply. 'Someone's coming. Get down.'

He pulled her to the ground behind a patch of reeds as the sounds of raucous laughter drew closer. A group carrying shotguns, machetes and baling hooks swaggered down the bank, and stopped just a few feet from their hiding place. They were ragged and mud-spattered and carried burning torches that dripped hot tar. India didn't recognise any of them.

The largest man carried a bulky sack across his shoulders like a haunch of venison. He delivered a kick to the spotty teen beside him. 'Go and get the boat, Charlie-boy. I don't fancy getting me feet wet.' The boy muttered something under his breath and hiked up his trousers as he waded into the shallows.

'Good pickings tonight,' said someone.

'It was just like the twins said. Northsiders are fat and weak. Just ripe for the picking.'

'Southsiders,' hissed India. 'I can tell from their accents.'

They're fat all right,' said a pinched woman with a voice like nails on glass. 'Look at this lump.' She prodded Cyrus's body with the toe of her boot. 'He looks a bit surprised, don't he?' The men laughed and one of them poked the body with the end of his shotgun.

'HOLD FAST. WHAT HAVE YOU GOT THERE?' an enormous voice boomed out of the darkness. It was deep and resonant and sounded as though it came from two places at once. The Southsiders fell quiet as two giant figures ambled out of the gloom towards them. When India saw them, she instinctively shrank back into the reeds.

The two men were the most enormous people she had ever seen. Their necks were thick columns of muscle, their heads were hairless and slick with sweat and their huge bulk was barely contained by their greasy black suits and long coats. Each man had an identical round face and they grinned from ear to ear so that they looked like nothing less than a pair of huge, malevolent babies.

'Mother of all riggers,' gasped Sid. 'That's the Pinkerton twins.'

'Who the hell are the Pinkerton twins?' returned India.

'Shh! They're bad news is what they are. The last I heard, they were running a people-smuggling ring in South-East Asia. I don't know what they're doing here, though.'

'Quiet,' hissed India. She pushed Sid's head down into the wet reeds as one of the Southsiders turned in their direction.

One of the Pinkerton twins looked at the sack slung across the Southsider's shoulders and slapped it with a fat hand. 'Good pickings?'

The man grinned. 'Fresh meat,' he said. 'It's just like you said, Brother Romulus. This'll fetch a good price in the market.'

'Well, just remember who you owe your good fortune to when you count your gold,' said the second brother. He rubbed his thumb and forefingers together. 'We expect everyone to pay their respects. Don't we, brother?'

'Indeed we do, Remus,' said the first brother. 'Because my brother hates it when people forget to pay their respects. Don't you, Romulus?'

'Indeed I do,' replied Romulus, grinning. 'And funnily enough, so does my brother. It makes us both feel quite... *disgruntled*.' They grinned at each other.

The man with the sack was starting to look nervous. 'I-I assure you, sirs,' he stammered. 'I would never dream of... I mean I've never...'

'ENOUGH,' barked the twins. 'GET THE PRIZES ONTO THE BOAT AND LET'S GET MOVING.' The two men spoke in perfect unison as though they were sharing the same thoughts. Every word, every breath, every inflection was identical. It was as though a single person spoke with two voices.

The effect was not lost on the Southsiders. They jumped if an electric shock had been passed through them and started wading out towards the remaining boats. The Pinkerton brothers paused beside Cyrus's body and looked down at it thoughtfully.

'Well, he's a plump one and no mistake, Brother Romulus.'

'Indeed he is, brother,' replied Remus. He took something from his top pocket and crouched down to jab at the corpse. India saw that what he was holding was a fork. 'Very juicy,' he said appreciatively. 'Make a good stew, this one would.'

His brother curled his lip. 'Always thinking of your stomach, Remus. Leave him behind; there's no room on the boat.'

Remus looked hurt. 'But he's a Londoner, Romulus. I've never tasted Londoner before.'

Romulus rolled his eyes. 'Well, I have and they're horrible. All gristle and no flavour. Now, if you want a proper stew, you need a Frenchman.'

Remus sighed blissfully. 'Oh, now you're talking, brother. I do so enjoy French food.'

'Come on, brother,' said Romulus, wading into the shadows. 'We have much business to complete and a long journey ahead of us.'

Remus gave Cyrus's body a lingering look and then returned the fork to his top pocket with a regretful sigh. 'As you wish, brother. But what would you say to a little trip to France when this is over, eh?'

The two men began to laugh. It was a high-pitched, chattering sort of noise that sounded like two jackals arguing over a piece of meat. It chilled India to her core.

They watched the departing skim boats carve a deep wake through the water before Sid rolled over on his back and let out a sigh. 'Damn! I thought they'd spot us for sure.'

India watched the boats retreating in the gloom. 'Who were those guys? Were they for real?'

'Romulus and Remus Pinkerton are about as real as it gets,' said Sid. 'They call themselves bounty hunters, but they really run one of the most brutal slaver gangs in the East. If they're working with the Southsiders, then your friends in the village are in big trouble.'

A cold wind blew off the water, making India shiver. 'What was that whole thing with the fork and Cyrus? They weren't really going to—'

'Eat him? Sure, how do you think they got to be so big? The Pinkertons are cannibals, India. They think eating their victims is a perk of the job.'

India felt her stomach flop over, but there was no time to dwell on the horror of the Pinkerton twins now. 'Come on, get up! We need to find Tom and Gilly now. Hopefully they've both have had the sense to lie low.'

They continued along the mudflats in the deepening gloom, helped by the orange glow coming from the direction of the village. 'Look! Over there. Someone's coming.' Sid pointed to a small figure stumbling towards them, coughing as he came.

'It's Tom,' said India.

She crouched down in front of the boy and took him by the shoulders. His face was grime-streaked and tear-stained. 'Tom, are you OK? Is Gilly with you?'

Tom looked her in the eyes and an awful fear closed on her heart. 'I found her down by the mudflats,' snivelled the boy. 'We were walking back to the village when we got spotted by Southsiders.'

The dread feeling grew. 'What happened?'

A tear ran down the boy's face, carving a fresh channel through the grime. 'Oh, India, it was awful. We had to run but Gilly don't run so good and she fell over and they... and they...' His voice choked in a sob.

'They caught her?'

They boy nodded miserably. 'They dragged her off to the skim boats,' he wailed. 'There weren't nothin' I could do.'

India cursed silently and looked out over the water, wondering how far away the Southsiders would be by now. But there was no sign of the skim boats and they were probably most of the way back to the Southside by now. She turned back to the boy.

'Listen to me, Tom. What happened isn't your fault. Do you hear me?'

The boy swallowed hard. 'What are we going to do?'

India bit her lip. The truth was she had no idea what they could do against such a well-armed group of raiders. She forced a tight smile. 'First, we're going to take you home to your dad, then we'll set about finding your sister.'

'Don't know why you're lying to the boy,' said Sid. 'If the Pinkertons have got her, she ain't never coming back. The kid might as well get used to the idea.'

India rounded on Sid, her eyes blazing. 'Just stay out of this, Sid. You may not give a damn about anyone else in this world but I do and if there's a way to get Gilly back then I'm going to find it. I know what it's like to leave a sister behind.'

'Please, India,' said the boy in a timid voice. 'There's something else.'

'What is it, Tom?'

'It was when the Southsiders caught Gilly...'

'Yes?'

'Well, the medic lady was there. She saw what was happening and she tried to make them let her go.'

'The medic lady? You mean Bella?' Cold fingers of fear closed around her heart. 'What happened?'

'They... they...'

'Tell me, dammit!' She grabbed the boy by the shoulders and shook him.

'They took her, miss,' he blurted. 'They took Bella and put her in a sack. The Southsiders have got her too.'

6

FIRST LIGHT

By first light, the fires were mostly out and a grey pall hung across the village, smelling of burned tar and death. The villagers moved around in the rubble like ghosts, salvaging what they could, repairing broken barricades and gathering the dead and arranging them in a long line along the main street.

In Vincent's house, the mood was sombre. A council of war met around the kitchen table with Vincent at its head. His broken leg was up on a chair. The bonesetter had done what she could but the limb was still horribly twisted and pain was written deep into the lines of Vincent's face. India looked at the crooked leg and knew that Vincent would probably never walk straight again. Bella would have done a better job. The thought made her catch her breath.

Bella.

As they had expected, the skim boats were long gone by the time the villagers had mustered any thoughts of pursuit. There was no indication which of the Southside factions might have been responsible for the raid but speculation was rife around Vincent's table.

'It's the worst loss we've ever experienced,' said an Asian man at the end of the table. He consulted a piece of paper in his hand, covered in pencil scrawl. 'We've got nine dead and six missing, including two children.' He hesitated when he remembered who one of the missing children belonged to, but Vincent remained impassive.

The man went back to his notes. 'Other than that, we've got fourteen in the infirmary. Machete wounds mostly but two of them were shot and are not expected to live.'

A woman at the back of the room spat on the floor. 'Southsider scum! They're not fit to live.' A ripple of angry agreement went around the room.

'What about our supplies?' said Vincent. His voice sounded strained.

'They took most of the livestock and killed what they couldn't take with them,' said the first man. 'We managed to hide some bags of grain and some dried meat but the truth is there's not enough food to take us through the winter.'

'Then we're screwed,' blurted another man. India recognised him as one of Cyrus's security team. He clutched the shotgun across his lap, his knuckles white with tension. 'Those bastards could be back at any minute to finish the job.' He glanced at the door as though he expected Southsiders to come bursting through it at any moment.

'We weren't ready,' said an older man. 'But next time we'll be readier. Southside's no match for Northside. Southside are wimps and pussies. Next time we'll be ready.' His voice trailed off as though he didn't believe any of what he was saying.

'Even if that was true,' interrupted the first man, 'we still don't have nothin' to eat. There's nothin' left for us here now. We've got to move out while we can before they come back.'

'Move out where?' yelled another woman. 'We were

driven out of our last place and the place before that. Wherever we go there's always someone wants to take everything we got. We have to make a stand sooner or later. I say we fight 'em.'

There was a cheer of approval from the men next to her and a dozen voices were raised in anger. Fingers were jabbed accusingly around the table and one man grabbed another by the lapels as though he meant to headbutt him.

The sound of Vincent's finger tapping slowly on the tabletop cut through the noise. 'That's enough.' Vincent hardly raised his voice but everyone in the room heard him. When he was sure he had their attention, he continued. 'Our first priority is to find those that got taken. We need to organise a rescue party.'

'Rescue party?' The woman at the back of the room looked at him incredulously. 'You may not have been paying attention, Vincent, but we just got our arses handed to us on a plate. Who were you thinking could lead this "rescue party"? Certainly not you with a busted leg.'

Vincent winced and laid a hand on his injured limb. 'It just needs strapping up. I'll be OK.'

'You'll be dead,' shot back the woman. 'And everyone who goes with you'll be dead too. You've led us long enough, Vincent. If we listen to you, we'll all end up hanging from trees. Our only hope is to clear out of here before they come back. Who's with me?'

Another cheer went up around the room as the woman turned and stormed out of the kitchen. She was followed by most of the people in the room until the only ones left were Vincent, India, Sid and the man who had first spoken.

'I'm sorry, Vincent,' said the man. 'But Betty is an angry woman. She's lost her husband and her son to Southsider raids in the last two years. I'm sure they'll come around when they've had a chance to calm down.'

Vincent shook his head. 'They're not going to come around, Sanjay,' he said. 'They've had enough of me. And now my leg's messed up, they'll be looking for someone new to lead them. I'm weak now and so I've got to go. It's the law of the jungle.'

Sanjay grimaced. 'I'm sorry, Vincent. I'll have a word with then and see what I can do.' He looked as though he wanted to say more but in the end he just gathered his papers and left.

'So that's it?' said India. She had been sitting at the far and of the table, glowering quietly while the meeting had gone on. Now she was angry. 'You're just going to let those sheep pack up and leave and forget all about what happened here.'

Vincent shrugged. He looked like a defeated man. 'I don't see as there's much else I can do.'

'You could show some balls,' snapped India. 'You could try and rescue your daughter and my sister and all those other people who got taken.'

Vincent slammed a fist down on the table. 'And how am I meant to do that? Betty was right, I'm useless and broken. Don't you think it burns my insides to know they've got my daughter? But if I go after them and get killed, then who's going to look after Tom? And it's no use asking anyone else here to help; they've all lost too much to the Southsiders already. No one is about to go charging over there on a rescue mission.'

'Well, I am.'

Vincent stared at her for long seconds then snorted. 'I believe you're crazy enough to,' he said. 'Well, good luck, but I guarantee you no one is going to go with you.'

'I'll go with her.'

They turned to look at Sid, who had been sitting in the corner of the room, cleaning his pistols. India shot him a grateful glance but he did not look up from his work.

'Well, great, that makes two headcases,' said Vincent. 'But at last count we got hit by over fifty Southsiders last night. They were well-fed and well-armed and they went through us as though we weren't there. And we don't even know where they make their camp. The Southside is a big place. You could be searching for days before you find them, that's if they don't find you first.'

'There's one way we can find out where they are.' They turned to Sid again, who was inspecting the gun chambers.

India rolled her eyes. 'Well, don't keep us in suspense. How?'

'That feller you laid out with a saucepan last night could tell us where their camp is.' He snapped shut the cylinder on one of the guns and spun it so that it rotated with the satisfying sound of well-oiled machinery. 'Of course, you'd need to give him the proper motivation.' He looked up and gave them a cold smile.

'Sid makes a good point,' said India. 'That guy could tell us everything we need to know. Is he still alive?'

'He's alive,' sighed Vincent. 'They're holding him in the cellar over at Betty's place. They were planning to string him up this afternoon.'

'Not until we've finished with him,' said India. 'We'll talk to him and see what we can find out. Then we'll decide what we're going to do next.'

They left Vincent staring morosely at his broken leg while they walked over to Betty's cottage. The bodies had been removed from the main street and a thick column of smoke rose from the scrubland beyond the edge of the village. India caught the sweet smell of burning flesh on the air.

They saw a family loading their meagre belongings onto a wooden cart. Then they watched as they climbed on top of their belongings and a tired donkey started to haul them away.

'I guess they're the first of many,' said India. 'They don't even care about fighting for what's theirs any more.'

'They care about staying alive,' said Sid. 'More than you do, it seems.'

She looked at him. 'Maybe. But I don't see any point in staying alive if you can't protect the people you care about. I can't stop thinking about Bella and what they might be doing to her. She...' India tailed off, finding the sentence too awful to finish. 'Anyway, thanks.'

'What for?'

'For saying you'd come with me. I appreciated the vote of confidence.'

Sid shrugged. 'It weren't a vote of confidence. If you get yourself killed, then who's going to pay me?'

India smiled. 'You always were a terrible liar,' she said.

They found Betty's cottage in the middle of the main street. It was larger than its neighbours and set back a little from the track. A man with a shotgun stood outside and challenged them as they approached.

'We need to talk to Betty,' said India. 'We want to question the prisoner we took last night.'

The man looked them up and down and grunted. 'You can come in. But you have to leave the guns outside.'

Sid raised his head just enough to fix the man with a stare from beneath the shadow of his hat. 'If you can take 'em, you can keep 'em,' he said in a soft voice.

The man swallowed and then stood back from the doorway. 'All right, go on in,' he said. 'But you'd best hurry. They're planning to string him up within the hour.'

They ducked through the door and found themselves in another kitchen, larger than Vincent's, where Betty was holding court around a table. She was a large woman with a thick tangle of curly red hair and a florid, wind-burned face. The men around her were all armed. *Vincent may be losing his job as village leader sooner than he thinks*, thought India.

As soon as she saw them, Betty stood up and came to meet them, standing, legs apart and hooking her thumbs in her belt as though to form a human barrier. 'Well if it ain't Vincent's hired killers,' she sneered. 'Has he sent you to deal with the opposition?'

'We're not Vincent's hired killers,' said India. 'Or anyone else's for that matter. I used to live in this village and my sister still lives here. She's the one who's been patching up your wounds and fixing your broken bones, if you hadn't noticed.'

The ferocity in Betty's face faltered a little. 'Yes, well... we were all sorry to hear about your sister. She was a good woman.'

'She's not dead yet,' shot back India. 'And I plan to keep it that way.'

Betty raised an eyebrow in surprise. 'You serious about planning a rescue?' She grinned. 'I underestimated you. You got more balls than most of the men in this place.' She looked at the men seated around her table to make her point. 'But you know you don't have a cat in hell's chance?

'So I've been told. But I want to try and even the odds a little. Vincent said you're holding the Southsider we caught last night. I'd like to speak to him.'

Betty went to a rough sideboard and picked up a bottle of evil-looking brown spirit. 'He won't tell you nothing,' she said, pouring a generous measure into a shot glass. 'Two of the boys worked on him most of the night but they couldn't get nothing from him. Don't see why you should be any different.'

'Just let me try.'

She drained the glass quickly and then slammed it down with a crack. She shrugged. 'Well, you'll need to be quick. He hangs within the hour. We're expecting quite a crowd.'

One of Betty's guards showed them down a flight of narrow stairs to a brick basement with no windows. The man who India had knocked out the night before was tied to a chair in the middle of the room. His body was limp and his head sagged onto his chest. Congealing blood spread down the front of his shirt and his lank hair fell across his face. Another guard lounged in the corner, cleaning his nails with a knife. He barely looked up as they entered.

'Is he awake?' asked India.

'Awake, asleep, it don't make much difference,' said the guard. 'He'll wake up soon enough when we string him up.'

Sid examined an array of objects on a small wooden table in the corner. 'This what you been using on him?' he asked.

India looked over Sid's shoulder and saw an assortment of household tools laid out on a dirty towel, sticky with blood. There were pliers, a hacksaw, a small hammer and a pair of heavy tinsnips. Strewn across the tabletop was a scattering of broken teeth, several of which had been yanked out by their roots. India turned away quickly.

'Can he talk?'

The guard shrugged. 'You can try. The boys worked him over pretty good last night, trying to find out where they took our people but all he'd tell us was that his name was Snitch. He kept babbling on about "the twins". Whoever they are I think he was more scared of them than anything we could do to him.'

India looked at Snitch's slumped figure and felt pity in her soul. He was probably no different from most of the people she had grown up with. The only difference was that Snitch was born on the other side of Lake London and that made him a Southsider. Then she remembered Bella, carried off to who knew where. When she thought of what might be happening to her sister, she felt a cold rage take hold of her and all thoughts of pity disappeared.

'I want to talk to him now.'

'Suit yourself but you're wasting your time. You'll get nothing out of him.'

'I know a way.'

She stepped up to the chair and pulled the man's head back by the hair so that he looked up into her face. He coughed and blinked in the light, then focused blearily on her face. 'Whasshup... Whaddya want?' His words slurred through the bloody mess of his mouth. 'I told you I ain't shaying nuffing to Norfshiders.'

'Where have they taken them, Snitch?' said India. 'Where's your camp?'

The man blinked as her voice cut through his clouded thoughts. He shifted uncomfortably in his seat and for a moment it looked like he would answer her question. Then he tore his head away from her grasp. 'Go shcrew yourshelf, bitch!'

India took a firmer hold of the man's greasy hair and yanked his head back again, hard enough to make him cry out. 'Where have they taken them?' she yelled into his face. 'My sister, and Gilly and the others. Tell me!'

'Leave it, India,' said Sid. 'You can't threaten a man that's about to die. He ain't going to tell you nothing.'

India leaned closer to the man's face and fixed him with her mismatched stare. 'Look at me,' she ordered. The man's eyes locked with her own.

'You will tell me what I want to know because I have the wind at my back, and the wind can sink ships.' Both Sid and the guard looked up when she spoke. Her voice seemed to have dropped an octave and had taken on a darker tone.

'I have earth beneath my feet, and mountains are made of the earth,' she continued. The man squirmed uneasily in his chair. 'And I have water in my blood and water can cut through stone.' She leaned in closer until her mouth was right next to his ear. 'And I have fire in my heart, enough to burn a man.'

The man did not look groggy any more; he was wide-eyed and scared. His mouth opened and shut like a fish but no words came out. All he registered was the girl's eyes, burning into him like twin jets of flame. And behind those eyes, he sensed something else, something older than the mountains and darker than coal. Something alive and, yet, not alive.

The darkness in the brick cellar seemed to close in around him until he was aware of nothing but himself and the girl. More than anything now he wanted to look away but he could not. He felt the darkness reaching for him, pulling at every secret he possessed. He tried to scream but, when he opened his mouth, the darkness rushed into his open mouth, filling his throat, his lungs with ancient horror.

'Glass Town!' He screeched out the words as if they had been pulled from him with wire. 'They've taken 'em all to Glass Town.' He tried to turn away his head but India tightened her grip.

'What are they planning to do with them?'

'Please...' Snitch blubbered and sniffled. A bubble of snot formed on his nose and popped. 'Please... no more...'

'Tell me!'

'The s-slave market...' he gasped. 'They're to be sold in the slave market.'

India shook his head violently. 'What slave market? I never heard of a slave market on the Southside. Tell me!'

'T-the t-twins,' he gasped. 'They arranged it all. They s-said they'd make us all rich s-slavers, like them. They s-said all we had to do was take 'em to Glass Town. T-that's all I know... honest it is. No more... *please.*'

He writhed out of her grip, arched his back and screamed. It sounded like the death-shriek of a bird caught in the jaws of a predator. Then it stopped abruptly as Snitch's eyes rolled up into his head and he went limp.

'Enough, India!' Sid tried to pull her away, but she turned on him, eyes aflame and full of savagery. Sid stepped back in alarm. 'Shit! What the hell was *that?*'

India turned away, her legs suddenly weak. She sat down on the edge of the table and buried her face in her hands. 'Something you weren't supposed to see,' she said quietly.

The guard in the corner was on his feet now, his gaze flicking between India and Snitch. 'I'm going to get it in the neck for this,' he gasped. 'I'm getting Betty.' He fled up the stairs, like a man escaping from a burning room.

Sid kneeled in front of Snitch's limp form and examined his eyes. 'What did you do to him, India?'

India took a deep breath and swallowed. 'Nothing,' she said quickly. 'I just asked him a few questions and he fainted, that's all. As soon as he wakes up we can start again.'

Sid shook his head. 'I asked plenty of questions in my time, but I never made anyone scream like that,' he said. He leaned forwards and raised one of the man's eyelids with his thumb to peer into a vacant eye. 'And you can forget asking him any more questions. Because this guy is stone-cold dead.'

IT TOOK them a while to negotiate their way out of Betty's cottage. Betty's followers were angry at having been cheated out of their hanging victim and for a moment, India was worried that they might try using her and Sid as stand-ins.

But when the guard who had been in the room told his story, Betty regarded India with fresh wariness, as if she was a dangerous animal. 'I heard of things like that, before,' she growled. 'They said the weirding women could reach into a man's mind and tear out his soul. Is that what you did to him?'

'She knows the old witch Cromerty,' said someone from the back of the room. 'She probably learned it from her. We should hang her afore she curses all of us.'

'You can't hang a witch,' said someone else. 'As soon as it gets dark, they'll climb down from the tree and come for your soul.'

'Shut up, you morons,' barked Betty. She turned on India and Sid. 'The pair of you, get out of here and don't come back. If you know what's good for you, you'll both leave town tonight.'

They did not need telling twice. As soon as they were back on the street, Sid laughed out loud. 'I've been accused of a lot of things in my time and most of 'em were true,' he drawled. 'But I ain't never been accused of being a witch before. I thought we were going to have to shoot our way out of there.' He looked at India thoughtfully. 'So, how did you really kill that guy? Was it really witchcraft?'

India could not bring herself to look at Sid. 'I don't know what you'd call it for sure,' she said. 'It was something I learned from Nentu when I was in Siberia. She could look into a man's soul and see what secrets he kept there. She showed me how to cast the spells to do it but... looking into someone else's mind... it's horrible, Sid. I swore it was something I'd never do again.'

'But you did.'

India laughed. 'Cromerty said I'd use my powers sooner than I thought, and she was right.'

Sid made a wry face. 'It sure is a handy skill to have. Maybe you could teach it to me, sometime?'

'Don't, Sid. Don't even joke about it.'

They walked on in silence for a while before Sid spoke again. 'So, what about this Glass Town? You ever heard of that before?'

'It's a settlement on the Southside,' she said thoughtfully. 'But it's tiny. We had a couple of skirmishes with them when I lived here but nothing like the raid last night.'

Sid shrugged. 'It sounds to me like the Pinkertons have been persuading your neighbours in Glass Town that there's more money in slavery than in farming. Reckon they're right too,' he added.

India felt a cold sickness in the pit of her stomach but pushed it away. If she was going to help her sister, she had to keep a cool head. 'So, all that stuff about a slave market? Do you think—'

'Yeah, I do.' Sid looked up at the sky and then turned up his collar. 'It sounds exactly like something the Pinkertons would do. They're slavers by trade and they're very good at it. You might as well forget about anyone who ends up in one of their slave markets.'

India's jaw tightened. 'My sister's in one of their slave

markets, in case you'd forgotten, and I'm not going to leave her there.'

Sid turned to face her. 'Oh yeah, and what are you going to do? You saw how well-organised that raid was last night. You seriously think you can fight them alone on their own turf?'

India frowned. 'We could organise a raiding party. I'm not the only one who's lost someone to those creeps. If we mounted a night raid, we could hit them before they realised what's happening.'

'You'd have no idea what you're walking into over there.' Sid spat on the ground to underscore his point. 'They might have a hundred people or a thousand. They might be armed to the teeth. They might have lookouts and see you coming from ten miles away. It's suicide, India. Face facts: your sister ain't coming back.'

'I don't like those facts!' For a moment he saw the same fire in her eyes he had seen when she questioned Snitch and it chilled him to the core. 'What I do know for a fact,' she continued, 'is that people will put their lives on the line for people they care about. I'm going to Glass Town and I'll take anyone who wants to come with me. The only question is: are you going to be one of them?'

Sid stared at her for a long time. 'Like I said, a raid like that would be suicide.' She waited. Then he blew out a sigh and looked up to the heavens. 'But if I don't come with you, you'll just get yourself killed and then I won't get paid. So I guess it's in my interests to make sure you stay alive.'

India stared into Sid's cold, pale eyes and grinned. 'Thanks, Sid. You're the best.'

Sid grimaced. 'Don't go reading anything into it that ain't there. I'm doing this for money. So, what's the plan?'

They had reached the narrow crossroads in the centre of

the village. 'I need you to go and talk to Vincent,' she said. 'Tell him to put the word around about the raiding party. See how many might want to join us. Make sure they're young and fit and properly armed, then get everyone to assemble by the lakeside at sunset. Vincent should be able to organise some boats to get us over there too.'

'And what are you going to be doing while I'm running your errands?'

India turned to look at the muddy track that led up the hill, away from the village. 'I've got a job to do first,' she said. 'I'm going to look up an old friend.'

7

CAM'EN TOWN

The old city lay stretched before her like a rotten carcass. Charred roof timbers splayed open like burned ribs and the clogged arteries of the city streets were sclerotic with mud and silt.

Where people had once gathered to laugh and flirt and drink cocktails the colour of gemstones, there was now only darkness and death and decay. London wore the curse of the Great Rains the way a corpse wears a shroud.

The old motorbike rattled through the decayed streets, shattering the silence like a lawnmower in a church. As she drove, India kept a watchful eye on the vacant stare of the old buildings on either side of the road, watching for signs of movement in the darkness.

Most lake dwellers had been brought up to avoid the old city like a plague. It was a place where rats ran in black rivers and dog packs a hundred strong might corner a man and tear him into strips. But what people feared most were the 'ghostmen', said to live beneath the city streets and who were the stuff of every child's nightmares.

The ghostmen might once have been men, or they might

be something entirely new, a mutated product of the Great Rains – no one knew. People who had encountered a ghostman and survived would talk of skins blanched to the colour of dead flesh and eyes with the pinkness of a lab rat.

The only thing anyone did know for sure was that there was no reasoning with ghostmen. They would tear living strips of flesh from your skin, suck the juices from your eyes and relish the moist tenderness of your tongue, all while you still lived. Of all the horrors that lived in the old city, they were the thing that terrified India the most.

She brought the old bike to a clattering halt in a main street where some long-subsided floodwater had washed the carcasses of old cars into an impassable barricade. She would have to leave the bike here and walk the rest of the way, which severely limited her possibilities for escape should the worst happen.

She wondered again if it would have been wise to bring Sid with her. His unshakeable calm and deadly accuracy with a pistol were what she really needed in a place like this. But she had been right to leave him behind. She didn't trust the villagers to organise themselves for the coming raid without Sid there to oversee the preparations. There was simply too much fear and resignation there and most would have been too ready to run rather than fight. If she and Sid had come on this mission together, they would most likely have returned to an empty village.

Besides, this was something she had to do alone. Somewhere in this dead town lay her friend, buried by Cromerty, and it was down to her to find him. She wondered again at how the frail old woman had managed to bring his body all the way to the old town and bury it here. But then Cromerty had always been a woman of extraordinary resourcefulness.

She shook herself out of her daydream. This was not a

place to let your mind wander, if you didn't want to get eaten alive. She dismounted the bike and reached into in her satchel for a small handheld device, held together by wrappings of tape. When she turned it on, a row of lights flickered awake and the box purred softly in her hand like a small mammal.

She turned slowly, pointing the device to all points of the compass and examining the readout for any change. But the lights remained stubbornly steady and she cursed under her breath and turned it off. Either she was out of range, or Cromerty's map was nothing but a lie – a final act of defiance from the grave.

She returned the device to her satchel, pausing to check that the plasma charger stored at the bottom of the bag was still safe in its cloth wrapping. Then she re-slung the bag and reached into the sidecar for Vincent's shotgun.

When he had learned of her plan to travel to the old city, Vincent had insisted she take the weapon. She had been reluctant at first. She did not share Sid's easy familiarity with guns. But now that she was here, feeling like a hundred pairs of eyes were watching her from the dead windows, she was glad of the gun's comforting feel in her hand.

She looped the gun over her shoulder and scaled a barricade of rusted hulks blocking the street. On the other side, the streets were less silted, allowing her to walk unimpeded along the centre of the street.

She kept a watchful eye on the ancient buildings for any signs of movement. At one time this street had been at the centre of local nightlife. There were paint-blistered signs for old drinking houses and dead neon tubes spelling out the names of long-forgotten nightclubs.

She came across a building with a tall brick façade and wide glass entrance that, at first, she took to be a church.

Inside, she found a wide staircase covered with the ruined remains of a red carpet. It was only when she saw the faded posters, hanging from the walls, featuring barely clad women and impossibly square-jawed men that she realised what this really was.

'It's a cinema,' she breathed.

She had been told about cinemas by her father when she was little, though even he had never seen one himself. He told her it was a place where people would go to sit in the darkness to watch magical stories that would take you to far-away lands and new worlds where you could have impossible adventures. She tried to imagine the people of the village sitting together to share an experience like that and couldn't. She decided that cinemas were just one more thing that had been washed away for good by the Great Rains.

At the bottom of the hill, she came to a large junction as wet and silted as an old riverbed. Broken street furniture and road signs littered the pavements, street lamps lay toppled like dead trees and ruined shop awnings hung in rags like rotten vegetation. She sighed; if there had once been an order to this chaotic jumble of streets, then she could not see it now.

She took out the map that Cromerty had given to her and frowned. At first the map appeared to make little sense but, when she turned it in her hand and compared the map with what she saw around her, she began to see something in the chaos. This line here was the street she had just walked down. This junction must be the brown spider in the centre of the map where Cromerty had drawn the words 'Cam'en Town' underneath a small red circle with a blue bar.

She scanned the other side of the street and crossed the

road to a dark brick building with wide arches and steel shutters pulled across a broad entrance. Every piece of glass in the building had been shattered and the hoardings around the entrance had long ceased to be legible. But one sign, made from painted steel, remained. It was formed of a red circle and a dark blue bar with white lettering across the centre. The sign was grimy, obscured by thick streaks of mud. She wiped it clear with her sleeve and traced out the letters with her finger.

Camden Town.

There could be no mistake, this must be the 'Cam'en Town' marked on Cromerty's map. At some point, the steel shutters covering the entrance had been forced open and there was now a narrow gap, just wide enough for a person to squeeze through. *Or a ghostman.* She pushed the thought away.

She squeezed through the gap, taking care not to jostle the contents of her bag, and found herself standing in a cavernous hall filled with watery echoes. And, once again, she was struck with the feeling of being in a church.

The crude torch picked out a tall hallway lined with glazed brickwork. A small glass kiosk stood at one end of the hall opposite four steep staircases that descended into the darkness. The torch beam alighted on sign on the wall bearing the word 'UNDERGROUND' in large white letters.

Her father had also told her about the Underground. He said that before the Great Rains, people had travelled on long trains that ran through tunnels under the earth. He said the tunnels ran all over the city, and that people could go anywhere they wanted without ever seeing the daylight. The thought made India's flesh grow cold.

According to the map, she was right on top of the place where Cromerty claimed to have buried the 'demon'. The thought of Cromerty bringing a body all the way out here by herself seemed far-fetched, but there was only one way to be certain.

She stood at the top of one of the staircases and looked down into the darkness. Her first surprise was that the stairs were made of metal and they fitted together like teeth. She realised that at one time they would have moved, carrying people relentlessly down into the darkness as though they were being fed into the mouth of a great machine.

The sight of the endlessly straight staircase disappearing into gloom made the hairs rise on her arms and on the back of her neck and she felt a primitive urge to turn and run. No one knew if the ghostmen were real or just tall stories spawned by home-made liquor. But if they were real, then this might be exactly the sort of place they would live.

A sudden noise made her spin around quickly. The torch caught a gleam of yellow eyes and greasy black fur as the rat skittered along a pipe and out of sight.

She forced herself to breathe slowly. This really would not do. She had seen what happened to people who lost their nerve. First came twitchiness that made them jump at every noise, then came the paralysing fear and, once that had set in, full-blown panic was not far behind. And when that happened, that was usually when people managed to get themselves killed. She was a tech-hunter, she reminded herself, and she had been in worse places than this.

She gathered up her satchel and arranged the shotgun so that she could hold it in front of her while still carrying the torch. Then she took a deep breath and started down the stairs.

Her boots echoed noisily on the steel treads. She moved warily, her torch barely penetrating the gloom ahead and, after a few minutes, she stopped and cursed under her breath. The stairs opened into a wide hallway with several smaller tunnels spidering off it into the darkness. The flood-waters had not entirely receded here, and the hallway was partially filled with an oily, black pool that smelled of sewage and rot.

She looked first at the map and then again at the foul waters and sighed. Surely Cromerty couldn't have brought the body down here? The old woman must have lied to her, and this map was no more than a joke from beyond the grave.

She pulled out the small device she had used earlier and the LEDs bathed her face in red light as she scrutinised the readout. But the lights remained stubbornly steady. She let out a relieved laugh that echoed away through the watery tunnels. That proved it. The old witch had definitely been lying.

She was about to turn and leave when the lights blipped.

It had been so quick that at first she thought she had imagined it. She panned the device around in a wide arc. When she aligned the device with the tunnel on the right, it happened again. Two of the lights on the box flared briefly.

It was the faintest of signals, but there could be no mistake: there was only one thing that could give off a signal like that. And that meant that Cromerty's map was real.

She returned the device to her backpack and adjusted the shotgun and torch. Then, steeling herself for what was to come, she descended the last few stairs into the filthy black waters.

The water was freezing, chilled by a hundred winters, and it stank. The smell was so overpowering that the bile rose in her throat. She spat the taste away and then continued her descent; this was no time to back out. Bella's safe return depended on what she was about to do next.

She kept descending until the freezing waters reached her waist. She looked longingly back up the stairs, then pushed the thought away. After another step, she mercifully found herself at the bottom of the stairs. She stood for a moment in the chest-high water, allowing her body to adjust to the cold, and then struck out along the right-hand tunnel.

It was slow progress, wading against the stagnant flood-waters. The stink was bad enough, but the surface was thick with floating rubbish, pieces of grimy plastic, chunks of wood and every conceivable piece of flotsam that had been washed down there over the course of a century.

The weak light from the torch sent weird patterns up the grimy walls, illuminating long-forgotten billboards. The faded pictures were filled with smiling, healthy people in clean clothes driving shiny cars along deserted country roads with no floodwaters or tyre-burners to be seen. Strangest of all were the adverts for something called 'perfume', which came in elaborate potion bottles and whose purpose she could only guess at.

The past was a different world to the one she knew. The people who lived there looked like they led perfect lives with literally everything a person could have wanted and none of them seemed to care about what was coming. Despite all the warnings, the Great Rains had still taken them by surprise and the fifty-year downpour had left nothing but starvation and desolation in its wake.

She felt almost sorry for them.

Mercifully, the tunnel came to some steps that led to a higher section. She ascended the steps and stood for a moment to let the thick water drain from her clothes. Signs directed her towards different platforms. She checked the detector again and picked up a signal on the left. She was getting closer.

She followed another tunnel and emerged onto a darkened platform. The sound of dripping water echoed through the darkness, telling her she was now in a much larger space. When she swung the torch around, she saw decay everywhere she looked.

Sodden roof panels sagged like rotten vegetation and electrical wires hung in swags from lighting and signage fixtures that had long been removed. The floor was thick with a paste of litter, mud and old rags and every surface was covered with thin green slime.

She walked cautiously along the platform, every step echoing through the vast cavern. She tried to imagine this place filled with people but she couldn't picture it; the sense of death and decay was just too overpowering.

At the edge of the platform, she looked down on a set of rusted steel tracks that disappeared into black tunnels at either end. Another check of the detector confirmed the signal was coming from the tunnel on the left.

Her heightened senses picked up a faint scratching sound behind her and she whirled around in a fright. The noise had been almost non-existent, but it stood out in the silence like a shout. She passed the torch carefully over the debris-strewn platform, but could see nothing out of the ordinary. *Probably a rat*, she told herself. But when she remembered the rat she had seen in the entrance hall, the thought gave her little comfort.

She paused briefly as the torch picked out a pile of rags heaped against the wall. Something about the shapeless bundle felt slightly out of context with its surroundings. She was about to turn away, when the bundle moved.

She watched with mounting horror as thin arms spidered from the bundle and a pale, domed head emerged from beneath the shreds of foul cloth. The thing hauled itself into an upright position and turned in her direction.

When she saw the face of the creature, she gasped and took a step backwards and it took all of her willpower not to scream. The skin was as pale and translucent as uncooked fish and the milk-white eyes reminded her of spiders' eggs. Pustulant sores the size of her palm had robbed the face of ears, nose, eyelids and lips and had pulled the mouth into a horror-show rictus grin.

There could be no mistake. The creature she was staring at could only be a ghostman.

8

THE TOMB

The horror scrambled to its feet, swaying slightly as though unused to taking its full weight on its spindly frame. It was emaciated, and hunched as if its very bones were losing their ability to keep it upright. The thin rags stretched over its body barely covered its naked filth and India caught a whiff of its rotten stench as the creature took a shambling step forwards.

She looked around for an escape route but the ghostman now stood between her and the exit. The head turned from side to side as though seeking something with its blind, white eyes and she realised, with another wave of revulsion, that it was sniffing the air like a dog. It was smelling her scent.

She took another step backwards and, at the sound of her boot on the concrete, the beast's head snapped in her direction. It might be blind, she thought, but down here in the darkness, other senses seemed to have compensated.

She took another step and immediately the ghost-creature dropped to a low crouch, bone-thin arms reaching at the air before it. It raised its head and made a series of sharp clicking noises with its mouth, as it panned from side to side. *Echo-location*, she thought, and some part of her brain marvelled at how the creature had adapted to a life of perpetual night.

With impossible speed, the creature scuttled towards her, halving the distance between them in less than a second and throwing out its arms in a fast grabbing movement that closed on thin air. India gasped. The speed of the movement had taken her completely by surprise. The way the creature's legs had moved reminded her more of a cockroach than anything human. Another lunge like that and she would be in its grasp.

She remembered the shotgun slung around her shoulders and, cursing her stupidity, she pulled it free and turned it towards the creature.

'That's far enough, ugly,' she growled, sounding more self-assured than she felt. 'Take another step and you'll get both barrels.'

If the creature understood what she was saying, it showed no sign. It sniffed at the air again, then it opened its jaws and hissed. The open mouth was blood-red and filled with rotten teeth, and the sound it made was filled with malice. Then it made another lunge towards her.

She could not have said whether she consciously pulled the trigger or whether fear had involuntarily tightened the muscles of her hand. The gun fired with a blast that reverberated endlessly around the tunnel walls. She had a vision of the creature's open maw coming at her face before the skull exploded in a wash of brain matter and bloody fragments and the wrecked body was flung to the floor.

She fought back the bile that rose in her throat and took another step backwards from the bloody mess. She almost didn't see the second creature as it lunged from the shadows. She caught a glimpse of the blood-red mouth and milk-white eyes as ragged fingernails clawed at her jacket.

She hammered the butt of the gun into the bridge of the creature's nose and it staggered backwards with a venomous hiss. The gun roared a second time, striking the ghostman full in the chest and hurling it backwards in a welter of blood and gore.

As the echoes of the blast died away, she gasped for breath and looked down at the corpses. Now that they were dead, it was clear that they had once been human. But the years of living in darkness had robbed them not just of their eyes, but of their humanity, until all that remained was the hunger and the relentless drive to feed on whatever strayed down here. They reminded her of the blind, white maggots that burrowed into the flesh of dead meat.

She turned away from the scene abruptly and vomited onto the ground.

She wiped her mouth, took a slug of water from her bottle and took stock. She would have to work fast now. It seemed sensible to assume that there would be more of the creatures and if so, the gunshots would almost certainly bring them running.

She consulted the detector again and was rewarded with a strong signal from the left-hand tunnel. She hopped down from the platform onto the tracks and started along the rails into the absolute blackness of the tunnel mouth. The weak, yellow torch beam penetrated no more than a few feet before it was swallowed up by the gloom.

Her heart began to hammer in her chest. For all she knew, she might be heading into an entire nest of those creatures. But, she reminded herself, she had a friend who was depending on her.

She stepped awkwardly along the unevenly spaced ties and tried not to think about the scuttling sounds that came from the darkness all around her. About a hundred metres into the tunnel, all six lights on the detector illuminated at once.

She allowed herself a small smile. There was only one thing that gave off a signal like that and it was close by. She shone the beam across the tracks and up the walls of the tunnel before alighting on an iron cover set into the brick-work of the tunnel wall.

The cover was about half a metre wide, secured in place by a series of large iron bolts around the edge. She frowned; how on earth had Cromerty managed to do those up by herself and, more importantly, how was she supposed to undo them? She cursed. Cromerty had been *really* deter-mined to keep this body hidden. Perhaps the old woman really had believed she was burying a demon.

Another search on the ground turned up a rusted iron spanner submerged in a filthy puddle, which she was relieved to find was the right size. Removing the bolts, though, was a different matter. Several years of rust had sealed the bolts into place and it took nearly an hour of heaving and grunting in the near darkness before she was able to remove the last one.

I must smell like a sewer by now, she thought as she wiped the sweat from her eyes. She stood back and regarded the cover carefully before taking aim and striking a blow with the spanner. The iron rang like a bell under the blow as the rust let go its hold and the cover clanged to the ground to reveal a dense black hole.

She leaned into the hole and cautiously shone the torch, half-expecting the gaping jaws of a ghost creature to come lunging out at her. Instead, she found a narrow brick chamber, musty but relatively dry compared to the rest of the station.

On the far side of the chamber, the torch picked out a long bundle of rags one wall. For a moment, she feared it might be another ghostman. But when she looked closer, she saw that this figure was taller and carried more bulk than either of the emaciated creatures she had seen earlier.

It was a squeeze to get through the narrow entrance but, once inside, the brick chamber offered more room to move around. She kneeled on the floor and inspected the body. It was cloaked in a long robe-like garment that was frayed with age and had been patched numerous times. That made sense, she thought. She knew he frequently travelled using the disguise of a holy man.

She felt carefully along the two long legs and tight midsection until she reached the head. Underneath the robe, the body was further wrapped with thick bands of linen that covered almost every exposed surface. She pulled at the wrappings around the head and quickly exposed a smooth-faced helmet. She looked on the blank expression and bit her lip. It was a long time since she had seen that face.

She linked her arms around the creature's neck and hauled the body into an upright position. It was heavier than she remembered, so much so that she had to brace her feet against the wall for extra leverage. But eventually, she managed to wedge the body against the bricks so that it stayed in place.

She used the water from her bottle to rinse the accumulated dirt from the face plate, then pulled back the wrappings and continued rinsing the chest and torso until she was looking at a smooth metal creature, taller and more powerfully built than a man and wrapped in a flexible metal skin that suggested a ripple of muscle beneath.

It was a creature that belonged firmly to that old world where people had seemed to live such perfect lives. But it was also a world where they had made weapons that could kill on an industrial scale. Weapons that thought for themselves, made their own decisions and which were virtually unstoppable.

Weapons like this one.

A sound from the tunnel made her glance over her shoulder anxiously. This was not the sort of place to wait around longer than you had to. She returned to the machine before her and fumbled with a catch at the front of its chest. A small panel slid aside with a whisper of pneumatics to expose a hole the size of her fist, sunk deep into the chest cavity. The hole was empty.

So that was how the old woman did it, she thought. She'd removed the power supply. It was just as well she'd thought to bring her own.

She found the cloth-wrapped tube nestling in the bottom of her bag and lifted it out with both hands. When she pulled back soft cloth, the brick chamber was suddenly filled with clear blue light that gave it the feel of an aquarium.

She swallowed hard. The sight of a plasma charger never failed to make her heart beat faster. A device like this had the potential to power a machine like this one for decades. But plasma chargers were one of the many things that the world had forgotten about and very few people knew what they were, let alone where to find one. It was why they were one of the most prized finds among tech-hunters.

She examined the glass to check that the seals were intact. The charger had taken her nearly a month to find and it had had a rough journey in her satchel. It wouldn't do to blow herself to pieces when she was so close to achieving her goal. Satisfied that the device was safe, she slid it into the creature's chest cavity with a hiss of expelled air. when she turned the handle, the device locked into place with a machined click.

She sat back and waited. For a long time, nothing seemed to happen. She bit her lip. After all she had done to get here, this had to work. It simply had to. Bella was depending on it.

Then she heard a faint clattering from inside the body of the creature, the faint whisper of electric relays and pneumatics coming awake. She sensed rather than heard the slight hum of contained power as electrons began to flow through its neural pathways. An electric shiver ran through the creature's framework and a faint blue light scanned once across the inside of the glass visor and back again.

And then it moved. A sudden simultaneous spasm of all its limbs that was immediately stilled. Then, very slowly, the head raised and turned in India's direction. The blue light scanned back and forth across the visor, absorbing visual imagery on a trillion wavelengths.

'Human,' it said eventually. 'Female. Approximately twenty-five standard years.' The creature paused and the blue light continued scanning. After several seconds, it spoke again. 'Bentley,' it said. 'India.'

She smiled. 'Hello, Calculus,' she said. 'It's good to see you too.'

The android regarded her for a long time, scrutinising her face. 'How long?' he said eventually. The voice was deep and resonant and sounded slightly mournful.

India chewed her lip. 'About two years. That old witch Cromerty told me she buried you down here. She had some idea that you were going to bring destruction on the village.'

The android took this information on board and was quiet. India could hear his internal relays ticking within the creature's skull as he ran computations, analysed available data and considered his next statement. 'That is correct,' he said. 'The old woman removed my plasma charger and sealed my body in here.'

India frowned. 'That's a pretty tricky thing to do to a war droid,' she said. 'Did you just stand by and let her?'

'Yes.'

'Why?'

'Because I asked her to and if she had not done as I asked, I really would have brought destruction on the village.' He examined the panel in his chest where India had inserted the new plasma charger. 'Shortly after I arrived here, I discovered that my old plasma charger had developed a leak. If I had stayed, the radiation would have killed everyone within a five-mile radius of the village.'

India stared at the android. 'So you asked Cromerty to shut you down?'

'Yes. She was surprisingly quick to agree. If you ask me, I think she does not approve of artificial life forms.'

'What happened?'

'She brought me down here and I instructed her on how to remove the faulty charger. After that, she was going to seal the chamber so I would not be discovered by other tech-hunters. She said she would dispose of the faulty charger in one of the deep shafts beneath the station, at some risk to herself, I should add.'

'Cromerty's dead,' said India flatly. 'She died last night.'

The android took this information on board. 'Quite possibly from the effects of the radiation exposure,' he said. 'She was a very brave woman.'

'I don't understand. If you knew you were a danger to the village, then why didn't you just leave?'

'You may remember, India, that when you sent me here you gave me a priority one order to keep close to your sister and make sure she wasn't in any danger,' said the android.

'I just wanted you to look out for her.'

'If I had stayed close as you instructed, I would have put her in great danger of radiation poisoning. But had I left, I would have been disobeying your direct order, which is forbidden by my core programming. Getting myself buried here was the only way I could stay close to your sister and at the same time ensure I did not endanger the village.'

India frowned. 'That's twisted logic, even for you.'

'Then perhaps, in future, you should be more careful when giving contradictory orders to an android,' he said. He sat up and examined his fingers, flexing them as though to banish stiffness. 'Thank you, for bringing a new charger with you,' he said. 'I would not have relished spending any more time in this hole.'

'You're welcome,' she replied with a frown. 'I figured something had gone wrong when I didn't hear from you. Bringing a spare charger was just a precaution. It cost me nearly four ounces of gold.'

The android thought about this. 'Then I'd say you were ripped off quite badly,' he said. 'But I will endeavour to repay your investment. I have information.'

'What sort of information?'

Calculus sat up and wiped the worst of the mud from his arms and torso. 'Before I was shut down, I witnessed a significant increase in Southsider activity.'

India rolled her eyes. 'Tell me about it.'

'When I saw how many raids Southsiders were carrying

out, I did some investigations of my own. I travelled to the southern shore to see what was happening.'

'You've been there? What did you find out?'

'The population of South London has grown hugely. It has become a trading centre for weaponry and old-tech as well as slaves and mercenaries. I believe there are now several thousand people living there.'

'Several thousand?' India's eyes opened wide in surprise. She had never seen more than a few hundred people in any one place around Lake London before.

'Yes, but that was over two years ago when I was last active. I think it is highly likely that their numbers have increased since then. I believe they may now pose a significant threat to the inhabitants of the Northside.'

'You might say that,' she said wryly.

The android looked at her curiously. 'Has something of importance happened since I have been inactive?'

She nodded. 'I've got quite a lot to catch you up on,' she said. 'But right now, there's only one thing you need to know.'

'Which is what?'

'Get yourself ready. We're going to war!'

9

THE AEROSTAT

B y the time they reached the surface, it was already well into the afternoon and the shadows were growing longer across the old city. India hurried them back through the shattered streets, anxious not to be caught in this place after sundown. They found the motorcycle where India had left it, picked clean of its wheels, engine, fuel tank and lights. India stared at the metal skeleton and cursed.

'I didn't think scavengers would venture this far into the old city.'

'Scavengers would risk a lot for a vehicle like this,' said Calculus. He had pulled up his hood and wrapped his cloak tightly around his body so that he had the appearance of a very tall monk. 'Perhaps you would like me to carry you back to the village?'

'Thanks, but I'll walk. I'm not sure arriving by piggy-back would do much for my credibility.'

'As you wish.'

It took over an hour to get back to the village, in part because they had to take a diversion to avoid a roaming pack of dogs. India took the time to fill in the android on what had happened since he had been deactivated.

'So, do you have any idea where they might have taken your sister on the Southside?' he asked.

'The man I questioned said they were from a place called Glass Town. But that doesn't make much sense. Glass Town was a tiny place when I lived here.'

'I believe the situation may have changed, India,' said the android. 'When I visited the Southside, I encountered several large settlements around the area known as Glass Town. It appears to have grown in size considerably and now seems to be an economic centre for slave trading as well as buying and selling old-tech.'

'That fits with what I heard about the Pinkerton twins,' said India.

'The Pinkerton twins?'

'I think they're slave traders and mercenaries.'

'I know who they are. The Pinkertons are notorious in the Eastern tech fields. I have to warn you, if they really have taken your sister then getting her back will not be easy. The Pinkertons are notoriously violent and ruthless with anyone who opposes them.'

India stopped walking and turned to look at him. 'So, what are you saying? You don't want to help?'

'I will do whatever you ask of me, India,' said the android. 'But, even with the assistance of a war droid, you will still need a significant number of people to ensure success in the venture.'

'Don't worry, Sid's working on it. He's organising some boats and rounding up the villagers for a raiding party. He should be ready to go as soon as we get back.'

'Sid?' Calculus looked down at her in a way that

suggested he might be peering over the top of a pair of glasses. 'You continue to have dealings with Sidney Stone?'

'He's good with a gun and I trust him.'

'May I remind you that Sid has not always proved to be the most reliable of individuals in the past. Indeed, you may remember that on our first encounter he shot me, in the chest, an injury that led to the death of my last body.'

'That was a long time ago, Calc. And Sid's changed a lot since those days. Don't worry, he can be trusted.'

'Sid works as a gun for hire, and since you have hired him to protect you, I would suggest his loyalty can only be trusted for as long as your money lasts.'

'All right, you've made your point. If you don't trust him, then trust me. Sid will have a raiding party ready to go when we get back.'

Getting back into the village proved more challenging than India had anticipated. As they approached along the track that led from the old city, they were met on the path by Betty and a posse of four men, all heavily armed. Betty stood in the centre of the track with her feet apart and her thumbs tucked into her belt as the men lined up behind her.

'Welcome back,' she said, sounding distinctly unwelcoming. 'Who's your friend?'

Calculus had pulled up the hood of his robe and tucked his hands into his sleeves so that no part of his metal skin was showing. From a distance he could pass as a man, albeit one that was nearly seven feet tall.

He's a friend of mine,' said India, 'a holy man. He's come to help find my sister. I'll vouch for him.'

Betty snorted. 'Is that a fact? Well, I'm still not sure who vouches for *you*, so I don't reckon that carries much weight.'

India frowned. 'I don't have time for this. Where's Vincent?'

'Haven't you heard? Vincent's out of action. *I'm* the authority around here now.'

India studied the woman thoughtfully. It hadn't taken long for Vincent to lose his grip on power. Still, she hoped that Betty would listen to reason. 'My friend is pretty good in a fight,' she called out. 'He's coming with us on the raiding party.'

Betty stuck out her jaw. 'I don't doubt he's good in a fight. I just don't want to be the one he's fighting.' The men behind her laughed openly and cradled their guns.

India sensed she was losing the argument. 'Look, I'm only trying to help here.' She held out her hands. 'Don't you want to get back the people who were taken?'

'None of them are my family,' said Betty bluntly.

'Is that all you care about?' India felt rage boil inside her and the blood flushed her face. 'You look after your own and to hell everyone else? When I lived here, this used to be a community; we looked out for each other.'

India took a step forwards and the four men immediately levelled their guns. She sensed Calculus readying for action behind her and cursed herself for allowing the situation to get out of control so quickly.

Fortunately, Betty did not seem quite ready to escalate. She watched Calculus warily and then stood down her men with a wave of her hand. 'All right,' she said. 'You can come back inside. But your holy man stays out here where we can see him.'

India was ready to argue but Calculus interrupted her. 'I think it might be diplomatic to accept her terms,' he said quietly. 'I am happy to wait out here until you are ready for me.'

India reluctantly agreed and Calculus sat down by the side of the track and crossed his legs in a lotus position. He bowed his head in the posture of someone in deep meditation.

Betty and her men seemed as taken aback by the android's behaviour as India but they parted to allow India to pass and then followed her inside. Once through the gates, India immediately noticed that the streets seemed even more deserted than they had earlier.

'Half the village has upped and left since this morning,' said Betty. 'If things carry on like this, we'll be a ghost town by sunset.'

India left Betty at her cottage and continued to Vincent's house. She found Sid sitting at an outside table with his pistols laid out on a cloth before him as he lovingly applied lubricant to their working parts.

'Don't you ever stop doting over those guns?' she said, still feeling agitated from her encounter with Betty. 'You're like a lovesick teenager.'

Sid looked up from his work. 'You find your friend?'

'Yes. But they made him wait outside the village. Betty didn't trust him.'

'They didn't trust a giant robot war-machine? Can't imagine why.'

India glowered at Sid and thought about what Calculus had said. Just how far would Sid's loyalty go if she wasn't paying him? 'So, what have you been doing while I was gone? How many do we have for the raiding party?'

Sid frowned thoughtfully. 'Including you, me and the metal man?' he said. 'Three.'

'What?'

'You heard right. None of these village hicks want to risk their necks to save your sister.'

India slumped down onto a rough wooden stool opposite Sid. 'But... what about their own people, what about the children?'

Sid shrugged. 'They told me it was better to be a live coward than a dead hero. They've got a point, too. There's not a rat in in a mincer's chance that we'd make a successful raid against the Pinkertons, even if the whole village was behind us. You might as well face it, India, your sister's as good as gone.'

She pressed her lips together tightly. 'That might be how you weigh up human lives, Sid. But Bella's my sister and sisters don't run out on each other. Now, I'm going to Glass Town with Calculus and we're either going to find Bella and the others or we're not. And frankly, I don't much care anymore whether you or any of these people come with me.'

Sid snapped shut the cylinder of the pistol he was cleaning and returned the gun to his belt. 'Now, just hold on to your cattle,' he said. 'I never said I wasn't coming with you. I just said I wasn't holding out too much hope of coming back.'

India swallowed. 'You're still coming? After everything you just said.'

He shrugged and tucked the second gun into his belt. 'You're still paying me, ain't you? Besides, I can't bear the stink of this place any longer.'

India bit her lip. 'Thanks, Sid,' she said.

They were interrupted by scuffling from the doorway as Vincent lumbered awkwardly out of the house. He looked pale and drawn. His leg was tightly splinted between two heavy wooden poles and he was using a crutch fashioned from a tree branch. The foot of his broken leg appeared twisted at a sickening angle and he winced with pain at each movement.

They watched him lower himself onto a seat beside the

door and fight to regain his breath. 'You're looking... better, Vincent,' offered India.

'I look like shit,' he gasped. 'But no one else is prepared to help, so here I am.'

'I already told you, you ain't coming with us,' said Sid. 'We've got enough to think about without having to carry a casualty.'

Vincent flinched but they could all see that Sid was right. Vincent was in no condition to travel to the Southside, let alone fight anyone when he got there. Nevertheless, India couldn't help feeling sorry for him.

'What we really need,' she said softly, 'is some transport. We have to be able to get to Glass Town without them seeing us coming. Can you get us a fast boat?'

Vincent shook his head. 'We don't have anything like that,' he said. 'But I've arranged for something better.'

Sid frowned. 'What's better than a fast boat?'

'I'll show you. Help me down to the town square; I can't do a damn thing for myself with this wretched leg.'

'The town square' was perhaps too grand a term for the patch of mud and cow dung in the centre of the village. In one corner, a large tyre furnace was being stoked by two men as it belched tar-thick smoke into the air. A short distance away was the remains of an old car, stripped of tyres, engine, axles, seats and even the roof.

The steel carcass was attached to heavy ropes and a tangle of nylon strings. The strings were attached in turn to heavy folds of tar-covered canvas, which lay in disarray on the ground, fluttering in the late afternoon breeze from the lake.

'This sure ain't no fast boat,' said Sid, examining the canvas.

'This is better than any fast boat,' said Vincent. 'Our

guys have been working on this as a way of getting to and from the towers more quickly. It's an aerostat.'

He grinned at India and Sid as if they were supposed to know exactly what this meant. 'What the hell's one of them?' said Sid.

'I know what it is,' said India. 'It's a lighter-than-air craft.'

'That's right,' said Vincent. He beckoned to one of the young men tending the furnace. 'Let me get one of the guys to explain it in detail.' The man came towards them, wiping his hands on a greasy rag.

'Lighter than air?' scoffed Sid. He kicked the toe of his boot against the metal chassis. 'This thing's heavier than a sack of bricks. And what's with the sail?'

'It's not a sail,' said the man as he approached. 'It's a balloon. We rig it up to one of the furnace valves and pump in hot air. When it's full, it'll carry you aloft, no problem.'

'This is Tobias,' said Vincent. 'He's one of our engineers.

Tobias patted the side of the car chassis affectionately. 'I did all the calculations myself,' he said, beaming like a proud parent. 'If the wind is in the right direction, we think it will take you across the lake in less than half the time of a boat.'

'You think?' said India. 'Have you actually tried this thing?'

'Of course.' Tobias looked offended. 'Last week we sent two goats up to five hundred feet.'

'I ain't no goat,' snapped Sid. 'What about people?'

Vincent shrugged. 'Tobias's father was the man who invented it. He flew the prototype.'

'All right,' said India. 'Where do we find him?'

'In the cemetery,' said Tobias. 'It turned out the ropes

Dad used weren't strong enough. But we fixed that. Don't worry, it's safe as houses now.'

'Forget it,' said Sid. 'We ain't risking our necks in this home-made contraption. Just give us a damn boat.'

'We don't have any boats to spare,' said Vincent. 'And it took me all afternoon to persuade Betty to let you have this. It's the aerostat or nothing.'

India and Sid exchanged glances. She could see Sid was not happy and even though the aerostat looked like a death trap, she was keen to end the conversation before Sid lost his temper. Besides, Vincent was right about one thing: the aerostat would give them the advantage of surprise.

If it worked.

'All right, we'll take it,' she said. 'How soon can it be ready?'

'Take a couple of hours to get her filled with hot air,' said Tobias. 'She should be ready for you before nightfall.'

It was decided quickly. Vincent gave Tobias instructions to ready the balloon and provide anything else that India and Sid needed for the journey, then he limped back in the direction of his cottage. As soon as Tobias had moved out of earshot, Sid turned on India.

'Are you crazy? Travelling in this heap is as sure as writing a suicide note and putting a gun barrel in your mouth. Them Southsiders will see us coming for twenty miles and by the time we run out of hot air they'll be waiting on the ground like a pack of hungry hyenas.'

'It's not that bad, Sid,' she pleaded. 'We'll be travelling in the dark and that balloon is as black as tar. There's no way the Southsiders will see it coming. Besides, it's the only help we're going to get from these people. They don't seem to care about helping anyone, not even their own families.'

'Yeah, well, I'm beginning to feel the same way.' Sid spat

on the ground. 'Every time I think about how much you're gonna pay me, it sounds less and less like its enough.'

'Well, it's all the money I have,' she shot back. 'So you can either clear out now or you can go and round up whatever weapons you can find to take with us. At this stage, I don't particularly care which.'

Sid grumbled under his breath but he didn't argue further and, to her great relief, he wandered away in search of weaponry. India remained in the square as Tobias connected a long, flexible hose to the home-made balloon and, over the next few hours, she watched as the great envelope swelled and fattened.

By sundown, the balloon had raised itself from the ground like a giant head and the support ropes began to tighten and take the weight of the car. The metal chassis creaked as it lifted into the air and then came to a stop as the anchor ropes held it fast, a few feet above the ground.

The balloon creaked and swayed in the evening breeze like an animal, straining to be free of its tethers. At one point, one of the supporting ropes snapped with a noise like a pistol shot and the car lurched to one side. India stepped back in alarm.

Tobias quickly moved to secure a new rope and in no time the car was level again. Sid returned a short while later, carrying two shotguns with half a dozen cartridges and a fresh box of ammunition for his pistols.

'I tried again to get some of 'em to come with us,' he said. 'But they're as scared as chickens in a dog fight. Looks like we're on our own for this one.'

As well as the guns, Sid had managed to secure two machetes and a lance with a sharpened metal tip. There was also a vicious-looking club with spikes on the end that he seemed particularly taken with and which he told her was called a 'morning star'. Lastly, wrapped in a burlap sack were two bottles of water and some bread and cooked meat. India thought that eating was likely to be the last thing on her mind but she was wise enough to know that this would probably change when the initial excitement had worn off.

When they were ready to leave, Betty was finally persuaded to allow Calculus into the village to join them. He arrived, with his hood still up, walking sedately and flanked by four of Betty's men. They held their shotguns at the ready and looked extremely nervous.

'Thank you, gentlemen,' said the android when they arrived. 'I am sure you all have other duties to attend to and I assure you I will be on my best behaviour whilst I am in your village. My intentions are not violent.'

The four men looked at each other with confusion on their faces. They were used to dealing with people whose intentions were generally very violent. They knew how to handle drunks, raiders, rustlers and thieves and any of the other many disturbances that regularly required their brawn and their weapons. But a holy man who spoke gently and assured them he would not cause trouble? This was something they were not equipped to deal with.

Reluctantly, they stepped back and drifted out of the square, throwing puzzled looks over their shoulders as they went. 'Master Sidney,' said Calculus when they were alone in the square. 'It is good to see you again.'

'Yeah, well, I can't say I feel the same way, robot,' drawled Sid.

'As I keep reminding you, Sidney, I am not a robot. I am an android. They are very different.'

Sid shrugged. 'Android, robot, it's all the same to me. You're a machine and I don't trust machines.'

'Really? I find that puzzling, Sidney. After all, at our first meeting it was you who shot me. If anything, it is I who should not trust humans.'

'All right, knock it off, you two,' said India irritably. 'This raiding party is going to be just the three of us against the whole of the Southside. I suggest we don't start fighting among ourselves before we even get there.'

Calculus turned to India and cocked his head in a strangely human gesture. 'Just the three of us? Do I take it that the villagers have no interest in assisting the rescue of their own people? That will make our task considerably more difficult.'

'Tell me about it,' grumbled India.

'In fact, I calculate that, even with my assistance, our odds of success against a gang of highly armed slavers would be less than one in fourteen thousand, six hundred and—'

'That's *enough*, Calc!' India ran her hand through her long hair in an exasperated fashion. For the first time, she allowed herself to think that maybe the villagers were right. Perhaps this was a hopeless cause.

Then she thought of Bella and what might be happening to her right now and she felt the cold fury taking hold once more. She drew herself up to her full height and addressed her companions. 'Listen up, you two. This rescue is going to take all our skill just to stay alive. Now, regardless of what you think of each other, I need both of you to watch my back. I have to know that you're thinking about the job in hand and not bickering with each other. Once we've rescued Bella, then neither of you ever have to speak to each other again. But until then, I need your word that you're going to focus on the job in hand.'

She glared at them with challenge in her eyes. Sid

shrugged and looked down at his feet. 'Sure,' he mumbled. 'I can play nice if he can.'

Calculus bowed his head graciously. 'And I give you my word that, whilst I am in your employment, I will carry out your orders faithfully and without distraction. And, as you know, an android's word is—'

'All right, let's get on with it,' snapped India. 'Get the last of the equipment in the car. I want to be underway before the sun goes down. Now where's Tobias?'

Tobias arrived with two helpers and they watched while he made some last-minute adjustments and topped up the balloon with hot air. Lastly, he tested the connecting ropes and, once he was satisfied, he stood back. 'All right, miss,' he said wiping his hands. 'She's good to go.'

India watched Calculus and Sid climb aboard and sit in opposite ends of the car as the ropes creaked under their combined weight. Then she crouched down and picked up a handful of dirt from the ground and let it sift through her fingers. She wondered just how long it would be before she was safely back on the ground again.

As she prepared to step into the car, there was a small tug at the back of her jacket. 'India?'

She turned to find Tom standing behind her. His face was pale and drawn and his eyes were red and tear-stained. Looking at him, she realised what hell the boy must have been through in the last twenty-four hours. She smiled. 'Hi, Tom. What is it?'

He seemed uncertain. 'I just wanted to say... I hope you find your sister...' He looked down. 'I hope you find mine, too.'

'I'll find all of them, Tom, don't worry,' she said with more confidence than she felt.

'And I wanted to give you this... for luck.' He slipped something long and cold into her hand.

She looked down at the small knife in her palm. It had a roughly hammered blade of around three inches, and a handle made from wrappings of old rag. It looked like something that might be used to peel fruit.

'I made it meself,' he said. 'Thought it might come in handy against them Southsiders.'

India wanted to laugh at the thought of trying to fight anyone with such a tiny implement but she nodded seriously and slipped it into her sleeve. 'Thanks, Tom. I'll keep it here for when I need it.' Tom nodded and stepped back and she turned away and climbed into the car.

As the seats had all been removed, there was nothing to sit on except for bare metal. She wedged herself uncomfortably against one of the doors, between Sid and Calculus. Sid had, once again, started to clean his guns while Calculus was looking out at the scene below.

Most of the remaining villagers had begun to gather in the square to watch the balloon depart and Calculus was attracting a huge amount of attention. Several small children ran around the car, trying unsuccessfully to attract the android's attention, while a crowd of men and women stood further back, pointing and muttering darkly behind their hands. She saw both Vincent and Betty among the crowds, standing apart and pretending not to notice the other.

When Calculus removed his hood, one or two of the crowd made signs with their hands that India knew were meant to ward off evil spirits. India supposed she couldn't blame them for being suspicious. After all, being suspicious of anything out of the ordinary was what had kept most of these people alive, and a war droid definitely fell into that category. All the same, the attention he was receiving was making her feel uncomfortable and she wished Calculus had kept his disguise in place until they were airborne.

When he had finished his checks, Tobias ushered away the children, and his assistants used axes to cut away the tether ropes anchoring the balloon to the ground. He paused, with his axe raised over the final rope. 'Best hold on to something,' he advised. 'With a full envelope, she'll go up like a rocket.'

'Bad choice of words,' muttered Sid under his breath.

'There's enough hot air in there to get you clean across the lake,' continued Tobias. 'She'll come down when she cools but if you want to descend earlier, just pull on that rope there.'

India checked the rope and made a mental note not to pull it by accident. 'OK. So, how do we refill the balloon for the journey back?' she asked.

Tobias made a face and shook his head. 'Only way to refill is if you got a furnace like this one. Otherwise, when this baby runs out of hot air, she ain't going anywhere.'

India sat up. 'Wait, what?' No one had suggested that the balloon was not good for the return journey. She began to get up to argue with Tobias but at that moment he swung the axe and severed the rope cleanly.

10

SOUTHBOUND

T rue to Tobias's word, the balloon launched into the sky like an uncaged animal. The supporting ropes snapped taut and the car was jerked skywards with such ferocity that India was thrown off her feet and would have fallen out altogether if Calculus hadn't caught her and pulled her back.

'That crappy double-crossing snake, Vincent,' she raged. 'He knew this trip was one-way and he never said anything. Probably afraid we'd change our minds, the bastard.'

'Relax,' drawled Sid. 'So what if we can't get back in the balloon? Southsiders got boats, don't they? We'll just take ourselves one of them.'

India was still fuming, but the view from the car as they rose into the air made it impossible to stay angry for long. She looked down at the upturned faces gathered in the square, growing steadily smaller beneath them. As the balloon rose higher, she had a complete view of the village, the mud tracks, the smoke from the tyre-burners and the damp stone houses, many now roofless and charred after the raid.

As their altitude increased, the balloon was caught by a stiff breeze that pulled them southwards. Beyond the village, they could see the ruined streets and shattered buildings of the old city spread out across the landscape like black mould.

The view across the lake on the other side of the car was significantly better. It was one of those rare evenings when the grey clouds had parted long enough to provide a brief glimpse of the sun as it sank in a blaze of red and gold. As the golden orb descended below the western horizon, London's usual watery tones were replaced for a brief moment by a dazzling display of orange and pink. The light sparkled like jewels on the water, transforming the tower blocks into pillars of ivory and yellow gold and, just for a moment, India thought this looked like the most beautiful place in the world.

And then, just as quickly, it was over. The horizon turned to the colour of a cooling campfire as greyness reasserted itself over the oily lake.

She looked up at the tar-black balloon that filled the view above them and checked the ropes securing them to the car. They seemed to be holding firm but India couldn't help thinking about Tobias's father. She imagined the sudden horror of seeing the ropes fail and of knowing that there was nothing you could do to save yourself. She quickly put the thought out of her mind.

Sid was leaning out over the front of the carriage, seemingly unconcerned by the vastness of the drop beneath them. 'Dang, they were right about one thing. This heap travels faster than any boat. We're already above them towers.'

India peered over Sid's shoulder and saw he was right. The balloon was nearing the centre of the lake and the city towers were directly beneath them, reaching up from the lake like broken fingers. She saw that the tallest of them was no more than fifty feet below them and realised it must be Cromerty's tower when she caught a brief glimpse of the open platform where they had discovered the dying woman.

When the cold wind became too much, they took shelter in the car. Sid glanced over at Calculus and nudged India. 'What's he doing now?' he said in a stage whisper. The android was sitting motionless at the far end of the car and had once again arranged his limbs into the lotus position. 'Has he shut down or something?'

'Actually, Sidney,' said the android suddenly, 'I was taking advantage of a few moments' peace to catch up on my meditation practice. I find it cleanses my circuits of unwanted data and enhances the clarity of my processing.'

Sid frowned. 'So, is that an android thing?'

'Not at all. It is a very human thing. I learned the techniques of meditation from a Buddhist master in Tibet.'

'Buddhist? You some kind of religious nutjob, robot?'

India shot Sid a look. She could sense trouble brewing again and she was not keen to have a fight break out in the confines of a hot-air balloon.

'I'm not sure what you mean by "religious nutjob", Sidney,' said Calculus loftily. 'However, I try to live by the principles of Buddhism. I do not steal, indulge in sensual pleasures, tell lies or take intoxicants. And I practise non-violence.'

India and Sid exchanged a look. 'So when you say you practise "non-violence"...' said India. 'What does that mean exactly?'

'I have learned that the violent ways of a war droid are a barrier to my spiritual growth,' replied the android. 'Therefore, I am committed to avoiding any actions that might harm another living creature, unless I am forced to act in self-defence.'

'You mean,' said Sid, 'you ain't gonna kill anyone unless they try and kill you first?'

'I believe that is what I said, Sidney,' said Calculus. 'You both seem a little perturbed by this news. Is something wrong?'

India frowned. 'In case it had escaped your notice, we're on a mission to rescue my sister from slavers.'

'I am aware of that, India.'

India rolled her eyes. She had forgotten how infuriating the android could be. 'Well, what are you planning to do when we get there? Force them into submission with harsh language?'

'Actually, that is quite a good idea,' said the android. 'I have often found that a violent situation can be avoided through negotiation. I advocate that we try that first.'

'Are you shitting me?' Sid stared at India with a horrified expression. 'When you told me you were bringing along a war droid, I thought it might be something that was actually useful in a fight. Not some cowardly, flower-waving... *peace freak*.'

'I assure you, Sidney, my actions are motivated by a concern for the sanctity of life, not by cowardice.'

'What's the damned difference!' yelled Sid. 'Either way it means you're going to be standing around, protecting your spiritual growth while we get our backsides kicked.'

'Please, Calc,' said India, trying to remain calm. 'Tell me you won't abandon us in a fight because of your principles. The odds are stacked against us enough as it is.'

'I will not make a promise I cannot keep,' replied the android. 'I am committed to coming with you on this rescue mission, but I intend to explore every avenue for a peaceful settlement of our differences with the Southsiders.'

There was nothing more to be said. While Calculus resumed his meditation, Sid turned away with his back to both of them and India buried her head in her hands. How could this be happening to her? When the villagers had refused to come with them, Calculus had been the one thing that gave her hope that they might succeed.

But it had been several years since she had last seen the android and it was clear that he was not the same person she had once known. All that she had with her to take on the Southsiders with was an angry young man and a Buddhist monk. *Surely*, she thought, *this can't get any worse. Can it?*

They sat in angry silence for the rest of the journey as the wind ferried the balloon southwards through the night. At one point India must have fallen asleep because she was woken by a nudge from Calculus.

'India, I believe we have nearly reached the far side of the lake. Look.'

They all stood up in the car and looked out over the side. The balloon was much lower now, and the black surface of the water was no more than two hundred feet below them.

About a mile across the water, they could clearly see the flickering orange flames of a dozen campfires strung out across the shoreline and the smell of burning tyres. Further inland was a brightly lit area that had the appearance of a chaotic market town, filled with rough wooden buildings and lit by burning braziers. The skeletal finger of a giant radio mast soared above the town, rising into the darkness, far above the height of the balloon. They could make out the figures of people moving around and the sounds of amplified music and thumping drums carrying across the water.

'I guess that's Glass Town,' muttered Sid.

'Indeed,' replied Calculus. 'Historically, this part of London was known as Crystal Palace, so named because it was once home to a cast-iron and glass structure built for the Great Exhibition of 1851 and which subsequently burned down in 1936. The transmission tower is over seven hundred feet high and—'

'That's enough, Calc,' snapped India. 'Can't you tell us something useful, like how many people are down there?'

There was a moment's pause, and they heard the whine of optical filters and lenses whirring into place behind the android's mask. 'I calculate there are approximately three hundred and eighty-five people in the main encampment with a further one hundred and fifteen in camps along the waterfront.'

'Five hundred?' India felt her heart sink. She had tried not to think about how many Southsiders they might encounter but she had hoped it would be a lot less.

'It may not be as bad as that,' offered Calculus. 'My sensors suggest that many of them are in a state of advanced inebriation. In addition, several more have been concentrated in one part of the main camp and appear to be held in a secure area with armed guards.'

India glanced up at the android. 'Prisoners?'

'That would be a reasonable conclusion.'

India felt a sting of fear. In her mind she had imagined Bella and the others being held by a relatively small gang. But this was virtually a whole town. There was no way they could fight so many.

'What about weapons?' she said. How many of the Southsiders have guns?'

The optics behind Calculus's mask whirred again. 'It's difficult to be precise,' he said. 'But as a rough estimate, I would say... all of them.'

'All of them?' India stared at the android, open-mouthed. Even the most well-armed settlements on the Northside rarely had more than a dozen guns in a whole village.

'Plus, I can see what appears to be an old anti-aircraft gun mounted near the radio mast. And I am detecting explosive devices along the shoreline. At a guess I would say the Southsiders have laid mines in the water.'

'So that's several hundred heavily armed hostiles,' said Sid. 'Not counting the booby traps and the heavy weaponry. So, are you thinking we should turn back yet?'

India swallowed. 'I'm not running out on my sister, Sid. You can turn back if you want to.'

Sid looked up at the balloon. 'It's not like I have a lot of choice in this thing.'

India looked down and realised they were now descending rapidly. 'Calc, is there anywhere we can put down safely?'

'Unfortunately, we have no means to steer the balloon,' he said. 'The best we can do is dump the remaining hot air and try to land somewhere where we are less likely to be seen. I calculate that on our present vector we will pass over a small wooded area to the west of the main town. The trees might offer us some cover.'

'Good enough,' said India. She grabbed at the rope Tobias had shown her. 'Tell me when.'

'This is not a precise art,' said Calculus. 'But I estimate that now would be as good a time as any.'

India jerked on the rope and there was a ripping sound from overhead as a panel tore free from the side of the balloon. The effect was immediate. The balloon began to drop like an anvil, leaving their stomachs behind with a sickening lurch.

'It's too fast,' cried India, clinging to a door handle for support. 'We'll be smashed to a pulp.'

'That is a possibility,' replied Calculus. 'However, I'm hopeful that the trees will—'

The car gave a colossal jolt as the car struck the first branch and threw them hard onto the metal floor. Then they were falling again, slamming into the thick boughs with a noise like an iron bell falling down a mine shaft. A particularly fierce blow sent the car spinning and tipped them at a terrifying angle so that Calculus had to catch hold of India to avoid her being thrown out.

They came to a halt with a neck-snapping jerk as the supporting ropes caught in the branches and arrested their fall. There was silence for several seconds as they swung freely in the branches with one end of the car tipped precariously towards the ground.

India raised her head carefully and checked herself. Apart from a few scratches, she seemed to be OK. 'Where's Sid?' she croaked. 'I can't see him anywhere.'

'Down here.' The voice came from the far end of the car. 'Can I get a little help here?'

Calculus disentangled himself from India and clambered down the car. He discovered Sid hanging from the end of the chassis with his feet dangling over empty air. The android grasped Sid's hand and quickly pulled him back inside the vehicle.

'You took your time,' was the only thanks Sid offered the android.

Calculus peered over the edge of the car at the ground. 'We are fortunate that the branches broke our fall,' he said.

'But we're still at least thirty feet above the ground. We will have to climb down the rest of the way.'

They gathered up the supplies they had brought with them but were disappointed to find that the machete and most of the food had been thrown out of the car and lay scattered on the forest floor somewhere below them.

'Damn. We'd have been glad of that before dawn,' said India.

'Still got this baby, though,' said Sid, brandishing the morning star before tucking it into his belt alongside his pistols.

When they had collected everything they could salvage, they began the climb down to the ground. India had been expert at climbing trees when she was younger but climbing out of a swinging car chassis in the pitch dark was something of a challenge.

Calculus led the way, reasoning that if a branch would hold him, it would hold any of them, and his illuminated visor provided them with some light. After twenty minutes of scrambling and a considerable number of additional scratches, they finally assembled on the forest floor.

'I can find no evidence that anyone detected our descent,' said Calculus.

'How far are we from the town, Calc?' said India.

The android paused and looked around, then pointed through the trees. 'The main town is about four hundred metres in that direction,' he said. 'But there are several small camps between here and there and I do not see how we can get there undetected.'

'We're not going to try,' said India, shouldering one of the shotguns. 'I figure that with this many people, there's no way that they can all know each other. And we don't look so different from the Southsiders we saw last night. As long as we have the right attitude, I reckon we can just walk through the middle of them.'

'Hide in plain sight?' said Calculus. 'An interesting and bold strategy, India. It might just work.'

'If they don't get suspicious at the sight of a seven-foot android, that is,' said Sid.

India looked Calculus up and down. 'There's not much we can do about your height, Calc, but put your hood up and keep that robe done up. If anyone asks, we'll just tell them you're a holy man visiting from Tibet and that you don't speak any English.'

'Oh sure,' said Sid. 'That'll throw them off the scent, for sure.'

'It will have to do,' said India. 'So, if we're all done with the chat, let's move out.'

11

GLASS TOWN

They forced their way through overgrown branches until they reached a small path that wound through the forest. Moving silently, they followed a network of muddy tracks meandering in the direction of the bright lights.

Keeping close to the forest edge, they passed the first of the campfires they had seen from the air. About twenty men and women were gathered around the fire, passing a bottle of brown liquid. Most appeared extremely drunk and one had passed out with his foot lying in the fire.

In a roped-off square of sand, a baying mob had gathered around a fight. The men in the ring faced off, bare-chested and clutching weapons. A man with the chest of a prize bull wielded a baseball bat with several nails driven through the end of it. His smaller opponent held a thick steel pipe like a samurai sword and weaved back and forth, looking for an opportunity to duck beneath his opponent's massive arms.

It was a one-sided fight. As they walked past the ring, the man with the baseball bat swung in a wide arc and the steel pipe was knocked into the undergrowth with a clang. The big man immediately followed up with a skull-crushing blow to his opponent's head and the smaller man folded like crushed paper. Their final view was of the smaller man being beaten to a bloody pulp as the crowd roared with approval.

'Nice people,' drawled Sid in a low voice.

'I expect we'll see a lot worse before we get out of here,' said India. 'So keep your wits about you.'

As they drew nearer to the glowing lights, the campfires became more numerous and crowds jostled along the narrow streets. Small market stalls lined the path on either side, selling fly-covered meats and rotten vegetables, while hanging chickens dripped blood onto the heads of passersby. 'Fresh cat,' bellowed a vendor who was roasting suspiciously small joints of meat over a brazier. 'Guaranteed no rats, rabies or mutations.'

A merchant with a hypnotic voice offered oils and balms that promised to cure everything from pimples to a broken neck while a group minstrels played tinny music on home-made instruments and collected coins in a tin. Sid paused to look over a stall selling guns, knives, helmets and other assorted weaponry.

'Ah, I see you are a man who knows his weapons, young sir,' oozed the stall holder as he eyed Sid's guns. 'Can I interest you in some body armour, perhaps?' He held up a vest with heavy steel plates sewn into large pockets around the torso. The vest was liberally stained with blood.

Sid curled his lip. 'Looks like your body armour ain't worth shit. You got any ammo?'

'Whatever you desire, young sir,' said the man with a bow. 'We have ammunition to fit all weapons, ancient and modern. If you'd like to step into the back, we can assess your needs.' He pulled aside a bead curtain at the back of the shop and invited Sid in with an oily smile.

India grabbed Sid's sleeve and pulled him away. 'What are you playing at? We don't have time for you to go shopping.'

Sid shrugged. 'You said we wouldn't attract attention if we had the right attitude. I'm just doing the same as everyone else.'

'There's such a thing as being too laid back, you know. Besides, we *are* attracting plenty of attention.'

Since they had arrived, Calculus's great height had been attracting more and more stares and comments. People pointed fingers at the robed figure and muttered darkly behind their hands as they passed along the street; several appeared to be following them from a distance.

'Keep moving,' hissed India. 'Perhaps we can lose ourselves in the crowds up ahead.'

'Not much chance of losing ourselves, with a seven-foot robot stomping along behind us,' muttered Sid. 'We're going to end up a target for every hired gun who wants to make a name for himself.'

'As I'm sure I don't need to remind you, Sidney,' said Calculus, 'I am an android and not a robot. However, I fear your conjecture is correct. I am aware that several young men are tracking our movements closely, and most of them are heavily armed.'

'Terrific,' muttered Sid. 'What great company you turned out to be.'

Calculus shooed at a small boy who had been trying to lift the hem of his robe to look underneath. The boy retreated a few paces and then made a rude gesture.

'How come you're so tall?' he demanded. 'I ain't never

seen a person as tall as you before. Who are ya? Are you a spy?'

Calculus stayed silent. His electronically enhanced voice would have given him away immediately. Dissatisfied with the lack of response, the boy turned his attention to Sid and India.

'How come he don't say nothin'?'

'He's foreign,' said India. 'A holy man. And he doesn't speak any English.'

The boy examined Calculus afresh and wrinkled his nose. 'Getouttahere!' he spat. 'He's a spy. I can smell 'em a mile off.'

If the boy believed Calculus was a spy, it did not seem to cause him any immediate concern. He fell into step beside India and Sid, squinting curiously at the pistols in his belt.

'Them your guns?' he asked with a sniff.

'Yes.'

'Kin I shoot one?'

'No.'

'Kin I jus' hold one, then?'

'No.'

The boy sniffed again and shrugged his shoulders. 'I don't give a cuss. They prob'ly got no bullets in 'em anyhow. You going to the games?'

India looked down at the boy. 'The games?'

'You know, *the games*,' said the boy, amazed at her stupidity. 'Last man standing gets to live. They had over fifty people in the ring last week. One bloke got his head cut off!' He grinned at the memory.

India swallowed. 'No, we're not here for the games.'

'Oh. Well, you must be here for the slave market, then?'

India stopped walking. 'There's a slave market?'

The boy clicked his tongue and rolled his eyes. 'What,

are you stupid or somethin'? It's a *Toosdee*. They always have a slave market on a *Toosdee*. All top quality, but you gotta get there early for the best ones.'

India and Sid exchanged a glance. 'Yes,' said India. 'You're right, we're here for the slave market. Can you show us where it is?'

The boy beamed. 'I knew it! Sure, I can show you where it is and I can show you the best place to stand so you can catch Ringmaster's eye.'

'You're quite the man to know around here,' said Sid.

'You bet I am. My uncle's the slave master so I can get you the best prices on the new batch.'

'New batch?' India crouched down to look the boy directly in the eye.

'The new batch. You know, the ones that come in yesterday from the Northside. Are you sure you're from around here?'

'Like she said,' said Sid. 'We're foreign.'

'You said *he* was foreign. You didn't say nothin' about where *you* was from.'

'Well, we're foreign too,' said India. 'So can you just show us where to find the slave market?'

'Sure, I *could*.' He gave them a gap-toothed grin and rubbed his fingers together. 'What's in it for me?'

It took several minutes of bargaining but finally, after India had rummaged through the assorted junk in her bag, they agreed he would take them in exchange for two dead batteries and a broken phone that India had been intending to repair.

The boy seemed delighted with his haul and quickly tucked them away into his own cloth bag. 'And I want a hold of his gun,' he added, wiping his nose on a sleeve.

'After you show us the slave market,' said Sid. 'Not before.'

The boy looked ready to argue but then thought better of it. 'OK, but don't go fergettin' now. This way.'

He led them towards the centre of the settlement where the market stalls became more crowded and they were reduced to a slow shuffle along the main thoroughfare. All the streets appeared to be converging on the soaring radio mast that loomed over everything and seemed to be the centre of all activity.

'This place never used to be any larger than our village,' whispered India. 'Now it's a like a small town. They've even got street lights.' She nodded at the pale globes strung between poles that lit the streets with an even yellow glow. Somewhere a generator clattered, out of sight behind some sheds.

Most in the crowd had the same ragged, mud-caked appearance that was the hallmark of lake dwellers all over London. But distributed among them were a few wealthier individuals wearing elaborate costumes of loose cotton and silk, fur cloaks, feather headdresses and heavy gold jewellery. Each one was accompanied by heavy-looking personal security guards with bulging muscles and battle-ravaged faces.

'There's no way all these people are from the Southside,' said India as they made the slow walk up a flight of steep steps near the base of the tower.

'S'right,' said the boy, who seemed able to hear every-thing they said, despite the noise of the crowd. 'We're famous now. Folks come from all over for a taste of what we sell here.'

'You mean slaves?' said India.

'S'right! We got the best there is. And there's no waste

either. Anything we can't sell gets used in other ways. You'll see.'

They reached the top of the steps and paused to take in the scene. Sid let out a low whistle. 'Son of a rigger, would you look at that.'

They looked down on a great amphitheatre, situated beneath the old radio tower. Huge fires burned at each corner of the tower and rows of tiered seating looked down on the space at the centre. The seats were already crowded with spectators, talking animatedly among themselves, bargaining with hawkers or gathered around three-card tricksters. Painted women with smouldering eyes swayed through the stands plying their trade and a man holding two ferrets was taking bets about how long he could keep them in his trousers.

The lower reaches of the tower's steelwork were strung with a complex tangle of ship's rigging and rope bridges where dozens of people clung to get a view of the proceedings. At the centre of the arena was a sand-covered area, stained here and there with sticky pools of crimson. A small crew was tossing buckets of fresh sand over the most heavily stained areas.

'Mother of all riggers, will you look at this set-up?' muttered Sid.

'What is this place?' said India.

'Told ya, it's the slave market,' said the boy proudly. 'Best there is. So now that I brung ya, let me have a hold your gun. That was the deal.',

'You didn't really think I was going to give my gun to a little thief like you, did you?' growled Sid. 'Get lost and don't come back.' He flicked out a hand and clipped the boy around the back of the head.

The boy flinched and backed off a few paces but his eyes

blazed with fury. 'That ain't fair,' he complained. 'We had a deal and you don't break deals in Glass Town, not if you know what's good for you. You wait till my uncle hears about this.' And with that he disappeared through the legs of the crowd.

'Nice going, Sid,' said India. 'That's not exactly keeping a low profile.'

Sid shrugged. 'No one's keeping a low profile in this place,' he said. 'This is the craziest collection of misfits I've seen since I was last in Sin-Sin.'

'What do you make of this, Calc?' said India.

'The boy suggested that this is where the sale of slave labour takes place,' said Calculus. 'But the bloodstains on the arena floor indicate that some form of gladiatorial contest may also be carried out here.'

'Gladiators?' said India. 'You mean like in ancient Rome?'

'I believe so,' said Calculus. 'It is interesting to note that throughout human history, when the rule of law breaks down, then some form of inhumane blood sport is usually present. Some researchers have hypothesised that—'

'We're not here for the gladiators,' interrupted India. 'I need to know where they're holding the prisoners and where they're planning to take them.'

Calculus turned to look back over the heads of the crowd and then back at India. 'Logically, the subjects of a slave auction would be kept in a nearby holding area,' he said. 'Though I am not sure where. As for what they're going to do with them, I believe the answer may lie over there.'

He pointed to an area about a quarter of a mile from the amphitheatre. From their vantage point at the top of the steps, they overlooked an expanse of flat ground, laced with the sinuous silver rails of a railway goods yard. The magnesium glare of dozens of floodlamps illuminated a long station platform where black steam locomotive squatted, breathing smoke and steam into the night air like a living creature. Men in overalls fussed around the engine like worker ants, loading trucks and fastening the couplings on a long string of carriages, goods wagons and flatbed trucks.

India knew about railways and she had seen the great Siberian goods yards and steam locomotives of Angel town and Salekhard. But she had never witnessed anything on this scale in London. 'They built their own train station?' she said incredulously.

'It would make sense,' said Calculus. 'Every commercial operation has to think about its supply lines. A rail connection would provide the slavers with the ability to ship their goods to any part of the country without delay.'

India shot the android a fierce look. 'Their "goods", as you put it, are human beings, who include my sister. So if you could manage to stop admiring the slavers for a few minutes, that would be much appreciated.'

'Something's happening down there,' said Sid. He to the arena, where the crew who had been sweeping the sand were now hastily quitting the area. The crowd had also sensed that something was about to happen. The hawkers and card sharps disappeared as people settled into their seats and an anticipatory hush fell over the arena.

A sudden fanfare of trumpets played over a crackling speaker system shattered the silence. At one end of the arena a large gate began to open and the mob in the rigging began to roar their approval. The roar was quickly taken up by the rest of the crowd and pretty soon the entire arena was in uproar.

'What's happening now?' shouted Sid over the din.

'I believe we are about to find out, Sidney,' replied Calculus. 'Look.'

A skeletal man emerged through the gate and paused in the centre of the arena with his arms raised to receive the approval of the crowds. The man looked like a Christmas decoration in human form. He was as thin and angular as a heron, with pinched features and black eyes that peered hawk-like from beneath the brim of a top hat, adorned with silver foil and feathers. He wore long boots of red leather and a glittering gold-coloured jacket, that caught the light of the flames and made it appear that he himself was alight.

'Who the hell is *that*?' muttered India as she stared at the apparition.

'That's Ringmaster, that is,' shouted a toothless man standing next to her. 'Now the *real* show's about to start.'

The man called Ringmaster signalled for quiet. Gradually the noise died down. When he spoke, his voice was amplified around the tinny speakers.

'Friends, traders and gladiatorial aficionados everywhere, welcome back to the second half of this evening's entertainment.' There was more cheering but this time he pressed on without pause. 'We have a fantastic line-up for you tonight, including our ever-popular events "Last Man Standing" and "Man versus Bulldozer".'

There was another outbreak of cheering and a hail of debris, including eggs, vegetables and coins began to rain down from the tower, none of which seemed to worry Ringmaster. 'So, stick around because we've got all of that to come. But before we get to the main event, here's a quick message from our sponsors.'

A hush fell across the crowd as Ringmaster adopted a serious tone. 'Many of you remember, as I do,' he began, 'how only a short time ago, this place was nothing more than a sleepy settlement, no different from a thousand others trying to scrape a living from the mud of Lake London. But look at us now.'

There was more cheering from the upper tiers. 'Now we are the centre of a noble world of commerce. We are the captains of cruelty, the sultans of suffering, the masters of mayhem and the profiteers of pain. We are the Southside Slaving Company!'

The crowd went wild and it was several minutes before Ringmaster could calm them down long enough to continue. 'But all of this is only possible because of the hard work and perseverance of the two men who brought us this great success. Two entrepreneurs who had the vision to make the Southside Slaving Company the cruellest and most feared organisation in the northern hemisphere. Ladeezangennelmen, please to put your hands together for our sponsors and benefactors...'

A tinny drum roll played over the speakers and a spotlight beam clanked on. It swivelled over the heads of the mob before settling on the high gantries of the radio tower where a painted theatre box, draped with bunting, looked down on the arena. Sitting in the front of the box were the two men India had seen the night before, grinning and waving to the crowds like a pair of malevolent babies.

'Romulus and Remus. The Pinkerton brothers!'

'Gotta hand it to them,' said Sid as the crowd erupted. 'Those Pinkerton boys sure know how to put on a show.'

When the applause had finally died away, Ringmaster continued. 'And now we come to our main event of the evening and I know this is the thing that many of you have come such a long way to see.' There was a ripple of acknowledgement from the finely dressed contingent in the front rows.

'Tonight, ladeezangennelmen, we will bring you the finest collection of slaves ever assembled from around the shores around Lake London. A superb collection of men and women and children in the prime of their lives, including several freshly rounded up only last night from the north shores.' India's heart began to beat faster.

'As always,' continued Ringmaster, 'the Pinkerton brothers guarantee delivery of your purchases to the location of your choice, using our secure private rail network.' The well-dressed contingent nodded their approval at this.

'And finally, may I remind you of our terms and conditions. All trades made in the slaving arena are to be settled by the end of the evening without exception. Acceptable forms of payment include gold, cut and uncut gemstones, working weaponry, food supplies and old-tech in good working order. And please remember, your life may be at risk if you do not keep up repayments secured on it.'

He paused to briefly remove his hat and wipe away the sweat that now coursed down his brow. 'And so, without further ado, let's see tonight's merchandise.'

The lights around the arena darkened until only the central area was illuminated. The gates opened once more and a line of people began to shuffle out, driven forwards by a man with a large whip. The men, women and children in the line blinked in the sudden light of the arena, looking around with fear and confusion on their faces. They were bound at the wrist and ankles and a long chain connected each one to the person in front. Many bore the signs of harsh treatment, and most were barefoot.

Ringmaster paraded around the frightened group, showing them off to the crowd as though they were a collection of livestock. 'Aren't they wonderful, ladeezangennelmen?' he barked. He began to move down the row, singling out individual people in the group for comment. 'Look at the teeth on this one,' he said, pulling back the lips on the youth at the front of the line. 'This young man is in the prime of life and will give you years of service in your mines.' He paused to stroke the cheek of a young woman. 'This female is intelligent and dextrous enough to undertake any task in your factories. These children will make excellent house servants.'

India cast her eyes along the row and then froze when she spied a slight figure near the end. She couldn't see her face at this distance, but when she looked closely, there could be no doubt. 'Sid,' she gasped. 'Over there. It's Bella.'

Ringmaster continued walking along the row and, at that moment, he stopped right next to Bella. He took some of her golden hair between his fingers. 'Now this one I'm sure will be of interest to our more discerning buyers,' he said. 'Because not only is she very beautiful, ladeezangennelmen...' He paused for effect. 'But she is also *a qualified medic*.' A murmur of approval ran through the crowd, as they considered the prospect of owning something as rare and valuable as their own medic.

India gritted her teeth. 'I'm going down there,' she said tightly. 'If I can get close to her—'

'That's a really dumb idea,' said Sid. 'They got armed guards all around here and there's more up in the tower.' He pointed to several figures crouched along the gantries, cradling long rifles. 'You'd be dead before you got five steps into that arena.'

India ground her teeth and forced herself to breathe deeply as she realised that Sid was right. She would be no use to Bella if she tried to go steaming straight in. Gradually, she felt the anger subside. 'All right,' she said eventually. 'What do you suggest?'

Sid did not reply at once. He seemed more interested in what was going on around the arena, squinting at each of the guards in turn and then casting a look back over his shoulder. 'If you want your sister back,' he said eventually, 'the best thing would be to wait until they move her. My guess is they'll be shipping her and the others out of here on that train we saw.'

'What are you suggesting?'

Sid shrugged. 'It didn't look like there was so much security down on that platform and there's likely even less on the train. I say we wait until the auction's over and hit 'em down there when they load up the train.'

India swallowed and bit her lip. 'All right,' she said after a few seconds' thought. 'Why don't we head down there now and scope out the area?' She looked back at the arena. 'I'm don't think I can watch this any longer.'

'I'm not sure we have the luxury of leaving just yet,' said Calculus suddenly. 'I am detecting several armed men closing in on this location. They seem to be headed towards us.'

India turned and immediately spotted two men with shotguns barging their way through the crowds towards them. Two more were coming from the other direction and another three were pushing their way up the rows of tiered seats. There was no escape.

'There they are! That's them, Uncle.' They turned to see the small boy who had brought them to the arena, leading a stooped man along the row of seats. The man wore a heavy leather apron and had a mouthful of broken, yellow teeth. 'They're the ones I told you about. We had a deal, and they broke it.'

Armed men closed in on them from all sides now and

the three of them drew closer together. Calculus spread his hands in a calming gesture.

'There is no need for violence,' he announced in a soothing voice. 'I assure you, we mean no you harm.'

'Speak for yourself, robot,' snarled Sid. 'I mean them plenty of harm.' He reached his hands behind his back and came out holding both pistols. But before he could shoot, a billy club struck him heavily from behind, bludgeoning him to the ground and sending his pistols clattering across the wooden floor.

As Sid hit the floor, India reached down to her boot and came up with the hunting knife. But a baton across her wrist sent it tumbling from her hand. An instant later, she was grabbed from behind and felt the cold edge of a blade at her neck. She struggled but then stopped as she felt the blade bite into the skin.

'Best stop moving if you don't want another scar to match the one on your face,' said a dark voice close to her ear. She stopped struggling and glanced at Calculus, who, had made no attempt to intervene.

'Calculus!' she hissed. 'Do something!'

Calculus turned his palms up in a motion that indicated his helplessness. 'As I have already explained, India, I am sworn to a life of non-violence. I cannot help you.'

'Non-violence, my arse,' spluttered India. 'I didn't dig you out of the ground so you could stand around looking pretty.'

The android shrugged in a very human gesture. 'I regret I cannot help you, India.'

India cursed out loud and brought her boot down hard on the instep of the man holding her. He grunted and his grip loosened just enough for her to sink her teeth into the flesh of his forearm. He shrieked and tried to pull away but India pulled him in tighter and dropped to one knee, executing a shoulder throw that sent him tumbling over the next row of seats.

She looked up into the barrels of four shotguns, all pointed at her face. The man in the leather apron leaned in close. 'I'm the slave master around here,' he growled. 'I get to decide who lives and dies. So I strongly advise you to give up if you want to live more than another five seconds.'

India took stock of their situation. Sid lay still in a pool of his own blood and Calculus clearly meant what he had said about not fighting. Reluctantly, she raised her hands and allowed herself to be hauled to her feet.

'What you gonna do to 'em, Uncle?' said the boy eagerly. 'Can I watch?'

The slave master turned long enough to clip the boy viciously behind the ear, then he turned to inspect Calculus. When he pulled back the android's hood to reveal his helmet and visor, the crowd let out a collective gasp.

'It's a demon!' someone shouted from the back of the group.

'Burn it!' shouted someone else.

'Shut up, you morons,' snapped the slave master. He examined Calculus's visor closely. 'I've seen something like this before, a long time ago. It's a war droid.' He poked Calculus in the chest. 'What are you, Hitachi? Bluestar?'

'I am a Matsushito 6000 all-purpose combat droid,' replied Calculus politely. 'I have a titanium chassis with a fusion-based power cell and a super-cooled quantum processing unit. Like all Matsushito units, I have a fully transferable consciousness and—'

'What kind of weapons are you packing?' asked the slaver cautiously.

'I can be equipped for a variety of combat situations,'

offered Calculus. 'But since beginning my studies as a student of Buddhism, I have removed all of my on-board weaponry.'

India groaned inwardly and a slow grin crept across the slave master's face. 'Perfect,' he said. 'Then I guess you're not going to be causing us any problems. Take hold of 'em, boys. The twins are going to want to meet this beauty and his friends as soon as possible.'

12

RINGMASTER

They were taken from the arena through a covered walkway towards one of the main legs of the transmission tower. India was shoved along in front of one of the gunmen while the still-unconscious Sid was hauled along by his armpits, the toes of his boots dragging through the dust.

The guards treated Calculus with more caution. Despite his insistence that he was unarmed and meant them no harm, they stayed well out of reach of his long arms and prodded him along gingerly with their gun barrels.

News of the war droid's arrest seemed to have spread right around the stadium and a crowd of onlookers lined the route to get a look at the strange mechanical man. They were brought to a halt at the base of the tower, where a long flight of crude wooden steps zig-zagged their way up the metalwork towards the wooden box they had seen from the arena.

'Wait here,' growled the slave master. 'Mr Romulus and Mr Remus will want a word with you two.'

While they waited, Calculus spoke to India in a low

voice. 'Are you all right, India? Did you receive any injuries in the fight?'

She turned and glared at the android. 'Fight?' she said. 'There was no fight, Calc. We got our arses kicked while you stood by and did *nothing*. Are you proud of yourself now?'

'The path of non-violence is not an easy one,' admitted the android. 'However, I am concerned about Sidney.'

Sid lay on the ground where he had been dumped, his eyelids flickering. India was also worried about him, but she was too angry with Calculus to think straight. 'What do you care?'

Calculus gave a human-sounding sigh. 'Just because I will not fight does not mean I am not concerned for my friends,' he said.

'Friends look out for one another,' she snapped. 'I don't know what you and me are any more but we sure as hell aren't friends.'

They both fell silent. India knew she was being unfair. Calculus had been her friend for over ten years and had saved her life on numerous occasions. But his failure to act at the moment they had needed him most, felt like the ultimate act of betrayal. And yet, for all her anger, the act of severing her friendship with Calculus had felt as painful as cutting off her own arm. She stared miserably at the ground.

'They are coming,' said Calculus.

She looked up to see Romulus and Remus Pinkerton descending the line of rickety steps, grinning and waving to the crowds as they came. When they finally reached the bottom they stood side by side to inspect the prisoners.

'Well, well,' said the first brother. 'What have...'

'...we got here?' said the second brother, completing his sentence.

The slave master whipped off his cap and bowed low.

'Begging your pardon, sirs. But we found 'em sneaking around the arena. We think they're Northside spies.'

The brothers stepped forwards, wearing the same expressions of gleeful maliciousness. They looked like an illusion created in a hall of mirrors. When they spied Sid lying on the ground, one of the brothers gave a cry of surprise and bent down, grasping Sid's chin to examine his face. 'My word, Brother Romulus,' he exclaimed. 'I believe I recognise this young man.'

The second brother crouched next to his twin and peered at Sid. 'My word, Brother Remus,' he cried. 'So do I. I do believe that is...'

'...Sidney Stone,' replied Remus, completing the sentence. 'This young man is responsible for an extensive series of thefts from tech mines throughout the Eastern states.'

'Including some of ours, as I recall,' said Romulus. 'Such a notorious outlaw would fetch a considerable bounty.'

'Perhaps,' said Remus, stroking his chin, 'but wouldn't it be more fun to put his head on a spike as a warning to others?'

'If you please, sirs,' said the slave master, touching his forelock. 'There's something else too. They've got a war droid with 'em.'

The guards parted to allow the brothers sight of Calculus. Romulus and Remus stared at the android curiously before turning to each other and smiling.

'My, my, Brother Romulus,' said Remus. 'I do believe that is...'

'A Matsushito war droid,' said his twin.

'This is most fortunate, brother,' said Remus. 'A creature like this will make a wonderful addition to our gladiator arena, don't you think?'

Romulus seemed delighted by his suggestion; his eyes widened and he waggled his fingertips. 'Ooh, the gladiator arena!' he exclaimed. 'A splendid suggestion, brother. Imagine the spectacle of a fighting robot.'

'With respect,' said Calculus mildly, 'I am an android. It is a very different thing altogether.'

The two brothers grinned unpleasantly. 'Robot, android,' said Remus. 'It makes very little...'

'...difference to us,' completed Romulus. 'Take him away and prepare him for the arena.'

The slave master was becoming increasingly agitated. 'Perhaps if I might make the *teeniest* suggestion, good sirs?' he said with a bow that brought his nose nearly to his knees. 'A functioning war droid would be worth a small fortune in the tech markets of Sing City. Perhaps we should...' The thought remained unfinished as he tailed off under the ferocity of Remus's glare.

'I have no doubt that such a creature is a rare and wonderful thing,' said Remus in a tight voice. 'But what you fail to understand, slave master' – his smile widened to a terrifying degree – 'is that my brother and I *enjoy* destroying nice things. Don't we, brother?'

'Indeed, we do, brother,' said Romulus, mirroring the smile so that the slave master's terror was doubled. 'It's absolutely our favourite thing to do. Besides, the crowds will flock to see a creature like this fighting in our arena.'

The slave master looked like he was ready to pass out from fear, but he had one more thing to say. 'I-I understand c-completely, sirs,' he stammered. 'But there is a small problem with making him fight.'

'And *what*...' said Remus.

'...is *that?*' added his brother.

The man trembled visibly. 'W-well, sirs,' he began.

'When we arrested these two, the android refused to fight us.'

The brothers turned towards Calculus in amazement. 'Refused to fight?' said Romulus.

'Whoever heard of a war droid refusing to fight?' added his brother.

'Said he was some kind of holy man,' said the slave master. 'He said violence was against his principles.'

'A holy man?' said Remus. 'Is this true, robot?'

Calculus inclined his head politely. 'That is correct. I am a practising Buddhist and I observe the principles of non-violence. I will not participate in your gladiator contest and there is nothing you can do to make me.'

The brothers' eyes lit up with delight. 'Did you hear that, brother?' said Remus, excitedly. 'He said we can't make him.'

'Indeed, he did, brother,' said Romulus. 'And we do so like a good challenge.'

'Challenges are our favourite thing,' added Remus. 'And we've never failed yet.'

'So I'm sure we can persuade you fight, Mr Robot. We just need to find the right...'

'...*motivation.*'

The brothers looked first at India and then at Sid, and then grinned at each other. 'Take the android for processing,' snapped Romulus. 'And put these two in the holding cage. We'll be seeing a lot more of them later.'

Without a further word, the brothers turned and headed back up the rickety stairs. India was shoved roughly from behind as the slave master led them away from the tower and back past the seating stands. He brought them to the far end of the arena, where a steel cage stood alone. Constructed of roughly-welded bars, it was large enough to accommodate two people but not high enough for them to stand up in. The slave master undid the bolt and pulled open a small door. 'In there.'

India ducked through the narrow entrance, and Sid's limp form was thrown in after her. As the slave master padlocked that door, one of the guards tossed a bucket of water over them both. India flinched and Sid let out a groan.

The slave master grinned through the bars. 'I wanted you to be awake for what happens next. You two are about to get the best view in the arena.' He jerked his head towards Calculus. 'Robot! You're with me.'

He turned and began to walk away but Calculus paused. 'I'm sorry about this, India,' he said. 'I really am. But I'm afraid I have to be true to my principles.'

India said nothing as he was led away. But as he disappeared into the crowds, she was seized with the terrible thought that she might never see him again. She called out but it was already too late. The android had gone.

Sid sat up and groaned as he felt his skull. He blinked rapidly and his eyes looked unfocused. 'Why am I always the one who gets knocked out?' he grunted. He looked around at the iron bars. 'And where are we? And why am I *wet*?'

'Long story,' said India. 'The short version is we got caught.'

Sid adjusted his position and took up the opposite corner to India. 'Yeah, I remember that much. I also remember your android turned out to be as much use as a ton of scrap iron.'

India looked away. 'I don't want to talk about him.'

'Suit yourself. But don't say I never warned you. You can't trust your life to a machine.'

They were interrupted by a guard who clambered on top

of the cage to attach a heavy chain to a ring on the roof. He jumped off and shouted to someone overhead.

'Now what?' said Sid.

With a sudden clanking jolt, the chain was pulled taut. A moment later the cage was jerked aloft, swinging from side to side as it went.

'What the hell...' spluttered India. 'Are they planning to drop us?'

Pulled by some unseen winch high above them, they continued their ascent up into the radio tower. As the cage rose above the rows of tiered seating, they had a view of the entire arena and hundreds of faces in the stands turned to look up at them.

'How high are they taking this thing?' said Sid, staring up into the darkness.

India clung to the bars and felt her palms grow sweaty as the ground dropped away beneath them. Even if they could get out of this cage, it was now far higher than either of them could safely jump. She closed her eyes and took a deep breath. 'Heights,' she said to herself. 'Why did it have to be heights?'

Jeers and catcalls broke out around the arena and some of the spectators in the highest seating levels began to lob objects at the cage. A hail of small items clattered off the bars: rocks, coins, rotten vegetables and things that India didn't want to think too closely about.

They came to a juddering halt, swinging back and forth above the arena like an erratic pendulum. When India opened her eyes, she saw that Ringmaster was ready to restart the auction.

Ringmaster called for hush and the arena fell silent again. The hail of objects slowed and stopped as the crowd settled back to watch the proceedings.

Ringmaster knew his job well. He moved along the line of chained people and began the bidding on each of the slaves in turn. He spoke quickly, with the rapid babble of an auctioneer, spotting bidders within the crowd by the merest raising of a finger or twitch of an eyebrow.

Most of the bidding came from a group of well-armed men at the far end of the stadium who looked rough and grimy and who India took to be mercenaries. They were mostly interested in the strong and healthy men in the line-up and India suspected they would likely be put to work in a slave mine or factory, to be worked until they dropped dead in their chains.

The women and children seemed to be of more interest to the wealthy and well-dressed merchants. India knew from her own experience that they might be employed in tech mines, where their smaller size was valuable for crawling into narrow underground passages to retrieve valuable tech. And if those passages collapsed on top of them, well, who cared? Slaves were expendable.

She spotted Bella, near the end of the row, still unsold. Ringmaster passed over her several times and appeared to be saving her until last. Finally, when she was the only one left in the ring, Ringmaster approached her wearing a large grin.

'And finally, ladeezangennelmen, our star buy tonight. She's beautiful, she's feisty and above all, she's *a qualified medic!*'

A ripple of approval ran through the crowd. The merchants seemed to be particularly interested and from her vantage point India could see several of them peering into their bags of gold to calculate how much they might have to spend on such a treasure.

'Just imagine it, ladeezangennelmen. Imagine the luxury

of having your own personal physician to take care of your diseases and skin sores with no fuss and no waiting lists. Well step right up, ladeezangennelmen, because tonight's highest bidder will get to take this treasure home. After all, you know what they say...' He paused for effect. 'Only the rich deserve to live.'

He swept back to the centre of the ring, all business now. 'So, what do you say? Shall we start the bidding at a thousand gold chips?'

There was a collective gasp at the audacity of the price. Several of the merchants were scandalised and looked at each other in disbelief. Never in all their experience had anyone asked such a sum. That much money would pay for a hundred regular slaves, they said. Such a price would surely put off the buyers.

The price, however, did not seem to put off all the buyers.

'A thousand gold chips!' cried a man in the front row. He stood out among the crowd like a peacock among a flock of sparrows. He wore an elaborate silk robe in brilliant blues and greens and an orange turban with a large ruby pinned to its centre.

Unsurprisingly, for a man with so much obvious wealth, he was surrounded by at least six personal guards, sporting the ugliest collection of broken teeth and scar tissue India had ever seen.

Despite the man's obvious wealth, there were others in the crowd who were prepared to match his bidding. To Ringmaster's obvious glee, the price escalated quickly, his machine-gun chatter speeding up with each new bid.

'I-hear-fifteen-hundred-do-I-hear-sixteen? Thank-you-madam. I-have-sixteen-do-I-hear-eighteen? Yes-I-have-eighteen-over-here-do-I-hear-nineteen?'

'Looks like your sister's pretty hot property,' said Sid, who had been watching the proceedings from the corner of the cage.

'Shut up.' India rattled the door in frustration as the auction rolled on.

'We ain't getting out of here until they let us out,' drawled Sid. 'So you might as well save your energy.'

Save it for what?' She turned to glare at him. 'So we can be thrown into their gladiator ring while Bella is sold off to become someone's personal property? Is that all we have to look forward to now? Slaves to the ones with most money?'

Sid gave a snort of laughter. 'Ain't that the way it's always been, India? Even before the Great Rains? The ones with money and the power get to do what they want. The rest of us just do what we're told.'

'I hadn't noticed you spent much time doing what you're told.'

Sid looked around. 'And now I'm in a cage.'

India fell silent. It was difficult to argue with Sid's fatalistic view of the world. But she couldn't accept that was all there was to life. She had to believe that the people of the village and thousands like them had the right to a peaceful life. All it would take was for a few to take a stand against—

'SOLD! To the gennelman in the snazzy outfit. Thank you for your custom, sir.'

Her attention snapped back to the arena, where Ringmaster was strutting around with his hands raised like a victorious boxer. In the front row of the stands, the wealthy merchant was also looking exceptionally pleased with himself as he was congratulated and backslapped by his entourage. India barely had time to catch sight of Bella's bewildered expression as she was led away.

'And that concludes tonight's auction, ladeezangennelmen,' barked Ringmaster. 'But don't go just yet, because we have a very special event for you tonight.'

'Here we go,' said Sid, coming to the front of the cage. 'This is where we get ours.'

Now that the slaves had all been taken from the arena, Ringmaster's personality seemed to grow to fill the space that had been left behind. He strutted around the arena, underlining his words with extravagant gestures that made the gold foil of his jacket flash in the firelight.

'Tonight, ladeezangennelmen,' he barked, 'we have a most special contestant in our arena.' He held his head high and placed a hand on his chest like a Roman emperor addressing the senate. 'Over the last two years, we have brought you some epic human battles, pitching the strongest and the bravest against each other for supremacy in the ring.'

A sense of excitement was building in the arena and the crowd hung on Ringmaster's words. 'We have brought you such greats as Barnaby the Barbarian!' A huge cheer went up from the crowd. 'Or how about Avril the Amazonian Queen.' A second cheer, louder than the first. 'And who could forget the master himself, Atticus Heart-Eater, the Butcher of Brixton!'

The crowd went wild. The mention of such great names told them that a really big announcement was coming. People cheered and hats were thrown into the air, the merchants in the front row were jostled and a small fight broke out when a bag of gold chips spilled onto the ground.

The Ringmaster pressed on. 'But tonight, ladeezangennelmen, we have something very special indeed. Tonight, for your delight and enjoyment, we bring you a warrior who is more than human.' A ripple ran among the crowd; they were interested now.

'A warrior with the strength of a thousand men who strikes terror into the hearts of all those who face him.' The crowd were buzzing now and even the merchants who had remained aloof for most of the evening couldn't hide their interest.

'Ladeezangennelmen, our champion for tonight is not from this world, but from a world before the Great Rains. He comes from a time when the fate of nations was decided by technology and the machines they built were like gods.'

Ringmaster paused, his hands up to the sky as the crowd held their breath. Their collective excitement was like an electric current running around the stadium. The air crackled with subdued violence and even the metal girders of the great transmission tower seemed to hum with the power of the crowd.

When Ringmaster spoke again, it was in a quieter, more dangerous tone. 'And so tonight, ladeezangennelmen, without further ado, allow me to introduce to you the most formidable warrior ever to set foot in this ring... a fully functioning Matsushito 6000 war droid!'

13

LET THE GAMES BEGIN

The twin beams of the spotlights swivelled around the amphitheatre and came to rest on the arena gates. Right on cue, the doors swung open and there was Calculus, picked out in the spotlights. He had been stripped of his robe and the lights gleamed on his flexible metal skin. His broad shoulders narrowed impressively to his tight mid-section and his powerful legs tensed and rippled with muscle fibre. He looked formidable.

The crowd gave a combined gasp. There were a few cries of 'demon' from the upper tiers, but most seemed delighted by the spectacle and animated conversations broke out in the stands.

Two men pulled him forwards by a long chain secured to a collar around his neck. They looked extremely nervous as they led him in, but the android did not put up any resistance. They spent a few moments attaching the chain to an iron ring, then they hastily scuttled out of the arena, anxious to be outside the android's reach.

India waved through the bars and cried out, 'Calc! Up

here!' On the far side of the stadium, the android looked up and inclined his head slightly in acknowledgement.

Ringmaster had allowed the excited chatter to continue for a full minute; now, he raised his hands for silence once more. 'Ladeezangennelmen,' he boomed. 'Well you might fear this monster, for this is a Matsushito combat droid. This mighty war machine can lift over eight tonnes in weight while its titanium body gives it the strength to tear a human being apart with its bare hands. It is equipped with a quantum neural processor and programmed with advanced strategic and martial combat skills. It can out-think, out-run and out-fight any human being on the planet and it is a merciless killer. Believe me when I say that if we let this beast loose, not one of you would be left alive within the hour.'

The audience were spellbound by Ringmaster's speech, gazing at Calculus with a sort of horrified reverence. India knew that almost none of the audience would have seen an android before but that many stories were told about these old-world machines and their near-mythical powers.

'But who, I hear you ask, could possibly fight such a demon? What challenger would be brave enough to risk being torn limb from limb? Well, tonight, ladeezangennelmen, we bring you not one but *two* mighty warriors prepared to do battle with this monster.'

He paused for effect, then continued. 'Ladeezangennelmen, I give you the first of our brave challengers tonight. He has been our undefeated champion for over six months with a total body count of one hundred and fourteen. You know him, you love him. Let's give it up for *Count Clubula!*'

From somewhere behind the scenes, India heard the sound of a heavy engine firing up and she caught the tang of diesel smoke on the air. Up in the tower, the Pinkerton twins lean forwards in their box with looks of obvious glee.

At the other end of the arena, a second set of doors yawned open to reveal a large, yellow machine, squatting on fat caterpillar tracks and sporting a gleaming hydraulic arm. With a roar of powerful engines, the machine lurched into the arena in a cloud of blue diesel smoke.

When India got a good view of the machine, she could it was a customised mechanical digger. The driver's cab was protected by an armoured steel cage and an iron club, studded with two-foot spikes, had been installed in place of the bucket scoop. When the driver manipulated the levers, the machine performed a series of rapid pirouettes in the centre of the arena before slamming its club into the ground. The force of the blow cratered the sand and shook the stadium, sending the crowd into an uproar.

'Holy crap,' muttered Sid.

Ringmaster started up again. 'But even the mighty Count Clubula could not tackle such a behemoth by himself. So we have been obliged to bring in reinforcements. Ladeezangennelmen, I am delighted to introduce our second champion tonight, freshly returned from his campaign of mayhem in the north. Will you please give a Glass Town welcome to the one, the only, the *Mighty Dozer!*'

The crowd reached new levels of hysteria as a second machine rumbled noisily into the arena. India recognised it as a giant construction bulldozer. Heavy steel armour had been welded to the machine's bodywork and the giant scoop at the front had been fitted with three steel spikes that projected forwards like the horns of a dinosaur India had once seen in a picture book.

As the crowd cheered, the two machines lined up in the centre of the ring, facing Calculus. If the android felt any fear, he did not show it, though the same could not be said for India. 'They're... not really going to make him fight those machines... are they?'

'Reckon they are,' said Sid. 'This should be interesting.'

India turned and slapped Sid across the face, so hard that it sent the cage swinging again. 'Don't you have any decency in you at all? Calculus is our friend.'

Sid rubbed his jaw. 'Your friend, perhaps,' he said. 'So far all he's done for me is stand around preaching love and peace while I get knocked out.'

'He's just... got things messed up in his head, that's all. He'll be back to normal soon, you'll see.' She turned away from Sid and bit her lip, not at all confident of what she was saying. Would Calculus try to protect himself at all when those two machines laid into him?

She did not have to wait long to find out. Ringmaster crouched down and pointed an accusing finger at Calculus. 'Know this, demon. You are a monster and we will not suffer your kind to live. For as the good Lord sayeth, "I will judge you according to your conduct and repay you for all your detestable practices. And you will know that I am the Lord when Count Clubula and the Mighty Dozer take vengeance upon you." Now...let the games begin!'

The digger revved its engine and lurched forwards, club raised high into the air. As it approached Calculus, the club came down with whiplash suddenness and the iron ball slammed into the earth. Calculus dived out of the way a fraction of a second before the impact. He rolled away to the limit of his chain and came up on his feet, just in time to meet a crushing blow from the bulldozer's giant scoop. The android's body was flung backwards, jerking to a neck-snapping halt on the end of the chain.

'They're trying to kill him,' gasped India.

Sid shook his head. 'I don't think so. That dozer could have run right over him if it wanted. I think they're just trying to make him fight.'

The next few minutes proved the truth of what Sid said. The two construction machines took it in turns to launch a barrage of brutal attacks on the android. A succession of pneumatic-powered blows rained down, forcing Calculus to take evasive action to avoid being crushed. At one point, the giant club swung a wide arc that caught him a glancing blow before demolishing a row of seats and sending spectators scrambling for cover.

'Why doesn't he fight back?' cried India. 'He can't keep dodging them forever.'

Sid nodded. 'Reckon you're right,' he said. 'My money's on the bulldozer.'

At a signal from Ringmaster, the two machines called off their attack and returned to the centre of the arena, idling their engines. Calculus lay slumped against the side wall, oozing blue fluid from a cracked plate in his shoulder.

'It seems,' said Ringmaster, through gritted teeth, 'that our android is refusing to put up a fight. The demon is denying you the opportunity to witness this epic battle.'

Boos sounded from the tiered seating and a hail of rotten vegetables began to rain down on the arena. Ringmaster held up his hand for silence. 'But have no fear, my friends,' he said smoothly. 'We will not let you leave this evening without a spectacle to remember. If the demon won't fight, we simply have to give it the right motivation.'

Up in the high gallery, India saw Romulus and Remus were grinning delightedly and a cold sensation took hold of her. Whatever happened next was not going to be good.

'It so happens,' continued Ringmaster, 'that we know the demon's weak spot.' He whirled suddenly and pointed directly at the cage containing India and Sid. '*There* are the demon's masters, the ones he is sworn to serve no matter what.' The chorus of boos increased. India flinched in the spotlight and wondered what was coming next. 'The demon may not be prepared to save himself, but the question is, will he fight to save his masters?'

At a signal from Ringmaster, four men rushed forwards to lift a series of metal covers set in the surface of the arena. Once removed, the covers revealed a steep-sided pit, around four metres on each side though India could not see how deep it was from her angle.

As she craned her neck to see further into the pit, the cage gave a sudden lurch. A series of dull clanks sounded from overhead, followed by the rattle of a chain as the cage began to descend.

'We're going down,' she said.

'Not just down,' said Sid. 'Across.'

The cage moved laterally out across the arena, cranking slowly over the heads of the crowd until it was suspended directly above the pit.

The crowd began to cheer again. 'I don't like it,' said India. 'What do you think they know that we don't?'

'Maybe that's your answer,' said Sid, pointing down. 'There's something alive in that pit.'

India looked down into shadows and saw Sid was right. In the darkest corner of the pit she could see a pale patch of grey. She leaned closer to make out the pale shape, then gave a start as it stirred. 'I think it's some kind of animal.'

'Whatever it is, I think we're about to get introduced.'

'Friends,' Ringmaster cried. He had now climbed up into the stands, well out of reach of whatever was about to happen. 'Tonight, we will conduct a simple experiment. At one end of the arena is a war droid, which refuses to fight. At the other are its masters, whose lives will shortly be placed in peril. All the android has to do to save them is to get past Count Clubula and the Mighty Dozer. If the demon refuses, then its friends will die. So let's see how keen it is to fight now!'

Two of Ringmaster's attendants came forwards holding burning torches that dripped hot tar, and threw them into the pit. For a moment, both torches guttered and looked like they would go out, then they flared back into life.

And for the first time, India and Sid had a clear view of what was waiting for them.

14

THE PIT

Crouched in the bottom of the pit was a creature with a broad head and a powerful body, covered in a thick coat of pale fur. Four muscular limbs ended in paws as wide as spades and the beast's short snout was pulled into an angry snarl.

India and Sid instinctively drew back as they looked down into the pit. Sid was clearly rattled by the sight. 'Holy shit, that's an ice-bear,' he cried. 'I seen 'em in Siberia. A monster like one that is strong enough to tear us both to pieces. Crap only knows how it got here.'

Maddened by the noise and the flaming torches, the bear raised its head and spied the two humans dangling overhead in a cage. Then it opened its jaws to an impossible angle, exposing black gums and an arsenal of ivory teeth and roared, shaking the air with its volume and ferocity.

India backed away as far as the cage would allow. 'What are we going to do? How are we meant to fight that?'

'There's only one sure fire way to kill an ice-bear,' said Sid thoughtfully.

'Which is?'

'Shoot it right here.' He jabbed the centre of his forehead with his index finger. 'Works every time.'

'Don't mess around, Sid, this is serious.'

'I'm being serious!' he snapped back. 'There's no way we can kill a monster like that without weapons. But they don't want us to kill it. They just want to throw us in there to find out if Mr Non-Violence will come to rescue us.'

'You mean...'

'I mean we're screwed, India.'

The bear paced up and down the pit, looking up at the caged humans as though they were low-hanging fruit. At one point it leaped up at them, swiping with a huge claw that only narrowly missed the floor of the cage.

Ringmaster was getting warmed up again. 'Ladeezangennelmen. Now we will see whether the war droid remembers what he is built for. Either he will come to the rescue of his friends or be forced to watch as they are reduced to a bloody pulp.' He raised his hands to the heavens and his eyes glittered madly. 'Let the mayhem commence.'

Several things happened at once.

The two construction machines lurched towards Calculus in a plume of diesel smoke to renew their attack. At the same moment, there was a dull clunk from the floor of the cage as hidden bolts sprang loose and the entire floor hinged downwards, sending India and Sid tumbling into the pit below.

They hit the dirt with an impact that knocked the wind from India's lungs. When she raised her head, Sid was already on his feet, snatching up the two burning torches and retreating to the corner of the pit.

'Get over here. We'll stand a better chance with our backs to the wall.'

India did not need to be told twice. She scrambled

across to Sid and took one of the sputtering torches from his hand.

Now that they were inside the pit, the bear looked much larger. Its giant paws were the width of India's two hands spread wide and ended in hooked black claws as long as her fingers. More terrifying still were the beast's teeth, sharp and gleaming as ivory blades, that looked like they would have no trouble shearing through meat and bone.

Despite its immense bulk, India could see the animal was in poor condition. Its flanks were drawn in against its ribs and ugly skin lesions leaked into its fur. It looked like it had spent a long time without any proper care or attention.

When they had fallen into the pit, the animal had retreated to the far end, wary of this new intrusion to its domain. It sniffed at the air and its dead black eyes gleamed with reflected torchlight.

'It's a young one,' said Sid in a hushed voice. 'A female, I think. She'll be naturally cautious but on the other hand she looks pretty hungry. Get ready. When the attack comes, it'll come quickly.'

Keeping her eyes on the bear, India slipped a hand towards her boot knife, which had been overlooked by her guards. When she brought it out, Sid looked alarmed. 'Careful how you use that. You stab her with that thing, she's liable to get really pissed off.'

'I'm not going to stab her,' she hissed. 'I'm going to get us some help.'

She rammed the hunting knife into the soft earth of the pit wall, right up to the hilt. Then, steadying herself with a hand on Sid's shoulder, she swung a boot up onto the knife hilt and used it as a step to pull herself up.

The pit was too deep to reach the top, but she could just

see the crowds in the tiered seating, laughing and pointing excitedly.

India filled her lungs and screamed. 'Calc! Help us, *please!* We're going to die in here if you don't do something quickly.'

The foothold gave way suddenly, pulling the knife from the earth and sending India tumbling back to the floor. At the far end of the pit, the great bear stirred and roared, giving them full sight of its fearsome maw.

'I hope he heard that,' said Sid as he pulled her up. 'Because now she's really pissed.'

At that moment, the bear launched its attack.

AT THE OTHER end of the arena, Calculus had his own problems. The excavator swung the club again, which he avoided by ducking and rolling. But this only brought him into the path of the bulldozer again and the crowd roared approval as one of the spikes punctured his shoulder armour and threw him to the ground.

Calculus knew that the injury was not serious, but that he would need time to initiate his repair sequences. And time was something he did not have. A few more attacks like that one and his performance would be severely compromised.

He was still evaluating his options when India's voice carried faintly over the noise of the crowd and the engines. He heard the tremor in her voice, calculated her stress levels and knew at once that her situation was critical.

He knew that the only way he could help her was to attack the two machines who stood in his way and incapacitate their drivers. But to do that he would have to break his vow of non-violence.

In the few microseconds it took him to process this information, he appreciated fully the ingenuity of Ringmaster's plan. Whether he helped his friends or not, then someone was bound to die and the crowd's lust for blood would be satisfied. The only question was: was he prepared to abandon his principles to save India and Sid?

The android had lost count of the number of people he had killed in his years of active service. Or rather, he had not really lost count, he just chose not to remember. The truth was, he could recall with perfect clarity every single one of those deaths. He maintained a perfect record of the spilled blood and gore, the screams of the dying and the awful silence that followed a victory.

And of all those battles, the last one had been the worst. It was the battle that haunted him still, like a black toad that had taken up residence in his soul. A battle that had brought the forces of all the world together at Har-Magedon. The battle at the end of the world.

There had been times when the torment had been so bad that he had thought to end his own existence. But the self-preservation routines coded into his neural pathways denied him even this basic freedom.

And so, he had vowed to forgo violence. He had removed his weapons and taken himself into solitude, spending hours in meditation. And slowly, the images of horror had retreated and he had found peace in the simple knowledge that he would never again need to harm another living creature.

Until now.

Two microseconds later, he had made his decision.

. . .

THE BEAST LEAPT at them with teeth bared and eyes that reflected yellow fire. It spread its paws wide to bring India and Sid into its deadly embrace as five hundred pounds of muscle and claws came down on them. One giant paw caught Sid a blow that tore deep into the meat of his thigh muscle.

He cried out and dropped to one knee, clutching the injured leg so that blood gushed between his fingers like hot soup. His torch dropped to the ground and went out.

As the bear pulled back for a second swipe, India lunged forwards and thrust the burning torch into the beast's snout. There was a brief hiss of burning pitch on flesh and the bear reared back.

The black eyes glared furiously as the bear paced the pit and India kept the flame held out before her. If Calc was going to do something, it had better be now, she told herself. She seriously doubted she would be so lucky next time.

THE BULLDOZER SHUNTED forwards to press its advantage. Moving quickly inside the armoured cab, the driver thrust the control levers forwards and the supercharged engines drove the iron spikes directly at the android's chest.

Calculus had been expecting the attack. He stood his ground until the last possible second, then, with a speed that reduced his form to a blur, he turned sideways and allowed two of the heavy spikes to slip either side of him.

The crowd came to their feet, convinced the android had been fatally speared. But as the driver turned the machine, they saw him, feet braced, pulling at one of the spikes.

The spike came free with a shriek of tearing metal, sending the android tumbling into the sand. Before

Calculus could recover, the driver turned the machine rapidly on its tracks and lined up for another charge.

The driver's reactions were fast, but an android is always faster.

As the bulldozer lurched forwards for another attack, Calculus hurled the giant spike like a spear. The projectile passed through the bars of the protective cage and penetrated the Plexiglas cabin. There was a sudden spray of arterial blood against the inside of the glass, and the bulldozer shuddered to a halt with its engine still running.

The second driver did not wait for the android to gather his strength. The iron mace came down with bone-crushing speed. Calculus barely had time to bring both arms up in an overhead block before the mace slammed into him. The force of the blow drove the android's feet backwards through the sand, but he remained standing.

The driver stared from his cab in shock and struggled frantically with the levers to enact a second blow. But this time the android was too quick for him. Wrapping an arm tightly around the end of the mace, Calculus wrenched the hydraulic arm sideways. For several seconds, the two machines were locked in a test of strength. Then, very slowly, the caterpillar tracks lifted from the ground as the digger began to tip.

Moments later, the machine's centre of gravity exceeded its base and it toppled onto its side with the slow relentlessness of a falling tree. Calculus cast the hydraulic arm aside and paused to gather his strength. The driver flung open the door to his cab and scrambled to safety but the android barely noticed. He had work to do now.

. . .

INDIA HAULED Sid to his feet and the two of them pressed into a corner in the hope of making a smaller target for the bear to strike at. The one remaining torch guttered in India's hand, threatening to plunge them into darkness. The bear hung back. It could smell Sid's blood and it knew that a kill was near. It paced, waiting for its moment.

'Sid,' hissed India. 'Talk to me!'

Sid slumped against the wall. The blood from his thigh soaked the front of his trousers and his usually pale face was now the colour of putty. India feared that he might collapse completely.

I said *wake up*, dammit!' She jabbed at him with her elbow and his eyelids fluttered. 'You've seen these things before. What should I do? Tell me how to deal with this beast.'

'You can't,' he said in a dry whisper. 'You get caught by an ice-bear without a weapon, then you're already dead and you just don't know it yet.' He looked at her with sudden intensity. 'Let it take me,' he gasped. 'I'm already half dead. Let it take me and maybe that'll give you a chance to get out of here.'

She stared. She had known Sid for years, but she had never thought of him as someone who would sacrifice himself for a friend; it just wasn't in his make-up. She shook her head. 'I'm not leaving you,' she said. 'Whatever happens next, we'll face it together.'

His laugh turned into a cough. 'I'll tell you exactly what's gonna happen next,' he croaked. 'We're both gonna get—'

The bear roared with the menace and of a thunderstorm. India held out the guttering torch before her like a last flimsy barricade against death but the bear had lost all fear of the fading flame. It crouched low on its haunches and India's legs felt like they might no longer support her.

'Before we die,' gasped Sid. 'I just wanted you to know...
I always—'

The bear leaped, jaws wide like a steel trap and time
slowed.

Absurdly, India found herself marvelling at the bear's
fine white fur, rippling in the air. She instinctively raised a
hand to her face as though that might protect her.

A heartbeat before the bear struck, a blur streaked
across her vision from above. Something slammed against
the creature's bulk and the bear roared as the impact sent it
sideways. An outstretched paw caught India in the side and
knocked her to the ground.

Pain burned in her ribs as she lay panting with dirt in
her mouth. She closed her eyes and waited for steel-trap
jaws to close around her body and claws to tear the flesh
from her bones. But they did not come.

Raising her head, she saw the bear wrestling in the dirt
with the silvery form of Calculus. The bear had its jaws
clamped around the android's head while Calculus's arms
wrapped around the bear's neck in a deathly embrace.

As she watched, the android succeeded in pulling his
head free of the bear's mouth with a shriek of teeth on
metal. He worked his way behind the bear gradually,
keeping his arms firmly clasped around the beast's throat as
the animal slashed at empty air.

India could see now that the bear was wearing a heavy
collar that had been buried within its fur. Calculus hooked
his fingers beneath the collar and then dragged the beast to
the end of the pit.

'Calc, don't kill it!' she cried out. She did not know what
had made her say it, but at that moment it felt important
that the bear did not become another victim of the
Pinkerton twins.

Keeping a firm grip of the bear's collar, the android reached his free arm beneath the creature's armpit. As a child, India had once watched the men of the village competing to throw a heavy barrel the furthest. The ones who achieved the greatest distance had used a technique of lifting the barrel with their arms while throwing their body-weight backwards, which was exactly what Calculus did now.

The android gave a mighty heave, and the bear was hurled up and out of its prison, its huge paws flailing wildly. The animal struck against the edge of the pit, sinking its claws deeply into the earth and began dragging itself up the wall.

India watched the bear with the distinct impression that it had spent long years waiting for this moment. No sooner had the creature obtained a purchase with its back legs than it scrambled out of the pit and was gone, followed by a chorus of screams from the arena.

'Calc!' gasped India. 'You came back...'

The android held up a hand. 'We are not out of danger yet, India,' he said. 'The bear will keep them occupied for a while, but we have to get out of here. Are you injured?'

India struggled to stand up and winced at a spike of pain in her side. 'Think I might have cracked a rib,' she gasped. 'I'll be fine. But Sid is hurt.'

Calculus crouched down in front of Sid. 'Your leg is seriously injured,' he said.

'I'll live,' grunted Sid. 'Just get me out of this pit before they decide to throw any more damned bears in here.'

Sid's face twisted in pain as Calculus picked him up and placed him over one shoulder. India retrieved her knife from the floor of the pit, then climbed onto the android's back.

Despite his load, Calculus climbed with ease, his metal fingers biting deeply into the pit walls as he hauled them out. At the top, they paused and surveyed the scene. There was panic in the stands as spectators shrieked and screamed and stampeded for the exits. One of fires had got out of control and a large section of seating was now ablaze with flames licking at the lower reaches of the tower.

They spotted the ice-bear, high up in one section of the seating, where it was swiping at anyone in its path. India saw several bodies swept into the air like straw puppets as people trampled each other in their desperation to get away.

India looked around the rest of the stadium. 'There's no sign of Bella or any of the others in the slave auction,' she said. 'They must have moved them out of here before the trouble started.'

Sid tore a strip of material from the end of his shirt and bound it tightly around his thigh to try and staunch the flow of blood. When he had finished, he looked up at the now empty wooden box, high up in the transmission tower. 'Looks like the Pinkertons have done a runner too,' he said. 'If I know them, they'll be looking to save their own hides at the first sign of trouble.'

A chilling thought occurred to India. 'If the Pinkertons are trying to escape, they'll be taking the prisoners with them. We need to get to that goods yard, quickly.'

'Whilst I don't disagree,' said Calculus, 'getting out of the arena may not be so easy. Our escape from the pit has not gone unobserved.'

He pointed to a lone figure at the far end of the stands. Ringmaster's top hat had gone, his golden jacket was missing a sleeve and one arm hung limply by his side, but his eyes burned with hatred.

He raised his good arm and pointed with a trembling

finger. 'There they are,' he cried, his still-amplified voice booming above the sound of screaming. 'The demon and the heretics are free. Stop them! I want their livers on a spike for what they've done.'

'That doesn't sound good,' muttered Sid.

'It's not,' said India. 'Look.'

The doors at both ends of the arena were blocked by grim-faced security men wielding shotguns and axes. The guards glared menacingly in their direction, although no one seemed to want to make the first move.

'There's no way out,' muttered Sid. 'Looks like we'll have to fight.'

'As I keep telling you, Sidney,' said Calculus, 'violence is not the solution to every problem. And, in my experience, there is *always* another way out.'

'The bulldozer,' cried India.

The others took her meaning immediately and all three began to run towards the abandoned machine with Sid limping along badly at the rear. Calculus was the first to reach the idling machine. He tore the armoured door from its hinges, wrenched out the metal spike that pinioned the driver to his seat and dragged out the body. 'Get in here, quickly.' He ushered India up the short ladder to the cab.

Ringmaster was now yelling at the guards, his voice rising to a shriek. 'What are you waiting for, you morons, get after them. I'll execute the last ten men to reach that bulldozer.'

The guards charged into the arena like a wave breaking over a dam. India slid into the driving seat as Sid reached the bulldozer and grasped hold of the ladder. 'Whatever you're gonna do,' he gasped, 'now's the only time you're gonna get to do it.'

India stared blankly at the array of levers and foot

pedals in front of her. 'How do I drive this thing, Calc?' she yelled.

'The control mechanisms on a bulldozer vary depending on the make and model of the machine,' said Calculus calmly. 'But most have common controls. The tracks are controlled independently by those two levers, transmission controls are on the right and the foot pedal on the floor is the throttle.'

A guard, wielding an axe, tried to climb into the cab. The android wrenched the weapon from the man's grasp before delivering a hammer punch to the man's face. As he fell away, Calculus turned back to India. 'However, in view of the urgency of the situation, might I suggest that you just try everything at once?'

15

THE GOODS YARD

India did not need telling twice; she pushed on every lever she could reach and stamped on the throttle. The supercharged engine bellowed like an awakened beast as the machine leapt forwards and several of the guards clinging to the outside leaped clear. There was a horrifying shriek as at least one man was crushed beneath the heavy tracks.

A hand clawed at her face as one remaining guard lunged through the door of the cab and attempted to pull her out. Sid landed a solid punch on the guard. They tussled briefly before the guard fell backwards dragging Sid out of the bulldozer with him.

'Sid!' she cried. 'We have to go back for him.'

'If we go back then you will almost certainly be killed,' said Calculus, looking through the cab's rear window. 'If you wish to save your sister, you have to keep going.'

India looked back but could see only dust and blood and the angry faces of the pursuing guards. And at that moment she knew that Sid was lost.

She pushed the throttle all the way to the floor and the

machine shuddered violently. India struggled with the levers and managed to keep the machine pointed in a straight line as the giant blade moved up and down.

'Aim for the stands at the far end,' said Calculus. 'They appear to contain the fewest people.'

As the bulldozer picked up speed across the arena, the tiered seating filled the forwards view. Only one person stood among the seats, a lone figure in a torn gold jacket. Ringmaster pointed at them and screamed something that could not be heard over the clatter of the engine.

The heavy blade slammed into the grandstand and Ringmaster disappeared in an explosion of splintering wood and metal. The poorly constructed seating was no match for the bulldozer; the blade ripped through wooden planking and scaffold poles and the relentless tracks ploughed over the wreckage with ease. A continuous roar filled the air as the upper levels crashed down around them, battering the bulldozer's armoured cab like a succession of heavy hammers.

Finally, the sheer weight of wood and metal overcame the machine's forwards momentum and the bulldozer ground to a halt with its blade embedded deep in a pile of debris. Silence filled the cab, eerie and unsettling after the chaos of the previous moments and broken only by the creaks and groans from the unstable wreckage.

Calculus helped India from the cab and they stood among piles of broken wood and twisted metal. None of the guards attempted to follow them from the stadium as they picked their way through the twisted debris and the sound of distant screaming suggested that the bear was still on the loose somewhere inside.

India paused and looked back over her shoulder. 'Calc, we have to go back for Sid. He's—'

'Sid is lost, India,' said Calculus. 'There is nothing you can do for him now. You must focus on what you came here to do. Find Bella.'

India realised the truth of what Calculus was saying even though the pain of losing her friend hurt like a knife in the chest. She took a deep breath and let it out slowly. 'All right,' she said. 'We keep going. But how are we meant to find Bella in this chaos?'

'Might I suggest,' offered Calculus, 'that we ask him.'

He pointed to a shambling figure in a leather apron who had just emerged from a tent carrying two large suitcases. 'It's the slave master,' said India. 'Calc, grab him.'

When the slave master saw the giant android bearing down on him, he dropped the suitcases with a shriek and tried to run. Calculus grabbed him by the scruff of his jacket and yanked him up off his feet.

By the time India caught up, the man was already on his knees, pleading for his life. 'Please, don't hurt me,' he wailed. 'I'm an honest working man, just trying to make a living the best I can.'

India looked at the snivelling wretch and felt nothing but disgust. 'Honest? You wrenched people away from their families to be sold in your slave market like cattle. I should let Calculus crush your skull.'

'Nooo!' wailed the man covering his head with his hands. 'Not that.'

India leaned down and grabbed the man by the collar. 'Then tell me where they've taken them. I'll give you precisely three seconds. One...'

'The goods yard!' he blurted. 'They've taken 'em to the goods yard. The brothers are planning to put all the slaves on a cattle train and escape with 'em tonight.'

India frowned. 'All of them? Including the slaves they've already sold?'

The slave master shook his head. 'The slave auction was just a con trick,' he gasped. 'The Pinkertons always meant to take the money and then keep the slaves for themselves.'

India frowned. Setting up a fake slave auction, stealing the money and taking the slaves with you was a bold and risky move but it fitted with everything she knew about the Pinkertons. 'Where are they going with them?' she said.

The man's eyes bulged with fear. 'I'm sworn to secrecy,' he gasped. 'They'll kill me if they find out.'

'I'll kill you if you don't,' said India. She pulled the man closer and held her face close to his. The slave master looked into India's mismatched eyes, and felt them burning into him like twin jets of flame. He began wriggling in an effort to get away.

But somehow her eyes held him where he was. He sensed there was something else behind her stare, looking out at him. Something that was ancient and older than the mountains and yet still alive... and *evil*.

Terror took hold of him. 'Stop it! Please stop it,' he wailed. 'I'll tell you. They're taking the train to the south coast. They've got a ship in the harbour, a big one. I heard they've got hundreds of slaves on board already and as soon as they get there the brothers are going to set sail for the East.'

'The East?' she said. 'You mean Sing City?'

The man nodded. 'The twins reckon they can get a better price for slaves out there. They were going to leave at first light-up but I reckon they've brought those plans forwards now, thanks to you.'

'Where's the train leaving from?' she said.

'The goods yard,' gasped the man. 'We had instructions

to get all the prisoners onto the train straight after the auction. It's all fuelled up and ready to go.'

'If he's telling the truth then we have very little time to lose,' said Calculus. 'The entire countryside between here and the south coast is filled with cannibal gangs and wild dogs. Once that train leaves here we will have great difficulty catching up with it.'

India shook the man roughly. 'How do we get on board?' she demanded.

'Y-you can't. The carriages are armour-plated and there's guards on the train and in watchtowers at both ends of the platform. The twins don't like nobody stealing from them.'

'Well, they'd better get used to it.' India let go of the man's lapels and pushed him away. He fell back and his coat fell open, revealing two pistols tucked into his trousers.

Before he could stop her, India plucked the guns from the belt and held them up. 'What do you know, these are Sid's guns,' she said, turning them in her hands.

India had fired shotguns in the past but had never handled pistols like these. They felt sleek and powerful and the urge to pull the trigger and feel them kick in her hands was overwhelmingly seductive.

The man licked his lips nervously. 'I was going to give 'em back,' he gasped. 'Honest I was. A fine pair of weapons like that belong with their rightful owner.'

India stopped admiring the guns and pointed one directly in the man's face. 'Thanks to your friends, he rightful owner won't be coming back for them,' she said. 'Perhaps I should even the score in his memory.'

Her finger tightened imperceptibly. It would be so easy, she thought, to squeeze the trigger and watch this man die before her eyes. She felt giddy with the power of it.

'India,' said the android's voice softly beside her. 'This is not a good idea.'

India continued staring down the barrel at the man. 'Why not?' she said. 'They killed Sid. It's only right that he should pay for it.'

'Killing is easy,' said the android. 'But living with the consequences lasts forever. Trust me on this, I know.'

'Sid killed plenty of people and he was OK with the consequences,' she said. 'Why shouldn't I be the same?'

'Is that what you aspire to, India?' said Calculus. 'You wish to become like Sid?'

India knew he was right. She was not cut out for killing in the same way as Sid had been. However much she might want revenge, she could not bring herself to kill another person in cold blood.

Very slowly, she uncocked the gun and lowered her arm to her side. The slave master slumped back to the floor and let out a sob of relief as a dark stain spread across the front of his trousers. India turned from him in disgust and walked away.

Calculus fell into step at her side. 'Now do you see why I took a vow of non-violence?' he said. 'If you kill another living creature, it destroys a part of you that you can never get back. If you keep on killing, then the person you used to be ceases to exist.'

India glanced up at him. 'You didn't look so "non-violent" back in the arena,' she said. 'So, what made you change your mind?'

The android gave a shrug. 'Sometimes, the needs of your friends are greater than your own,' he said. 'If I had maintained my vow then you and Sid would be dead. I thought about it for a long time and decided that I could not allow that to happen. I guess I will never be anything other than a war droid.'

'I'm sorry you had to make that choice,' said India. 'But I'm very glad you did. Thank you.'

'You are most welcome, India.'

'So, how long was it?'

'I beg your pardon?'

'You said you thought about it for a long time before you made the decision. So, how long was it?'

'Approximately four microseconds,' said Calculus. 'Which I assure you is a very long time for an android.'

India gave him a small smile as she tucked Sid's pistols into her belt. 'Well, I'm glad you gave it some serious consideration,' she said. 'Now, let's find that train.'

They fought their way through the last of the crowds fleeing from the burning arena and climbed a slope behind the transmission tower that overlooked the goods yard.

The brightly-lit goods yard marked the boundary between the outer reaches of Glass Town and the desolate blackness of the countryside beyond. A small forest of industrial lights on metal pylons glared down on an cranes, oil tanks and maintenance sheds and a gleaming tangle of steel rails criss-crossed the site like filigree.

They saw at once that it would be very difficult to approach the goods yard undetected. The long platform was now very crowded with people and armed guards patrolled with their weapons held tightly as if they expected to come under attack at any moment. Beyond the platform, the rest of the goods yard was dark but powerful search lights directed from the watchtowers swept over the area every few seconds illuminating even the darkest hollows in harsh brilliance.

Just as the slave-master had said, the iron-black locomotive looked ready to leave. The drivers' cab was bathed in fierce orange light from the furnace and the train hissed and snorted like an angry horse waiting for the start of a steeplechase.

Behind the engine came a luxurious passenger carriage with varnished wood panelling and warm yellow light spilling from its lace-curtained windows. The rest of the rolling stock was considerably more industrial in appearance. A metal-sided boxcar with steel grilles in place of windows followed by a series of cattle trucks, flatbeds and goods carriages.

'I guess that must be the Pinkerton's train,' said Calculus.

'It figures,' said India. 'They get to travel in luxury, while the poor souls they buy and sell ride in the cattle trucks. Is there any way to get on board?'

'The train appears to be heavily fortified against attack,' said Calculus. 'The trucks are reinforced with steel plate and there is a piece of heavy artillery mounted on the last carriage.'

India looked along the line of carriages and saw that the last carriage was a converted flatbed truck with a small field gun mounted on a turntable. At least a dozen heavily armed guards milled around the rear of the train, stamping their feet and blowing on their fingers.

India let out a low whistle. 'It looks like they're expecting an army.'

'That would make sense if they're intending to take this train across the South Downs,' said Calculus. 'The area is rife with bandit gangs. But once that train gets rolling it will be difficult for anyone to get near that cargo.'

'Including us,' said India. 'The only way we'll stand a chance of rescuing Bella is if we can get to her before they put her on the train.'

'I fear we may be too late for that.' Calculus pointed to a line of people, chained hand and foot, being led onto one of the armoured box carriages by guards wielding heavy clubs. 'It seems that the Pinkertons brought their captives straight from the arena.'

'I can see Bella,' cried India. 'There at the end of the line.' She pointed to a small figure, too far to see clearly but with a banner of golden hair that marked her out from the rest of the line.

She heard the whirring of optical filters behind Calculus's mask. 'It is her,' he said. 'And I think she is still with the others from your village.'

India pulled one of Sid's pistols from her belt. 'All right, enough talk. Let's get down there.'

'Might I advise caution, India. By my estimate there are at least a dozen armed guards on the platform, not to mention those in the watchtower. Even if you could get to Bella, I seriously doubt you could free her and escape safely. In fact, I would put your odds of success at less than one in —'

'All right, I don't need to know the odds. Well, what do you suggest?'

'Perhaps a stealthy approach might be more successful,' he said. 'The guards are all watching the platform but they appear to be disregarding the other side of the train. If we approach from the direction of the maintenance sheds, we would stand less chance of being seen.'

'And then what?'

'Then I suggest we try and find a way into one of the carriages before it leaves. If we are lucky, there may be fewer guards on the train. We might be able to overpower them and make our escape without being detected.'

India sighed. 'There are a lot of "ifs" and "mights" in that sentence,' she said.

'The odds of success are stacked against us. However, the odds in favour of my suggestion are marginally better than yours.'

'All right, we'll try it your way,' said India. 'I guess we've got nothing left to lose.'

Calculus led them down the slope towards to the goods yard. They crept through scrubby bushes around the edge of the site keeping to the shadows of the maintenance sheds then picked their way across the railway lines, approaching the train on the far side of the platform.

They paused briefly behind an oil storage tank while Calculus peered out to get a better look at the platform. He ducked back quickly as a powerful beam swept across the area, turning the shadows to sudden, harsh daylight.

'Those beams are a problem,' he said. 'By my calculation, they sweep the area approximately every fifteen seconds. I could make it from here to the train in that time if I was on my own, but...'

'Don't worry about me, I can run pretty fast.' India's tone made it clear that there would be no further discussion on the matter.

The android inclined his head politely. 'In that case, the next sweep will be in five seconds. Get ready to run.'

As soon as the searchlight swept past the oil tank, they dashed from their hiding place. Calculus was swift and sure-footed in the near darkness but India, struggled to see her way. After twenty paces, her foot caught on a rail and crashed onto the clinker, scraping the skin from the palms of her hands. Before she could protest, Calculus scooped her up and sprinted for the shadows.

They reached the cattle trucks and ducked into the space between two carriages just as the fierce light swept through the darkness. 'I guess I'm not as fast as I used to be,' gasped India.

'Sadly, that is true for many of us, India.'

India looked along the length of the train. Now that they were close to it, the locomotive looked even more like a slumbering beast, reeking of coal smoke and hot oil. The boxcars and cattle trucks had been heavily modified with sheets of iron bolted to the outside and long spikes jutted from the rooftops, like thorny metal collars.

She pressed her ear to the wall of the carriage. 'Nothing,' she said. 'There's no one in this one. They must be further along.'

They made their way along the train, listening at each carriage until they reached a metal-clad cattle truck where they could hear the sounds of murmured conversation and sobbing from inside. India tapped on the metal armour with her fingernails. 'This must be the one, but how are we meant to get them out?' she said. 'This metal looks like it's half an inch thick.'

The android examined the metal sheathing and then peered beneath the carriage to examine the underside. 'As I thought,' he said. 'Only the walls and roof are protected. The underside is just thin sheet metal. I could cut my way in there without too much difficulty.'

'Who's that?' An urgent whisper sounded in the darkness. 'Who's out there?'

India gave a start and looked up. About halfway up the side of the carriage, a narrow slit had been cut in the metalwork to provide some ventilation. A disembodied mouth was pressed to the slit. 'Where are you from?' hissed the mouth urgently. 'Are you from Brixton or Putney? There's Brixton people in here. Can you get us out?'

'We're from the Northside,' replied India. 'We're going to get you out if we can. My... friend thinks he can cut through the carriage floor.'

Bless you, lady,' said the mouth. 'There's children here too. The raiders took us almost a month ago. Please get us out of here. We're afraid we'll never see our families again.'

'We'll try,' said India. 'I'm looking for someone from the Northside. Her name's Isabella Bentley. She goes by the name of Bella. Is she in there?'

Urgent whispering came from inside and the sounds of scuffling as people changed places inside the crowded truck. Then a new mouth pressed to the slit. 'This is Bella. Who's out there?'

'Bella, it's me, India.'

There was a gasp from inside the carriage. 'India? It's really you?' There was some more hushed whispering from inside. Then Bella returned to the slit. 'What are you doing here? How did you find us?'

'It's a long story, Bel. Right now, we need to get you out. Are the other Northsiders with you?'

'Yes, we're all here,' said Bella. 'But we're not the only ones. There's nearly fifty of us in this carriage. They've all been taken from different places.'

India bit her lip. 'I can't help that. There's only two of us. We can't rescue everyone.'

'Either help all of us or no one,' insisted Bella, her voice suddenly steely. 'I'm not leaving anyone behind.'

India sighed. 'Be reasonable, Bel,' she said.

'No, you be reasonable, India. How do you ever expect us to make peace with our neighbours if we don't help each other out? The people who kidnapped us are the enemy but the people inside this carriage are victims, the same as us. It doesn't matter where we're from; take all of us or take no one.'

'Now look here, Bel—'

'India,' interrupted Calculus. 'May I remind you that we are in danger of being discovered at any moment. If we are going to get anyone out, then I need to start now.'

India sighed and rolled her eyes. She knew from long experience that once Bella had made up her mind about something, she rarely changed it back again. Somehow she had to find a way to do as Bella asked.

'All right,' she said eventually. 'We'll do our best. Calc is going to cut through the floor. Keep everybody away from the centre of the carriage.'

The mouth at the slit smiled. 'Thanks, sis, you're the best.'

Calculus opened a small panel in the back of his hand and ignited a cutting torch that hissed with a sky-blue flame in the darkness. 'It should take about twenty minutes to cut through,' he said in a whisper. 'I could do it more quickly but that would make too much noise. Keep an eye out here.'

Calculus ducked beneath the carriage as India shrank back into the shadows. From beneath the carriage, she could hear the gaseous hiss of the cutting torch while, on the platform guards barked orders and doors were being slammed. It sounded very much like the train was getting ready to leave.

She crouched down beside the carriage. 'How's it going, Calc?' She could see the tiny blue flame of his cutting torch moving back and forth.

'It's slow work,' he replied. 'At least another ten minutes before I can remove the floor panel.'

'Hurry it up, will you?' she whispered. 'I don't think we have that long.'

She watched anxiously as the cutting torch resumed its motion, willing the work to move faster. Then somebody coughed behind her.

India's reactions were fast. She whirled around, simultaneously drawing one of Sid's guns and levelling it at the shadowy figure standing behind her.

'Bloody 'ell. D-don't shoot, lady!' From the slightness of build she could see it was a young boy. His eyes opened wide as he held up his hands in surrender. 'I wasn't doing nuthin'. They told me to check the train before it left, that's all.' He sniffed loudly and wiped his nose on his sleeve.

India relaxed and lowered the gun and looked more closely at the boy. The matted black hair and urchin face was familiar. It was the same boy they had met on their way to the games.

'I know you,' he said suddenly. 'You're one of them Northsider spies that caused all that trouble in the arena.' He looked past India at the blue flame of the cutting torch, clearly visible beneath the carriage. 'What are you doing under there? That ain't allowed, that ain't. I oughta call someone. I oughta—'

'Don't!' said India quickly. 'Don't call anyone. We're just... just doing some repairs, is all.'

The boy looked sceptical. 'And why would they ask a Northsider to do repairs? It's like I said, you're spies, aintcha?'

She looked desperately up and down the platform. No one else seemed to be coming. All she had to do was keep the boy from raising the alarm before Calculus was finished.

'Do I look like a Northside spy?'

'Yeah, you do.' He stared at her defiantly. Then his shoulders drooped and he bit his lip. He looked around quickly to make sure no one else was listening. 'But if you was a Northside spy, you could take me with you, couldn't ya?'

India blinked. 'Take you...with me?'

'Back to the Northside,' he elaborated. 'I heard they got everything on the Northside. 'They got proper houses that don't let in the rain and all they can eat too. Bread, meat, fresh milk, anything you want. Enough to bust your guts. That's what I heard.'

'I, er...' India thought quickly. 'Well...suppose I did agree to take you with me. You'd have to promise not to give me away.'

'I promise,' he said at once. 'Cut me froat and spill my guts if I'm a liar.'

There was scuffling beneath the train and Calculus appeared. He was streaked with grime and oil and his visor glowed with the reflection of the cutting torch. 'What's going on, India?' he began. 'I heard a noise and—'

He was cut off mid-sentence as the boy let out a shriek of terror. He stepped back and tripped over a rail, then continued scrambling backwards, pointing a trembling finger at the android. 'It's the robot!' he shrieked. 'He ain't no holy man; I saw what he done in the arena. Keep him away from me! Don't let him eat me. Help!'

India tried to silence the boy before his terror brought others running, but it was too late. Heavy boots sounded on the gravel at the far end of the train as a group of men rounded the last carriage. Torch beams flared on and sought them out.

'What's goin' on back here?' growled an ugly voice. 'Sniffer, is that you doing that yelling?'

'It's me,' yelled the boy. 'Help me, I bin caught by Northsiders and they got that robot with 'em.'

One of the torches picked out India and she flinched in its beam. 'There's one of 'em,' shouted a voice.

The shot was as sharp as the snap of a dry stick. Something zip-cracked past India's ear and punched a coin-sized hole in the metal behind her.

Calculus leaped from beneath the carriage and stood in front of her as four more shots clattered against his body armour. 'I think it's definitely time to abandon this plan, India,' he said. 'Come on.'

Before she could protest, the android picked her up and slung her across his shoulder as he began to run back across the yard, leaving the gunmen and the boy to stare after him and wonder at the speed of his movement. Twin searchlights swung across their path and a dozen more shots clattered from the watchtowers, spattering the clinker into flinty shards.

'Calc! Put me down,' yelled India. 'We've got to go back for Bella. We've—'

Calculus ducked behind an open-topped wagon piled high with sand and lifted India down from his shoulder. 'We will go back for Bella,' he said earnestly. 'But we cannot help her if we get killed doing it.'

He looked out from behind the wagon and was rewarded with half a dozen shots that clanged against the metal sides and forced him back behind the wagon. 'There are at least eight armed guards headed in this direction,' he said. 'Their weapons are relatively low calibre and will do me little harm, but you are vulnerable. I need to create a distraction that will allow us to escape.' He crouched down and hooked his hands under the truck.

'What are you doing?'

'Delaying our pursuers, India,' he said. 'Might I suggest you stand back a little.'

India watched with growing astonishment as the android tightened his grip on the underside of the truck and straightened his knees. The metal framework creaked under the strain and axles groaned. Very slowly, India saw that the wagon was beginning to tip as the wheels lifted from the rails.

'Calc...' she began before falling silent.

As the android stood upright, the angle of the wagon increased. The steel rails under the carriage pinged and began to buckle as the sand shifted to one side of the carriage.

When he was standing straight, he continued to raise his arms until the edge of the wagon was level with his chest. Then, with the power of a weightlifter, he shunted the immense weight above his head, to execute a perfect 'clean and jerk'.

The wagon seemed to hold still at an impossible angle for an instant, until, very slowly, it began to topple. The carriage hit the ground with the sound of a small explosion and a tidal wave of sand rushed out across the tracks towards the approaching gunmen.

India had barely time to register surprise on the faces of their pursuers as the sandwave surged over them and they were lost in a cloud of dust and grit. Before she could react, Calculus grabbed her hand again and they were running full tilt in the other direction.

'Where are we going?' she gasped.

'That sand should throw our pursuers off for a few minutes,' he said. 'But we should find cover before they resume the search. There are several warehouses on the other side of the yard. They might offer a place of concealment whilst we consider our next option.'

Once across the railway sidings, Calculus pulled her into

a labyrinth of storage tanks, crane gantries and maintenance sheds separated by narrow pathways, choked with weeds. When India looked back over her shoulder, she could see no signs of their pursuers.

'OK, time out,' she gasped, wrenching her arm away from the android. 'You might be tireless but I'm ready to lie down and die.'

She collapsed behind a stack of oil drums arranged against a wall. The spot was well hidden in the space between two maintenance buildings but also gave them a clear view back across the goods yard.

She took stock of her injuries, exploring her arms and legs with her fingers and wincing visibly each time she found a fresh source of pain. Apart from the minor scrapes and scratches that seemed to cover every exposed part of her skin, the pain in her side had turned to a dull ache and felt like a cracked rib. She had a cut on her forehead that she suspected she had picked up in the bulldozer and the entire left side of her body felt beaten and bruised.

Now that she was sitting down, her eyelids felt suddenly heavy and every fibre of her being wanted to close her eyes and sleep for days. She slapped herself in the face a few times. She could not think about sleeping, not while Bella was depending on her.

She turned to Calculus and caught sight of four cleanly punched bullet holes in the metal skin of his back. 'You're injured!' she said. She sat up and examined the holes, which were leaking a sticky blue substance.

'It's just minor ordinance damage,' he said. 'My auto-repair mechanisms will deal with it. However, if our rescue attempt has taught us one thing, it's that the Pinkertons have invested heavily in security. I suggest we do not make another attempt to reach the train just yet. Perhaps we can try again in a few minutes.'

The sound of the steam whistle carried across the goods yard, like a lost soul in the darkness. India stood up and stared as the train took up the slack along its length with a clanking jolt. 'Oh no,' she said. 'I think we're too late for that, Calc. The train's leaving.'

16

LONDON ROAD

The train came awake with a burst of steam. Steel shrieked against steel as connecting rods clanked into action and shoved the engine forwards. The mighty wheels spun briefly against steel tracks before finding traction. Each rotation of the mighty wheels was accompanied by a great exhalations of smoke and vapour that quickly enveloped the engine as the beast shunted out of the station.

'It's leaving, Calc. What are we going to do?'

'There is not much we can do,' said the android. 'For now, we will have to be content to let it go. Perhaps there will be another opportunity to find your sister before she is taken abroad by the Pinkertons.'

The train accelerated noisily out of the station, trailing steam behind it like tattered silk. India watched it go and felt despair fill her heart. Calculus was trying to be optimistic for her sake, she could see that. She knew that once her sister had been swallowed up by the dark lands to the south of London, her chances of finding her sister again would be close to zero.

As the last of the carriages disappeared into the gloom, the remaining crowds on the platform began to disperse. India stared after it for a long time, listening to the fading sound of the engine, before she let out a sigh. She would not cry, not here and not now; that was a luxury she would only allow herself when she could be alone with her own thoughts. For now, she had to focus on the task of getting Bella back, however impossible that seemed right now.

Her thoughts were interrupted by the sounds of gunfire coming from the direction of Glass Town. The skeletal framework of the old transmission tower now looked like a vast burning torch, lit up from below by the raging fires in the arena. There was more gunfire and she could hear panicked shrieks in the distance as the last of the citizens of Glass Town fled for their lives.

'Now that the Pinkertons have left town, it seems that there is no one left to keep order,' said Calculus. 'I suggest we continue carefully from here. If Glass Town was dangerous before, it will be even more so now that the mob is in control.'

India sighed. 'We really have lost our way, haven't we, Calc?' she said. 'If people start killing each other just because they think no one is watching, then there's nothing left to live for. It's the end for all of us, isn't it?'

The android shrugged. 'There have been many predictions about the end of human civilisation,' he said. 'There are examples in the Talmud, the Qur'an, the Bible and the prophecies of Nostradamus.'

'What's your point? Are you saying it'll never happen?'

'No. My point is, sooner or later, one of those predictions is bound to be right. Perhaps that time is now.'

India looked at the android's blank visor. Even after ten years she still had no way of knowing if Calculus was joking, or even if he was capable of making a joke. She gave a wry smile. 'It's a good job I didn't bring you along on this trip to improve morale, isn't it?'

The android did not answer. He turned and stared into the darkness as though listening to something that India could not hear.

'What is it?' she said after a pause.

'There's something coming this way. A large truck, hauling a container.' He paused and cocked his head, listening. 'It sounds like the container is only partially full.'

India could hear it now too, the sound of a ragged diesel engine grinding gears as it approached along a service road. A few seconds later the truck came into view, a pre-rains articulated lorry, battered and pock marked with steel grilles across the windows. It hauled steel container that clanked and boomed as the truck bounced over potholes.

'They're coming this way,' said Calculus. 'I suggest we take cover behind these oil drums.'

India narrowed her eyes as she stared at the lorry coming up the path towards them. 'India!' said Calculus more urgently. 'I must insist that you take cover.'

'How fast could a truck like that go?' she said absently.

Calculus paused. 'That is a MAN TGX long-haul vehicle with a fifteen-litre engine. A truck like that would have an unloaded top speed of over ninety miles per hour, although considerably less than that on poor road conditions. If you are interested in trucks, India, I would be happy to tell you everything I know another time but for now, I strongly suggest we get out of sight.'

She looked at the android and grinned. 'Yeah, you might say I'm interested in trucks,' she said. 'All right, listen up, I've got a plan.'

They took cover behind the oil drums and India peered

out at the vehicle. The truck came to a stop with a hiss of airbrakes, beside the warehouse where they been standing a moment ago. The door clunked and a woman jumped down from the driver's seat. She was short and stocky and with a mean look in her eye that said she was on a mission. She stood in front of the truck, surveying the warehouse by the light of the headlamps.

She was joined by a man who climbed down from the passenger seat and shambled over to her, blowing on his fingers. The man was as gangly and skinny as the woman was stocky and looked like he might blow away in a strong wind.

'I don't understand what we're doing here, anyway,' he complained in a whiny voice. 'Fossburg told me some of the guys had broken into the storerooms and were handing out whisky. We should be over there getting our share and not standing out *here* freezing our butts off.' He paused and looked around as though taking in his surroundings for the first time. 'Where are we, anyway?'

The woman spoke without looking at him. 'This is the twins' storage depot,' she said, staring up at the warehouse. 'It's where they kept their *personal* supplies. I delivered some boxes here once; you wouldn't believe the stuff they keep in here. Food, fuel, old-tech... *gold*.' She let the word hang in the air.

The man's eyes suddenly widened as though an electric current had passed through his body. He licked his lips and looked back over his shoulder as though he was afraid they might be observed. 'The twins!' he said. 'I don't know about this, Marge. Stealing stuff from the food stores is one thing, but stealing from the twins... Those guys are monsters. Do you know what they'll do to you if – *oof!*'

He broke off sharply as the woman's meaty fist planted

heavily in his stomach. 'Do you know what *I'll* do to you if you don't stop whining and start using your brain?' she snarled. 'The twins are gone. They've left town on that train. They took their slaves with them and I heard they ain't never coming back. That means all this stuff is just there for the taking.'

The man looked dubious. 'Yeah, I know but...'

'Suit yourself,' she snapped. 'You can stay here and get drunk with that dumb piece of slime, Fossburg if you like. By morning Glass Town will have been burned to the ground and all you'll have to show for it is the mother of all hangovers. And then what, Doug?'

Doug frowned, trying unsuccessfully to summon a counter-argument. 'I... er...'

'I'll tell you what you'll do,' she continued without pause. 'You'll go straight back to being a useless bum, scraping around in the mud looking for useless old-tech that you hope you might be able to sell for a drink some-where. Well, not me. I've got ambition, see? I'm going to break into this warehouse and fill the truck with everything I can carry. I've already got ten fifty-gallon drums of diesel in there that'll fetch a fortune in the Bristol tech markets.' She turned and gave him the full force of her ferocious glare. Can't you get it through that dense bone skull of yours? Now that them Pinkerton creeps are gone, there's a chance to make some really big money here. So you can either stay and get drunk with your buddies or you can help me. It's up to you.'

Doug licked his lips and his frown deepened as he processed this new information. Then he shrugged. 'All right, Marge, whatever you say. But...' He looked over his shoulder at the orange glow coming from the direction of the town. 'When we've finished, perhaps we could swing back past the storerooms and see if there's any whisky left?'

'Just shut up and follow me, Doug.'

Marge pulled a pair of work gloves from her back pocket and turned to the warehouse. Then she stopped. Where there had been no one a moment before, there now stood a young woman, dressed in a leather jacket and boots. She had long hair and a scar down one side of her face and, there was something *weird* about her eyes...

'Who are you?' demanded Marge. 'What do you want? This is *our* warehouse. We saw it first.'

The woman gave a thin smile. 'I don't want your warehouse,' she said. 'I just want your truck.'

Before Marge could react, the young woman reached behind her back and pulled out a long-barrelled pistol that looked too big for her to hold. 'What is this?' snarled Marge. 'You trying to hustle us? I eat little girls like you for breakfast.' She took a step towards India, but the girl's grip tightened on the pistol.

'Just leave the keys and step away from the truck,' said India. 'No one needs to get hurt, here.'

Doug licked his lips nervously. 'Maybe we'd best do as she says, Marge,' he hissed in a stage whisper. 'Looks like she means business.'

'Means business does she?' scoffed Marge. 'Well, she ain't the only one. Listen here, girly, I own this rig and I'm taking what's mine from this warehouse, so don't try stopping me, see.' She was thoughtful for a moment. 'I tell you what, though. You look like an enterprising sort. Give us a hand to get the truck loaded and I'll cut you in for five per cent of the deal. That's got to be better than the other option.'

'What other option?'

'This one, honey.' Moving with surprising swiftness for someone of her build, Marge dropped to a crouch and reached into her coat, coming up with a sawn-off shotgun on a shoulder strap.

India jerked the trigger instinctively. The pistol discharged into the night with a kick that nearly knocked to the ground. But the shot was snatched and the bullet sang away into the darkness. Marge stood up and grinned.

'That was your one shot, honey,' she said. 'And it's all you get, I'm afraid. Now suck on this.' She raised the shotgun to her shoulder and took aim.

In the same instant, a pair of hands reached from the darkness behind Marge and Doug and slammed their skulls together with the dull crack of bone on bone. Marge groaned and Doug let out a feeble gasp before both of them sank to the ground like sodden towels.

Calculus studied the unconscious bodies for a moment before looking up at India. 'If you're going to start pulling that pistol on people, might I suggest you learn to shoot first,' he said. 'By my estimate, that bullet went at least three feet over the head of your intended target.'

India scowled as she returned the pistol to her belt. 'Yeah, well, she took me by surprise. Besides, what kept you? You were supposed to be my back up. That woman nearly had me cold.'

'It took me a moment to get into position,' said the android. 'After all, you did say you probably wouldn't need any help.'

She glared at the android. She had said that, it was true, but somehow, she couldn't shake the feeling that Calculus had been trying to teach her a lesson. 'All right,' she said. 'Let's get out of here before they wake up. Grab the shotgun and see if there's any more ammunition. I'll see if the keys are in the truck.'

While Calculus searched the bodies, she hauled herself into the driver's cab and was pleased to find the keys swinging from the ignition, attached to a lucky rabbit's foot. 'Not so lucky for you, Marge,' she murmured under her breath.

The fuel gauge showed half a tank of diesel and a quick inspection of the glove compartment disclosed an ancient road map, coming apart at the seams, and small sack containing some bread and sausage. There was also a pair of handheld radios, held together with thick wrappings of sticky tape and which looked like they might have spent some time underwater.

She tore off a chunk of sausage and chewed it while she consulted the map. When Calculus climbed in beside her, she grinned and jabbed her finger down on the map. 'Marge has done us a big favour,' she said. 'She's marked the map with every passable road and bandit encampment between here and the south coast.'

The android parked the shotgun and a handful of shells on the parcel shelf. 'I'm not sure how that helps us,' he said. 'Might I ask what your plan is exactly?'

India rolled her eyes. 'You now, for someone with a quantum processor for a brain, you can be a bit slow on the uptake sometimes. This map shows the Southsiders' main supply routes to the south coast, avoiding all the worst bandit areas. And look at this,' she traced a finger along an inked-in line that spidered across the map. 'Railway tracks.'

'I still don't see how that helps us, India.'

'Because look at this. The tracks head west before they turn south. I'm guessing that when the Pinkertons built the line, they wanted to avoid the cannibal gangs on the South Downs.'

'Not an unreasonable assumption. So, what's your point?'

'Well, look at this. It's the old London to Brighton road. It runs directly south and then meets the railway line here, at a place called Balcombe. After that, the road and railway line run side by side.'

'I see. So, you're suggesting that if we took this road, we could arrive at Balcombe before the train.'

'Hallelujah! Finally, he understands.'

'There are just two small problems with that plan, India.'

'What's that?'

'Firstly, we will have to drive through the area that the Southsiders were specifically trying to avoid. It will take us directly through cannibal territory.'

India shrugged. 'So? We've got guns and one of us is a war droid. We should be more than a match for any cannibals. What's the second problem?'

'Well, supposing you manage to avoid getting eaten long enough to catch the train. What are you proposing we should do then?'

'I haven't got to that part yet,' said India. She grinned and turned the key in the ignition. The fifteen-litre engine thundered to life and the vibration ran through the length of the rig. 'But if I drive this rig flat out, I reckon it'll take us about an hour to get there. So that gives you plenty of time to figure out how we're going to stop the train.'

The android's body language suggested alarm. 'Flat out? Are you sure you wouldn't prefer me to drive, India? I'm qualified to drive all forms of heavy goods vehicle, up to and including a battle tank.'

'Yeah, and you drive like my grandmother. Just concentrate on the map and figure out what we're going to do when we get there. I'll do the driving.'

'Have you ever driven a truck like this before?'

India shrugged. 'Not exactly, but I drove a bulldozer for the first time about an hour ago. How different can this be?'

She slammed the engine into gear and the truck kangerooed forwards as she manoeuvred past the warehouse and turned back towards the service road. It took several minutes for India to get the hang of the gears, during which time she managed to scatter a pyramid of oil drums and turn a small maintenance shed to matchwood. At the bottom of the hill, the rough track met an ancient road. The surface was pitted and cratered but still significantly easier to drive on. India accelerated up through the gears and, gradually, the rail yard buildings fell away behind them until Glass Town was just a faint orange glow in their mirrors.

They passed through streets of blackened, shattered buildings, indistinguishable from the ones that India was used to seeing in the North. At one point they came across a flaming barricade of wrecked cars that had been dragged across the street, but the truck ploughed straight through, scattering flaming wreckage in its wake. A shadowy group emerged from shop doorways as they passed and hurled broken bricks at the truck, more in protest than with any real hope of forcing them to stop.

After that the roads were quieter, gradually giving way to open fields and ancient highways that had seen little in the way of maintenance for over a hundred years. India was pleased to be away from the city and the threat of barricades and hijacks, but the roads out here were long disused, as pitted as the surface of a forgotten planet. She gritted her teeth and steered the straightest line she could manage between the worst of the fissures, trying to ignore the fierce stab of pain in her ribs every time she turned the wheel.

A pothole the size of a bomb crater appeared suddenly in the headlights, too close to avoid, and the truck shuddered violently as the axles tried to absorb the impact. For a moment, the truck tipped dangerously to one side and threatened to spill into a ditch. India wrestled with the wheel as the truck slithered and fishtailed before coming back under control.

'You are fatigued,' said the android, looking at her carefully. 'You should really let me drive for a while so you can get some sleep.'

India rubbed her eyes and refocused on the road. 'I can't sleep, not while Bella's still missing. At least driving gives me something to do.'

Calculus did not pursue the point but continued to observe her closely. 'Were you and your sister very close when you were young?'

She looked at him sharply. 'That question's a bit out of the blue. Why are you asking me that now?'

'I believe it is called "small talk",' he offered. 'I observed that you are struggling with fatigue and I calculated that engaging in light conversation might help you to retain your focus. I determined that the topic of conversation should be neither too frivolous nor too serious and considered several different possibilities before settling on a discussion about your family relationships. If the subject is too personal, I could select a less meaningful topic if you like?'

She laughed. 'And there was me thinking you were actually interested,' she said. 'But since you ask, yeah, we were pretty close. After Mum died, I sort of took on responsibility for looking after Bel but, to be honest, she was always the more responsible one.'

'Why does that not surprise me?'

India gave a rueful smile and continued. 'When Dad was away, we were pretty much inseparable. We spent a lot of time hanging around the shoreline, fishing, digging up old artefacts, even poking around in the old city if we were feeling brave enough. I was always the one that wanted an adventure, but Bel was the one who wanted to learn. She had a million questions about everything and she'd write it all down in notebooks. Once she found out a fact, she never forgot it. She was kind too, just like Mum. I'm not surprised she trained to be a medic.'

'So, what happened between you?'

India threw the android a look. 'What do you mean?'

'I understood from Sidney that there was friction between you and Bella when you returned to the village. It seems that you did not remain as close as when you were children.'

India frowned. '*This* is your idea of small talk?'

'Not really. But I have observed that humans frequently lose touch with people they were once close to and I was curious to know why. Is it because humans care less about their family as they grow older?'

India sighed. 'No, not really. It's complicated. People change over time; they want different things and sometimes the people around them don't recognise that. When I was growing up, I wanted adventure more than anything. And when it came along, I grabbed it with both hands, even though it meant leaving Bella behind.'

'I see. And she resented the fact that you had gone off without her?'

'Yes, but I don't blame her. I'd got so used to thinking

about her as a little girl that I didn't realise she'd grown up while I wasn't looking. When I finally did come back, we didn't have that much in common anymore.'

'I see. So, this rescue mission is really an attempt to reconcile the guilt you feel about abandoning your sister?'

'No! It's an attempt to save someone I care about more than anyone in the world, Calc. If Bella doesn't want to know me after this is over, I won't blame her, but at least I'll know she's safe.'

The android was silent for nearly half a minute before he spoke again. 'Curious. Just when I think I am beginning to understand the algorithms that govern human relationships then I discover another variable that I hadn't accounted for.'

'Perhaps you should stop thinking of them as an algorithm and just go with it,' she said. 'Besides, I think you understand the meaning of relationships pretty well, Calc.' She turned to look at him and smiled. 'I never thanked you properly for coming back to save us, when we were stuck in the bear pit.'

The android shrugged. 'It's what any friend would have done,' he said.

'Yes, but it cost you a lot, personally. You had to break your vow of non-violence.'

'I had to make a choice. In the end, helping my friends was more important.'

'So, are you going to re-take your vow?'

Calculus shook his head. 'I suspect the same thing would happen again. I have to face the fact that I was built to be a war droid and I will never escape from that destiny. From now on, I will use my abilities in the best way I can, but I know I will never be able to avoid the killing.'

India blew out her cheeks. 'I guess that's the world we

live in,' she said. 'Perhaps all we can do is try and make it better for other people.'

A sign flashed past in the headlights and she turned her head sharply. 'Hey, map reader, wake up! That was the sign for Balcombe.'

Calculus turned his attention to the map. 'According to this, the road meets up with the rail line near here. There's a level crossing about five miles ahead and then they run in parallel until they reach a viaduct. After that they separate again. If we are going to stop the train, it will have to be before the train crosses that bridge.'

'Then that's our chance. We'd better not mess this up.' India accelerated, feeling the truck fishtail briefly behind her as she took the bend.

'I would advise caution, India,' said Calculus. 'We won't be much use to Bella if we end up in a ditch.'

'Or if we miss the train,' she shot back. 'How much further to the level crossing?'

'About another mile.' He glanced over his shoulder and then at, India. 'I suspect I know what you are planning to do, India,' he said. 'I think you are planning to use the truck to block the level crossing.'

'Ten out of ten, Calc.'

'I must advise against that course of action. The woman called Marge said she had ten fifty-gallon drums of fuel in the back of the wagon. If that is true, then the resulting explosion might injure the prisoners being transported on the train.'

She turned to look at him and her mismatched eyes flared briefly in the darkness. 'We don't have a choice. None of the weapons we have with us are anything like powerful enough to stop an armoured train. This truck is the only thing we have. Besides, the prisoners are near the middle of the train and I'm banking on the explosion being confined to the front.'

'That is more wishful thinking than anything else, India.'

'It's our only shot. If you want to get out, just say so now.'

'No, that's all right,' he said. 'I suppose part of me is curious to see what will happen.'

'I guess boys always like to see things get smashed up, eh? OK, hold up, it looks like we're here.'

They passed through a wooded area and rounded a bend to be confronted with a white gate across the road with a faded 'stop' sign at its centre. A second identical gate was visible a dozen metres away and between them lay a set of gleaming steel rails. The rails snaked out of the darkness and cut across the road before plunging into a railway tunnel a quarter of a mile up the line.

India pulled to a stop, and they clambered out of the cab. They looked up the line towards the mouth of the tunnel. 'The tunnel goes right underneath that hill,' said Calculus. 'According to the map, it emerges only a couple of miles from the viaduct. Once the train has entered the tunnel, we will stand little chance of catching them in the truck.'

'Then this is where we make our stand,' said India. She rattled the gate and swore under her breath. 'Padlocked,' she muttered. 'We'll have to take it out with the truck. Get in.'

They climbed back into the cab and India gunned the engine. The rotten wood offered little resistance to the truck, cracking and splintering with ease as India drove through first one gate and then the other. When the trailer was parked squarely across the tracks, she applied the handbrake.

'How long do you think it will be before the train gets here?' she said, looking up the line.

'Despite your erratic driving, we made good time on the journey here,' said Calculus. 'Judging by the distance shown on the map and my estimate of the train's top speed, I calculate that it will reach here in the next fifteen minutes. Might I suggest we unhitch the trailer and take the cab to a safe distance? We may need it later.'

'Do you know how to unhitch this thing?'

'Yes. Once I have disengaged the trailer, take the cab to the top of that rise, by the trees. That should give us a good view of the train without the risk of being hit by debris.'

India drummed her fingers impatiently on the steering wheel while Calculus disconnected air hoses and cables and removed the safety clips from the coupling bar. When he was finished, he slapped twice on the side of the cab.

The trailer disengaged smoothly and remained behind as she pulled forwards. She took the cab to the top of the rise as Calculus had suggested and looked back at the trailer straddling the line. The metal-sided trailer looked flimsier from a distance and she bit her lip. Would it be enough?

Calculus remained beside the trailer with his head cocked slightly. After a moment, he kneeled down and pressed his ear to the track, then sat up, alarmed. 'India, I'm afraid I have miscalculated,' he called out. 'I am picking up frequencies in the rails that could only be made by an approaching engine. The train is here.'

17

ACROSS THE ROOFTOPS

India's mouth went dry. Her plan to stop the train had been contrived on the spur of the moment. But all her bravado hadn't prepared her for the moment when a fast-moving train carrying her sister and a hundred other souls would slam into the barricade she had set up across the road. And when it did... then what?

She glanced at the trailer and then back at the cab. Was she far enough away? Should they get further into the trees? What if the collision harmed the hostages? A dozen thoughts crammed in on her at once, shouting for attention.

She could hear the train now. The insistent hiss of vibrating steel as the tracks picked up and amplified the frequencies of the approaching train. 'Calc,' she cried. 'Get up here quick.'

The android sprinted up the short rise to the cab and the two of them looked down on the lines. 'Calc, tell me I'm doing the right thing,' she muttered.

'I'm afraid there are too many variables to give you an accurate answer to that question. However, if it is any help, I judge the odds of the trailer having sufficient mass to stop the train as approximately one in two hundred and seventy-five.'

'Thanks,' she muttered. 'That's not really any help at all.'

The sibilant hiss of the rails reached a crescendo and the vibrations increased exponentially. They could hear the locomotive now too, an insistent chuffing accompanied by the rumbling of steel wheels moving at speed.

India fixed her eyes on the bend in the tracks until the train swung into view. The locomotive was a giant muscular presence exhaling great gasps of steam and completely black save for a single lamp at the front. It moved much faster than its bulk had suggested when they had seen it in the goods yard, closing the distance with frightening rapidity.

'It's travelling faster than I anticipated,' shouted Calculus over the oncoming roar. 'Perhaps it would be prudent to seek cover before—'

His words were lost in the sound of approaching thunder as the train closed the final distance, trailing thick clouds of white steam as it bore down on the crossing. The ground shook beneath the soles of India's heavy boots and the night was filled with the squealing of metal wheels and clank of metal couplings.

'It's not stopping,' yelled India over the din. 'They haven't seen the trailer.'

As India recalled the incident later, there was a moment of pure stillness, just before the crash. A point where the metal and the steam and thunderous rattle of the carriages seemed to stop and the whole scene became a frozen tableau.

And then the collision happened.

The impact shattered the night like an explosion in a bell factory. The truck trailer disintegrated under the force of the collision, flying apart in a blizzard of twisted metal that bore no resemblance to what it had been and spraying debris into the trees at high velocities.

An instant later came the explosion. Liquid fire blossomed from the wreckage like a huge and deadly flower. A fountain of flame erupted into the air, spraying burning fuel into the trees and back along the length of the train. A great wash of heat passed over India and she instinctively held out her hands to protect her face.

But still the train did not stop. As the conflagration blossomed outwards, the locomotive burst from the flames like a mythical beast. Burning wreckage clattered down through the trees and liquid flame streaked the sides of the carriages, making the train look like a visitation from hell.

But still the train did not stop.

'It didn't work,' yelled India, as the flame-streaked carriages rattled past them. 'They didn't even slow down.'

'They may be used to bandit gangs trying to block the line,' shouted Calculus over the din. 'Maybe that's why the train is so heavily armoured.'

They watched the train thunder away, still trailing ribbons of flame as it headed for the mouth of the tunnel. India stared after it, feeling the despair rise in her chest again as she saw the last hope of rescuing her sister getting away.

'I am sorry, India,' said Calculus as the sound of the train faded. 'I'm afraid there is no chance of catching them now.'

She clenched her fist and punched the side of the truck with a roar of frustration, hollowing the door panel. 'NO!' she screamed.

'India, I understand that you are—'

'NO!' she yelled again. 'I won't let this be the end. I'm not giving up on Bella.'

'But, India, I—'

'Get in the cab!'

Calculus watched her climb back into the cab and, after a brief pause, he followed. India was already fumbling with the keys.

'India, I'm not sure what you hope to achieve by—'

'There's still a chance to catch them. We're going after that train.'

'I don't like to contradict you when you are upset, India. But there is no chance of catching them. It's nearly four miles by road to around that hill, whereas the tunnel goes straight through. They will be a long way ahead of us by the time we get there.'

'We're not taking the road,' hissed India. 'If that train can follow a straight line, then so can we.' She reached for the belt hanging from the door pillar behind her. 'Put your seat belt on; this is liable to get bumpy.'

'India, I believe I know what you are planning and I must advise against this course of—'

The rest of his words were lost in the rumble of the diesel engine coming awake. India gunned the engine and ground the truck's gears as they pulled away. A short distance along the road, she found what she was looking for, a turn-off from the main road, blocked by a five-bar gate.

'There,' she said triumphantly.

The android sounded concerned now. 'India, that is just a rough track. If you are planning to pursue the train by driving over that hill, I must advise against it. It is highly unlikely that this truck will be able to navigate the path safely.'

'Who gives a damn about "safely",' she shot back as she turned off the road. 'What's the matter, Calc? You're not afraid, are you?'

'I am incapable of fear, as you well know. And whilst I am unlikely to be harmed if this truck crashes, the same is not true for you.'

'That's my problem. Now shut up and let me drive.'

The gate offered no resistance and was crushed to splinters under the truck's wheels. As they headed up the track, India wondered whether she had made a mistake. Calculus had been right: what she had taken for a narrow road that led over the hill was little more than a stony path. The truck lurched dangerously from side to side as she gunned the engine over the uneven ground. When they entered a wooded section, the low branches hammered the roof and windshield of the cab, shattering the screen so that Calculus had to punch out the remaining glass with his fist.

At one point, the vehicle tottered precariously on two wheels as they skirted the edge of a steep slope before mercifully slamming back to level ground. The trees finally fell away as they approached the crest of the hill. India changed gear and the truck slithered along the grassy hilltop.

Calculus consulted the map and gave her shouted instructions over the wind rushing through the cab. 'Take a straight line heading slightly south-west,' he yelled, indicating the direction with his hand. 'Provided we don't meet any obstructions, we should arrive at the tunnel exit on the other side.'

The journey down the slope on the far side was even more terrifying than the route up. The ground was steeper and the truck picked up speed quickly. When India tried to apply the brakes, the truck just slithered uncontrollably and threatened to overturn. Her only option was to keep them pointed directly downhill and try to avoid the large rocks and trees that loomed out of the night with little warning.

At the bottom of the hill, the ground levelled out and became softer so that progress slowed and the wheels began to slip in the mud. Finally, they came to a field where the ground dropped away in a near vertical escarpment, protected only by a thin wire fence. Faded signs in red paint warned of the dangers of the sheer drop.

India pulled the truck as close to the edge as she dared, and they peered down at the drop. Directly below them they could see the silver tracks emerging from the hillside and snaking away into the night. There was no sign of the train.

India looked at Calculus with a quizzical expression. 'This is the tunnel so, where's the train?'

The android shrugged. 'Perhaps they stopped in the tunnel to assess the damage before they continued their journey. We could go down and look, but it will be a difficult climb down to the tunnel entrance.'

There was a faint rumble from below and a tremor ran through the cab. 'No need to check,' said India grimly. 'It's here.'

A moment later, the locomotive exploded from the end of the tunnel in a burst of steam and smoke that engulfed the hillside on which they had parked. As the locomotive sped away into the night, a stream of armoured carriages unspooled from the tunnel entrance and clattered away down the tracks. Some of the trucks still trailed flames in their wake as the last of the fires burned themselves out.

'Stay here,' said the android, opening the door. 'I will attempt to jump onto one of the carriages as they pass.'

'What and leave you to have all the fun?' India restarted the truck's engine. 'We're in this together, Calc, so hold on to your hat.'

Realisation dawned on the android as to what was about to happen. 'India, no, don't!' He reached for the steering wheel, but he was already too late. She floored the throttle and the truck's wheels spun briefly before finding traction and lurching towards the edge.

The truck tore through the flimsy fencing and launched itself over the edge of the escarpment. The android reared back and braced in his seat and India threw up her hands for protection. She had a last glimpse of the carriages thundering away beneath them as the cab tumbled sickeningly and crashed nose-first into the centre of a passing carriage.

The effect was like falling down a lift shaft while imprisoned inside a steel drum. The collision slammed India against the seat restraints as splintered wood and glass fragments smashed their way into the cabin. An airbag exploded to life, striking her in the face as it absorbed the impact and her head cracked painfully against something hard.

The noise of the collision gradually settled as the last pieces of broken glass tumbled from the smashed windows. India found herself hanging face downwards, suspended by her seat belt. The air was filled with choking clouds that made it hard to breathe and a white fog filled the cabin, blurring her vision.

She raised her head painfully too look around her. Several soft and heavy bags had been pushed through the windscreen and had burst open, swamping the cabin with soft white powder. Calculus was extracting himself from the debris that had smashed into him at the point of impact. He pulled aside the last pieces of broken wood and scrambled across the cabin towards her.

'Can you hear me, India?' he asked as he peered into her face. She opened her mouth to reply but all that came out was a strangled growl. 'Don't try to speak,' he said. 'You appear to have a broken nose but I can find no signs of serious injury.'

She coughed and tried again to sit upright. 'The train... are we?'

'The truck is lodged in the roof of a goods carriage about halfway along the train,' replied the android. 'Against all the odds, you appear to have succeeded in getting us on board.'

She heaved one of the burst sacks off her lap, sending more clouds of powder into the air. 'This white stuff... what *is* it?'

'It appears you have crashed the truck into a carriage containing sacks of flour,' said Calculus. 'As it happens, that was remarkably fortunate. I believe most of the other carriages are filled with pig iron and fuel drums. Had we struck one of those, we would almost certainly have been killed. Or at least you would.'

'Well, I guess I'm just a regular lucky charm.' She groaned as she tried to free herself from the tangle of seat restraints and the remains of the deflated airbag. Then she wiped the cloying mess of flour from her face and eyes.

'The hostages,' she grunted. 'Which carriage?'

'The carriage containing your sister and the other prisoners is located three carriages forwards of here,' said Calculus. 'There are no connecting passages between the carriages. I believe the only way to reach them will be via the roof.'

They heard the sound of someone shouting over the rattle of the train, coming from somewhere behind them. The shout was followed by the sound of rapid gunfire and a quick rattle of shots that spattered against the metal of the truck.

'Someone's shooting at us,' said India.

'As I recall, there is a guard carriage and a gun emplacement at the far end of the train. No doubt the guards have seen the truck and believe they are under attack.'

Another volley of bullets clanged against the truck's bodywork. India stirred herself and pulled at her seat belt until it sprang apart. 'We can't stay here; we're sitting targets. Help me out here.'

The truck was lodged into the carriage roof, nose downwards, at a forty-five-degree angle and both cab doors were wedged tight against the sides of the carriage. The only possible exit was through the windscreen, which no longer held any glass but which was now jammed with several large bags of flour.

Calculus cleared them a path through the windscreen, pulling aside the heavy bags until they were both able to crawl free. The crash had torn away most of the carriage roof but by standing on top of a pallet of flour, India was able to look along the roof of the train.

The sky was losing its blackness as the dawn approached, turning the sky a leaden grey. She narrowed her eyes against the wind and the smoke and counted the engine plus five carriages ahead of them. Through the half-light she could see the elaborate passenger carriage at the front of the train, trailing lace curtains through its shattered windows. Two carriages further back, she saw the cattle truck containing Bella and the rest of the prisoners from Glass Town and was relieved to see that it bore only a few black scorch marks from the explosion.

The view to the rear of the train was blocked by the truck, sticking out of the roof like an abstract sculpture. Every few seconds, more gunfire sounded from the rear of the train and the truck's metalwork would ring out as the bullets found their mark.

'We need to get forward to the cattle truck,' shouted

India over the rushing wind. 'If we can unhitch the carriage from the rest of the train, we might be able to get the prisoners out.'

'Disconnecting the carriage will do little good unless we can also stop the guards at the back of the train,' shouted Calculus. 'May I suggest that you make your way to the front of the train whilst I deal with the guards?'

India nodded. 'That sounds like a fair division of labour.' She paused and leaned back through the truck's windscreen, emerging clutching the two radios. 'Here, take one of these so we can stay in touch. Let's hope Marge kept these things charged up.'

The train shuddered and leaned as it took a bend in the track. India reached out to steady herself and, for a brief instant, they caught a view of the gun emplacement at the rear of the train. A guard on the rear carriage spotted them at the same time and unleashed a volley of hurried shots before the train straightened and shielded them from view again.

'Are you sure you want to go back there?' said India. 'You don't have any weapons.'

'The guards are mostly using small-calibre rifles and the occasional shotgun, which are unlikely to cause me any significant harm. My only concern is if they try to use the big field gun. My armour is not built to take a close-range impact from such a weapon.'

India nodded. 'If we try to get the prisoners out while that gun is still working, we'll be open targets,' she said. 'Do what you can to take it out.'

The android nodded once and turned away towards the end of the carriage. 'And Calc...' she added. 'Try not to get yourself killed.'

'I will do my best, India. I have been killed many times

in the course of active service and it is never a pleasant experience.'

The android gave her a brief nod and she watched as he turned and climbed nimbly over the wreckage of the truck before disappearing from view. Her cracked rib had now turned into a steady ache and her nose throbbed unpleasantly. She wiped the blood from her face with her sleeve and looked towards the front of the train. There was no time to worry about her injuries now. Bella was depending on her.

She steeled herself for what she was about to do. Running across the roof of a moving train was something you read about in adventure stories, but when she looked along the rattling, swaying carriages and thought about falling onto hard clinker or being dragged under steel wheels, her legs turned to jelly.

She forced the intrusive thoughts to the back of her mind; none of this was going to help her sister. Moving carefully, she pulled herself fully out of the hole and found an unbroken portion of the roof where she could stand up. The wind felt twice as strong up here, buffeting her body as though it would carry her off like a scrap of paper. Several times the swaying of the carriage nearly pitched her sideways until she got the hang of keeping her body steady as if she were standing on the deck of a moving ship.

When she felt stable enough, she tried a tentative step forwards and immediately had to fight to regain her balance before taking another. She quickly found the best and safest method was to crouch low and keep moving, using forward momentum to keep herself stable. This worked well until she reached the end of the roof.

The gap to the next carriage was a distance of no more than eight feet but it loomed like a canyon before her. She

looked down at the gap between the wagons and considered
for a moment the possibility of climbing down and then
back up again. But a moment's consideration told her that,
with nearly a dozen carriages to cross, this would take far
more time than she had available. She would have to jump.

She braced herself, placing one leg behind and tensing
for the jump. Then, abandoning all considerations of
personal safety, she leaped. He legs pedalled the air as she
crossed the distance and she had a brief glimpse of greasy
grey couplings and steel tracks flashing beneath her before
she came down on the other side, hitting the roof in a low
crouch.

She stayed still and low until she regained her balance,
then proceeded cautiously along the roof of the next
carriage. She made more rapid progress this time, taking
short, sure steps, timed to coincide with the swaying of the
train. The leap across the couplings was easier too and she
continued almost without breaking stride. When she
reached the carriage containing the hostages, she paused
before leaping.

The Pinkertons obviously valued their slaves more
highly than the goods in the previous wagons. Heavy
armour and steel spikes had been riveted to the sides of the
carriage and thick swags of barbed wire were nailed crudely
around the roof to prevent anyone attempting to climb up.
She took a short run-up to clear the wire but her trousers
caught in the barbs, slamming her down face-first. The
swaying of the train sent her rolling across the roof and she
barely caught a handhold before she reached the edge. For a
moment, her legs swayed precariously out over the moving
track until she managed to haul herself back.

She lay for almost a full minute trying to catch her
breath before getting up and staggering to the centre of the

carriage. A heavy trapdoor had been set into the roof, secured by an iron bolt, presumably to check on the prisoners or pass down food and water. She pressed an ear to the wood but could hear nothing inside above the rumbling of the train.

Praying that the Pinkertons hadn't decided to place an armed guard inside the carriage, she drew back the bolt and heaved open the trapdoor. An iron grille covered a dark hole and, in the darkness below, a dozen faces stared up at her like hungry sparrows.

'Who is it?' called a voice from below. 'Who's up there?'

'Have we arrived yet?'

'What was that explosion? Are we being attacked?'

India held up her hands for quiet but struggled to make herself understood to the panicked crowd below. Then a familiar voice cut through the clamour. 'India? Is that you?'

Bella's face appeared in the square of upturned faces, staring up at her sister. 'How did you get up there? The train's moving!'

'It's a long story, Bel. But I'm here to rescue you.'

Bella squinted up at the opening. 'Can you get us out of that hatchway?'

India shook her head. 'Not this way. These bars are solid and the walls are reinforced with steel plates. I'm going to try and disconnect this carriage from the rest of the train.'

A ripple of excitement ran through the group at the prospect of escape. Some began to cry while others began shouting and demanding to be released immediately. Finally, Bella managed to make herself heard again.

'India, there's something you need to know. As we were being brought onto the train, I saw your friend, Sid being carried on board.'

India's eyes widened. 'Sid's *alive*?'

Bella shook her head. 'I'm not sure. He was on a stretcher and he looked like he was in a bad way. But I heard one of the guards saying they needed to keep him alive because he had a price on his head.'

India thought quickly. She remembered Sid telling her he was wanted by some of the gangs he had dealt with in the East and that many were prepared to pay handsomely to have him captured alive. She looked down at Bella again. 'Where did they take him?'

'They put him in the prison van,' she said. 'It's the carriage in front of this one.'

India cursed silently. If she went ahead and disconnected Bella's carriage as she had planned, then she would be leaving Sid to the mercy of the Pinkertons. And if that happened, then who knew what horrific things the gangs in the East might do to him. She bit her lip and looked along the train. All the people in the carriage down below were now depending on her to set them free. If she went to help Sid, then there was a definite chance that she might get caught and they would all be doomed. But if she abandoned her friend...

She tried to think what Sid would have done in her position and realised immediately that was not a good way to judge the situation. She looked down at Bella again. 'Sit tight,' she said. 'I'll have you all out of there in just a bit.'

'Where are you going?'

India felt a constriction in her chest and found she could not look Bella in the eye. 'I'm sorry, Bel,' she said. 'I need to go and help a friend first.'

18

REMUS

The android made his way swiftly along the train roof, without hesitation or falter. The micro-muscles within his limbs made over a million adjustments a second, ensuring that his frame remained stable, and his targeting sensors remained rigidly focused on the gun emplacement on the last carriage. It was just a shame, he thought, that he had no weapons to use when he got there.

As he approached the last two carriages, he paused. The last carriage was the flatbed truck carrying the gun emplacement. The carriage in front of that was boxy and plain-sided and he suspected it was being used to house more guards. He could see no sign of whoever had been shooting at them and he suspected they had now retreated inside the carriage. He should proceed with caution.

He looked around for India but his view was largely blocked by the truck, sticking from the roof. Looking further ahead, he followed the line of the rail tracks through the forest until the trees gave way to a broad green valley, about three miles distant. The tracks continued across the valley on a tall brick-built viaduct, with many arches like an army of long-legged giants.

Beyond that, he knew, lay the South Downs, swarming with cannibal gangs and bandits, and a slaver ship that waited in a harbour for the Pinkertons to spirit away their human cargo. Calculus knew that if they could not stop the train before they reached the Badlands, their chances of rescuing India's sister would be close to zero.

As he turned back to the rear of the train, a guard emerged from the guards' van and stood on the gangway directly below him. The man carried a heavy rifle and wore nothing but a set of long underwear, crusted with filth. He reared back in shock when he saw the android looming over him on the roof and he snatched a hurried shot. Calculus flinched as the slug struck his visor and buzzed away like an angry bee.

The man did not get the chance to deliver a second shot. The android dropped from the roof, landing with feline grace on the small gangway. As the guard fumbled with his weapon, it was snatched from his hands and torn in two before being hurled away. A moment later, a steel hand caught the guard around the side of the head and smashed his skull against the door post.

As the man's body slipped soundlessly from the gangway and disappeared beneath the crushing steel wheels, the android stepped through the door. The carriage beyond was little more than a plain boxcar in which a dozen cots had been arranged for sleeping. Some men sat on their bunks, seemingly unaware of what had just happened while others were already priming their weapons and backing away from the door as the war droid advanced into the room.

Calculus held up a hand against the first volley of shots

as one might shield themselves against a driving rain. As half a dozen men cocked their rifles for a second shot, Calculus swiped a rifle from the nearest man and swung it, club-like, around his head. Three skulls cracked in quick succession and bodies collapsed in spreading pools of crimson. A fourth man, wielding a gleaming sabre, screamed and charged at Calculus in a berserker-frenzy. The sword sparked on the android's armour and glanced off, a moment before a steel fist smashed the man to the floor with a rattle of broken teeth.

By now the remaining guards were backing out of the far door, keeping their weapons trained on the android. The door was slammed shut and heavy bolts were drawn from the other side. Calculus covered the length of the carriage in three strides, pausing to pluck a pump-action shotgun from one of the cots.

A swift kick from the android reduced the door to splintered wreckage. On the far side of the door, three guards immediately unleashed a barrage of gunfire. There was a moment's pause as the gunsmoke cleared. Inexplicably, the guards found themselves staring at an empty doorway. The carriage beyond looked very empty, still littered with blankets and weaponry abandoned in the fight.

'He's gone,' said one, peering more closely at the doorway.

'Maybe he ran away,' said another hopefully. 'Reckon we scared him off.'

'Steady, lads,' said an older man. 'That creature is still hiding in there somewhere, waiting for us to come and find him. Keep your wits about you.' He glanced back at the heavy field gun where two men were frantically cranking the elevation wheel to lower the barrel down towards the doorway.

A full minute passed.

The men licked their lips and glanced at each other nervously before the one who had spoken first took a tentative step towards the doorway. His colleagues tightened their trigger fingers as they waited.

A shadow cut across the sky above them. One of the guards looked up to see a figure on the carriage roof, two metres tall and silhouetted against the dawn sky. He let out a strangled cry. 'It's up there. The robot's on the r—'

His words were sliced off like a razor across a throat as the android dropped into their midst. A furious whirl of well-targeted blows rapidly laid all three men in a heap at his feet. Calculus looked down at the bloody mess of limbs and then dropped the gun he was holding. The fight had taken no more than three seconds.

Then he looked up and, for the first time since the encounter began, he experienced surprise. At the end of the flatbed, a nervous teenager squatted behind the huge field gun. His eyes were wide with fear and beads of greasy sweat rolled down his forehead. 'Stay back, robot!' he commanded. He licked his lips and tightened his grip on the firing lever. 'Stay back or I'll blow you to bits!'

And, for the first time, Calculus realised that the muzzle of the field gun was pointed directly at his chest.

INDIA TORE herself away from the pleading faces below the trapdoor and resumed her passage along the roof. If Sid really was being held captive in the next carriage, she would find him and free him. Then the two of them would uncouple the hostage truck and they would free the hostages and—

She stopped at the end of the carriage and looked down

at the gangway below. If Sid really was down there, then there was no guarantee as to what condition she would find him in. According to Bella, he'd been in a bad way. What if he was unconscious or unable to walk?

She shook the thoughts away as she lowered herself between the carriages and onto the narrow platform. Every fibre in her body told her that she should be freeing the other prisoners. But she also knew if she abandoned her friend, the thought that he might have died because of her would haunt her for the rest of her days.

She examined the walls and the door of the prison carriage. While the other wagons had crude metal plates, bolted onto the wood to protect them from attack, the prison carriage was purpose-built to be impregnable. The walls and the door were made of riveted steel with heavy bolts. Thick iron grilles were set high in the walls in place of windows and a medieval collar of iron spikes projected down from the roof. It was clear that the Pinkertons reserved this carriage for their most valuable prisoners.

She examined the door handle and wondered what she would find on the other side, then let out a curse when she remembered that she had forgotten to bring the shotgun from the truck. But there was no time to go back for it now. Whatever might lie inside this carriage, she would have to face it unarmed.

She tried the door handle without much expectation of success and, to her surprise, discovered it was open. Clearly the Pinkertons' own security was not as tight as it first appeared.

The door opened soundlessly on well-oiled hinges. She stepped inside and closed the door quietly behind her. The sudden muting of the noise from outside was like the peace of a library after her hectic her passage across the rooftops.

She let her eyes adjust to the dim light and saw she was standing in a narrow corridor that ran down one side of the carriage. The only light came from narrow thin slit windows high up on the wall. Dust motes played in the weak sunbeams, illuminating a row of individual prison cells, each one secured by vertical steel bars across the front.

Most of the cells were empty, their doors ajar, but in a cell near the end of the row, the crumpled form of a young man lay beneath a threadbare blanket, a black hat lying beside him. In the dimness of the carriage, India could not tell if he was breathing.

'Sid!' She rattled the bars, glancing anxiously along the carriage in case someone came in. The figure shifted under the blanket and groaned. 'Sid, wake up. It's me, India. I'm here to get you out.'

Sid lifted his head from beneath the blanket and squinted at her. India inhaled sharply. Sid's face was puffy and swollen; both eyes were blackened and the left one was nearly closed. His clothes were torn and there was congealed blood down the front of his shirt.

'Sid, are you OK?'

The man coughed. 'Oh, sure,' he said weakly. 'I'm just peachy.' He grimaced, unable to disguise the pain with his light-heartedness.

She inspected the cell door, which was made of hardened steel bars with a heavy lock and frame. 'Sid, do you know where the keys are?'

He shook his head and was immediately seized by another bout of coughing. 'Not in here,' he gasped. 'Took 'em away when they locked me up.'

The sound of cheerful whistling made India turn just in time to see the door at the far end swing open. A young boy stood silhouetted against the open doorway, fumbling with a bunch of keys. When he looked up and saw India, his whistling stopped as suddenly as if someone had cut off his air supply.

For a moment India was afraid the boy might bolt out of the door again, but he stayed where he was, staring at her with wide eyes. Then he blinked, sniffed and wiped his nose on his sleeve and she realised who it was.

'Sniffer?' she said.

The boy blinked again. He glanced at the door to Sid's cell and then back at India. 'You ain't s'posed to be in here,' he said. 'It ain't allowed. You ain't s'posed—'

His words were cut short when India pulled Sid's gun from her belt and levelled it at him. 'Get away from the door,' she hissed. The boy licked his lips and did as she told him.

'Now draw those bolts, top and bottom.' The boy moved quickly to draw the bottom bolt but was too short to reach the top one. 'It doesn't matter,' said India. 'Have you got the keys to this cell?'

He sniffed again and dug his hands into his pockets defiantly. 'Might have. What's it worth?'

India bristled. 'I'm the one holding the gun. Work it out for yourself.'

'G'waaaan! You ain't gonna shoot me. I'm just a kid.' He employed the sleeve to wipe his nose again.

She stared at the boy and thought about doubling down on her threats. But one look at the scorn on his face told her it was a useless endeavour. She uncocked the gun and returned it to her belt. 'Alright,' she said. 'I'm not going to shoot you. So, do you know where the keys are or not?'

The boy sniffed, this time with the air of someone who knows they have the upper hand. 'Yeah, I got 'em. The Mr Pinkertons trust me with 'em. They told me to go and check on the prisoner. When they heard the explosion, they was afraid someone was tryin' to bust him out. Seems like they was right too.'

India looked the boy up and down. Despite his confident air, his frame was angular and stick-thin, his cheeks were drawn and there was a fading yellowish bruise down one of them. 'I notice you're not running to raise the alarm,' she said.

'I might do yet,' he declared. 'I ain't decided. Depends what you got to offer me.'

'And why should I do a deal with you? Last time we met, you gave me up to the guards.'

'I 'ad to, didn't I,' he said with another defiant sniff. 'The guards found me talkin' to you. I had to cover my backside somehow. But it's different now; there ain't no one else here.'

India sighed. 'All right, what do you want?'

The certainty faded from the boy's face for a moment and he glanced over his shoulder. His voice dropped to a conspiratorial whisper. 'I already told you, didn' I? I want you to take me with you.'

India frowned. She had assumed the boy had just been spinning her a line. 'Are you serious?'

'Sure.' He stepped closer; there was pleading in his eyes now. 'It's like I said, Northsiders live in luxury. Got all the food they want, that's what I heard.'

'Well, it's not quite like that...' she began.

'I don't care!' A look of sudden desperation crossed the boy's face. He grasped at the sleeve of her jacket. 'I've got to get away from here. From... *them...*' He looked back over his shoulder. 'I could do stuff for you on the Northside. I could find things that you need. I'm good at finding things. Everyone says that's what Sniffer's best at.'

'Sniffer?'

'That's what they call me.' He wiped his nose on his sleeve again to illustrate his point. 'So, what about it? You gonna take me with you or what?'

India looked around in exasperation. 'What about your uncle? The slave master. Won't he be worried about you?'

The boy gave a particularly long sniff. 'He ain't my uncle. He was jus' someone I used to find things for. I try to be useful, you know? If you ain't useful around here then they...' He shuddered and fell silent.

India sighed. The last thing she needed right now was to acquire any more needy children. 'Look... Sniffer. I think you've got the wrong idea about the Northside. It's not much better than the Southside and—'

'But, they don't beat up on kids there, do they?' Sniffer's eyes were suddenly filled with tears. 'I'd be safe there, with you, wouldn't I?'

'Sniffer... I...' India found herself lost for words. 'You need to understand. We're a long way from the Northside and I'm not sure how I'm going to get back myself.'

'But if you took me with you, I could help, couldn't I.' He looked eager now. 'I could help you get home. And then I could come and live with you on the Northside and find things for you there. I'm good at finding things.'

India sighed and her shoulders slumped. She knew when she was beaten. 'All right,' she said. 'I'll take you with us back to the Northside. But I can't guarantee what'll happen after that. Now, have you got those keys or not?'

Sniffer broke out in a grin that threatened to engulf his entire face. 'You won't regret it,' he said gleefully. 'You won't believe how much use Sniffer can be. Here, look.' He fumbled in his overall pockets and pulled out a bunch of iron keys on a large ring, then held it out to her.

India tried several keys before she found the one that

fitted. The lock was well-oiled and turned smoothly and she wondered how regularly these cells were used by the Pinkertons.

'Sid, wake up!' While India had been talking to Sniffer, Sid had drifted back into unconsciousness. She shook him. 'We've got to get out of here.'

Sid groaned but did not open his eyes. India was about to try again when Sniffer picked up a tin mug of water from beside the cot and threw it in Sid's face. The reaction was instantaneous. Sid exploded awake, swearing and spluttering as he sat up and glared murderously at them.

'Dammit, India Bentley. Are you trying to kill me?'

'See!' said Sniffer delightedly. 'Works every time. I told you I was useful.'

India scowled at Sniffer, then turned to Sid. 'Sorry about that,' she said. 'But we need to get you out of here quickly. Here, I'll help you up. Sniffer, get the other side of him.'

Sid shook his head and then focused on the boy. 'Who's that?' he growled.

'Name's Sniffer,' said the boy cheerily. 'I find things.'

'It's a long story,' said India. 'Don't ask.'

Working together, India and Sniffer managed to get Sid on his feet and the three of them staggered the length of the narrow hall. They had almost reached the door when someone began pounding on the other door and rattling the handle.

'Sniffer, open this door, you little wretch. I sent you out here half an hour ago.'

Sniffer's face turned suddenly pale. 'It's Remus Pinkerton,' he whispered. 'He's come to find me. Please, we gotta *hurry!*'

The rattling on the far side of the door stopped and the door shook from a massive blow. The iron bolt at the bottom held the door firmly but, despite its thickness, the top half of the door bowed inwards and made splintering noises.

'He's coming in,' wailed Sniffer. He let go of Sid and backed against the wall. Sid immediately slid to the floor with a groan. India bit her lip. Her plan to find Sid and escape without being detected was totally shot now. She removed one of the pistols from her belt and held it steady in both hands as she aimed it towards the door.

A second kick from outside splintered the frame and made Sniffer shriek again. At the third blow, the iron bolt gave up its grip on the wood and the door burst open to hang loosely on one hinge. The bulk of Remus Pinkerton filled the doorway, blocking the light from outside. 'Sniffer, you little wretch,' he roared. 'Get out here or I'll—'

He stopped talking when he noticed the open cell door. Then he spotted India, Sid and Sniffer in the gloom at the far end of the corridor. Remus pulled himself up to his full height and regarded them for several seconds. India did her best to keep the gun steady and wondered if he could see her hands shaking.

Then Remus Pinkerton smiled. It was a terrifying smile that split his wide baby face and revealed a perfect set of white teeth. She shuddered as she remembered what Sid had said about the Pinkertons' predilection for human flesh.

He took a step into the room. 'Stay back,' growled India. 'I don't want to shoot you, but I'll use this if I have to. Just let us walk out of here and nobody needs to get hurt.'

The smile on Remus's face widened. 'Unfortunately, my dear, somebody always needs to get hurt. How else could men such as myself and my brother stamp our authority on the world unless through the medium of violence? Of course...' He gave a high, tinkling laugh that sent icy fingers down her spine. 'It helps if you really *enjoy* violence.' He took another step forwards.

'This is your last warning, Pinkerton. I won't let you make slaves of those people.'

He raised his eyebrows in surprise. 'Slaves? You misunderstand. These people are not destined to become slaves; we have a much higher purpose in mind for them.'

India tightened her grip on the pistol. 'Enough of your bullshit. I'm walking out of here now and I'm taking those people with me and neither you nor your brother are going to stop me.'

Remus adopted an expression of mock sadness. 'Oh, that is so unfortunate, my dear,' he said. 'You see, I was really hoping you'd join us on our little pilgrimage to the East. But now...' He let the sentence hang in the air. 'Now, I'm just going to have to kill you.'

He lunged towards her.

The gun exploded in her hand and a wave of compressed energy echoed round the steel walls. Remus Pinkerton flinched as the shot went high and splintered a wooden beam above his head. Then he lowered his head like an angry bull and charged the length of the narrow corridor towards India.

Remus moved fast for a man his size and India fumbled with the gun, trying to pull back the hammer for another shot. A second blast echoed round the carriage but missed as Remus ducked and rolled nimbly across the floor. He came up quickly and grabbed the lapels of India's jacket before slamming his bony forehead into her face. She dropped the gun and reeled backwards as a wave of pain blotted out everything and her eyes filled with tears.

But Remus wasn't done with her yet. He grabbed her by her long hair and began to drag her back along the carriage.

In the centre of the wall was a loading door that slid open on tracks. Remus undid several bolts with his free hand, then wrenched back the handle. The door shrieked open on greased rails, and daylight and noise suddenly filled the carriage.

India gasped when she saw the scenery rushing past in a blur, just feet from where she was standing. Reading Remus's intention, she tried to pull back, but the big man was too strong for her. Gripping her hair tightly, he delivered a sharp kick to the back of her legs that brought her to her knees as he pushed her towards the open door.

India grasped the door frame and gritted her teeth as she looked down on a blur of railway ties and sharp clinker. The frame cut into her fingers, but it didn't do much good; inch by inch, she was being pushed relentlessly through the doorway.

At one point she fumbled for a better grip and her hand brushed against something slender and firm in the sleeve of her jacket. As her muscles burned with the effort of holding on with one hand, she managed to reach into her sleeve and pulled out a small blade, about three inches in length with wrappings of old rag for a handle.

Tom's knife.

With renewed hope, she twisted in Remus's grip and, gripping the rag-handle tightly, she rammed the blade backwards. There was a brief jag of resistance as the knife plunged deeply into Remus's knee, shearing through flesh and ligaments. Remus screamed in pain and the pressure was immediately released from her neck. He fell back, screaming like a burned animal, the knife still sticking out of his kneecap.

'My knee. You bitch!' he spat. His eyes gleamed with madness now. The baby-faced grin had been replaced by a look that seethed like something unholy. Snarling and grimacing with pain, Remus pulled himself upright using the cell bars. He looked down at the knife and grasped the handle tightly. Then, glaring at India all the while, he pulled the blade free from his knee with a thick sucking sound.

The pain must have been intense, but Remus made no sound. His eyes burned into India and his snarl intensified as though all of his pain and anger was being projected towards her on a beam of pure hatred.

'I will kill you for this,' he hissed. He tossed the blade aside, then reached into his pocket for a slim cut-throat razor with a handle in mother-of-pearl. The sharpness of the silver blade seemed to sing in the half-light. The manic grin returned to his face.

'Do you think you can take a blade to one of the Pinkerton brothers and live?' Thin flecks of spittle formed on his lips as he spoke. 'You have crossed a line and entered the kingdom of hell. I will nail your hands and feet to the floor. I will cut off your nose and make you watch while I eat it. I will—'

He broke off mid-sentence and lunged, swinging the blade in a wide arc at her face. Remus was fast, but India's reactions were faster. As the blade curved towards her, she clutched the doorframe and arched her body backwards right out of the open door. The razor passed an inch from her face, and she jerked herself back into the carriage, simultaneously landing a vicious kick directly onto Remus's injured knee.

The big man screamed with renewed agony as fresh blood spurted from the injury. The razor skittered across the floor as Remus sank to his knees. Still using the doorframe for leverage, India swung herself up and over the man's kneeling form. Before Remus could register what had happened, she jammed her boot into his back and shoved his body straight out of the open doorway.

There was a brief shriek as Remus fell from the train, trailing his black coat like a ragged crow, and then he was gone. India looked out after him but could see no sign of the body beside the track. When she turned back, she saw the boy staring at her in shock and Sid, still slumped in the corner, regarding her through half-lidded eyes.

'Not bad, tech-hunter,' he said weakly. 'We'll make an outlaw of you yet.'

19

ROMULUS

The android stared down the barrel of the field gun and spent several microseconds considering his options. An instant later, his decision was made. Moving faster than the human eye could register, he ducked and rolled beneath the gun's elevation. As he came upright, he slammed the barrel upwards so that it pointed safely away from the train. The young man behind the gun reared back in fright, involuntarily pulling the firing lever.

The howitzer announced itself with a bellow that scattered a flock of starlings from the trees. White smoke furled from the end of the gun into a perfect ring as the fifty-pound shell punched a hole through the air and screamed away on its upwards trajectory.

As the smoke cleared, the young man behind the gun stared at Calculus and swallowed. He began to back away from the android, stumbling backwards over spent shell casings and ammunition boxes, Calculus held up his hand.

'Stop. I will not harm you. Put down your weapons and you will be—' He stopped mid-sentence as the young man turned in terror and threw himself soundlessly from the back of the train.

Calculus looked over the end of the train but the man was already lost from view, swallowed up by the gloom of the retreating landscape. The android was still looking when a dark rumble cracked the air somewhere in the distance, like a breaking thunderstorm.

He turned just in time to see a gout of flame and dust rising from the centre of the viaduct where the shell had found its mark. The roar echoed around the hills as the explosion sent a dusty column of debris high into the air and showered the valley with broken masonry, twisted rails and shattered railway sleepers.

As the dust cloud began to drift on the wind, Calculus had a clearer view of the remains of viaduct. One of the arches spanning the valley had been destroyed entirely. Where once there had been a continuous line of track, there was now broken brickwork, rails twisted like liquorice and a gap, fifty feet wide that looked down on the valley floor a hundred feet below.

A gap where the train would be arriving in approximately two minutes.

'Oh, crap,' he muttered.

INDIA AND SNIFFER staggered from the prison van, supporting Sid's weight between them and deposited him on the small gangway outside. India glanced up at the roof ladder then crouched down in front of the semi-conscious outlaw.

'Sid, you have to try and get up that ladder and onto the roof. I'm going to disconnect these front carriages so we can get the hostages out of here.'

Sid grunted and his eyes rolled up into his head. Sniffer shrugged. 'I don't think he's all there, miss. And he weighs a ton too. You sure we can't leave 'im behind?'

Before India could answer, the walkie-talkie slung across her shoulder crackled to life. 'India, can you hear me? It's urgent that you...'

The remainder of the message was lost in a blizzard of static. India turned the channel selector back and forth and then thumped the handset with her free hand. She placed her mouth close to the microphone. 'Calc, say again. There's too much interference.'

'...bridge has been destroyed... two minutes... disconnect carriages.'

The radio set crackled again and went dead. 'There's only one bridge between here and the coast, miss,' piped up Sniffer. 'And that's the one coming up about now.'

A sick dread took hold of India's stomach. She looked up at the carriage roof. 'Wait here,' she said. 'I'm going to take a look.'

She scrambled up the ladder and peered along the track and saw at once what Calculus had been talking about. The viaduct was still about a mile distant, but even from here she could see it was enveloped in a thick cloud of brick dust and smoke. And, through the dust, she saw the missing archway like an unexpected gap in a mouthful of perfect teeth.

'Shit!' she gasped. 'We're going over the edge.' She slid back down the ladder and held out her hand. 'Sniffer, help me get Sid up there,' she yelled. 'I don't care how we do it; we've got to get him onto this roof.'

The boy managed to pull Sid into an upright position so India could grasp his collar. Then with Sniffer shoving and India heaving, and some small help from Sid, they dragged the young outlaw to the top of the ladder. When they reached the roof, Sid managed to pull himself over the lip and then collapsed in a dead faint.

India had no time to worry about Sid. She helped Sniffer up the ladder then started back down. 'Stay here with Sid,' she yelled. 'Make sure he doesn't slide off the roof. I'm going back to disconnect the train.'

At that moment, the engine driver became aware of the danger they were in and slammed on the steam brakes. The locomotive's steel wheels squealed in protest as they lost traction against the brake shoes and the carriages rattled and jerked, their combined weight threatening to derail the train entirely. A dense cloud of sparks burst from the smoke-stack and the air was filled with the sounds of tortured metal and the smell of sulphur.

The sudden slowing of the train broke India's grip on the ladder and sent her crashing into the gangway, where she narrowly avoided slipping between the trucks and onto the track. She struggled to regain her balance as the train continued to scrub off momentum, but managed to brace her feet firmly against the ladder. Holding onto the rungs with one hand, she leaned over the tracks as far as she dared, to examine the mechanism joining the two carriages.

The mechanical coupler was black with grease and shaped like two huge steel fists, gripping each other tightly. A steel pin as thick as her wrist held the coupling secure. The pin could be lifted by means of a heavy lever which was currently locked in the 'down' position.

She grasped the lever and heaved upwards but the coupler pin remained tightly wedged, stuck fast by the pressure of the braking carriages behind. She tried again, using her legs for leverage and pulling until her arms felt they would be ripped from their sockets. She shouted all the curses she could think of at the top of her voice but still the pin stubbornly refused to move.

The train was slowing now and the pressure between the carriages was diminishing. It was now or never. She seized the handle again and heaved and her heart leapt as she felt the pin shift half an inch. She was about to try again when the carriage door opened and she looked up into a giant baby face, wearing a manic grin.

For a moment, she thought that Remus had somehow managed to climb back onto the train. Then she realised the awful truth. This was Romulus; identical in every respect to the brother she had just killed, and oozing hatred from his every pore.

At the back of the train, Calculus looked towards the ruined the viaduct and then down at the rails thundering past. The train was still braking hard but a rapid calculation told him the truth: they were never going to stop in time. In less than thirty seconds, the engine would plunge over the edge of the abyss and drag every carriage with it to the valley floor.

Further calculations told him that while he could do nothing to stop the engine from going over the edge, it was just possible that he might be able to lessen the consequences of the crash. But that would only work if he was prepared to risk fatal damage to himself.

It was a simple choice: either he abandoned the train and lived, or he sacrificed himself and other people did. There was nothing in between. It was not a choice at all, really; he knew what he had to do. The decision took nearly three full microseconds. *But*, he reflected as he jumped from the back of the train, *serious issues like this can't be rushed.*

. . .

'YOU!' Romulus's voice was a reptilian hiss over the squealing of the brakes. He held up the gleaming razor. 'This was my brother's razor,' he growled. 'Where is he? What have you done to him?'

He stepped onto the gangway and she scrambled away, trying to reach the ladder. But Remus was too quick for her; he lunged forwards and slammed her against the carriage wall before planting a huge knee on her chest. She gasped for breath, thinking her ribcage might collapse under his weight as he grabbed her hair and forced her head back.

'If you've harmed my brother, I'll slice you to ribbons,' he screamed. His teeth were drawn back into a wild dog snarl and flecks of white, foamy spit sprayed from his lips. He held the razor up and let the light flash from its surfaces as he turned it in front of her face. 'Tell me!'

He slammed her head back against the wood so that she saw stars. 'Staying silent on me, eh?' he said. 'Well, I'll just have to give you the proper motivation to talk. Shall we see how much you value your scalp.'

India thrashed in Romulus's grip, fighting vainly against the hand pinning her as surely as an iron claw. The sound of the shrieking brakes filled her ears as the grinning face of Romulus leered at her and pressed the blade against her hairline.

She gasped as she felt the sting of the razor as it began to bite and the grin on the face of the big man widened. Was this it? Had all of her efforts been for nothing? She closed her eyes and waited for the end.

The world lurched beneath her.

Every carriage along the length of the train seemed to buck and jump at the same time. The screeching of the brakes was suddenly overwhelmed by other sounds: the clang of heavy iron, the screech of steel on steel and the roar of the locomotive as it tipped into the abyss, dragging a dozen carriages after it.

The air filled with smoke and dust. The hand pinning her to the wall was promptly released and India felt the world tip on its axis so that what had been 'forwards' suddenly became 'down'.

She screamed as her legs slithered from the gangway and she grabbed blindly for a handhold, grasping a rung of the ladder as her legs dangled in space. As the smoke cleared, she blinked away the grit from her eyes and realised the enormity of the situation.

The great engine had managed to scrub most of its speed by the time it arrived at the viaduct, but not all. When it reached the break in the tracks, the engine had pitched over the edge and had immediately pulled the passenger carriage and the prison van after it. India could see the engine and the derailed carriages dangling like a Christmas paper chain, over a hundred-foot drop to the valley floor.

The third carriage, containing her sister and the other hostages, teetered on the edge of the precipice, creaking ominously as the engine swung back and forth below them. India clung to a handrail, her feet dangling as she looked down into the doorway of the prison van.

The impact of the crash had thrown Romulus through the door and he now clung to the bars of one of the holding cells inside the carriage. As she looked down at his dangling form, he sensed her gaze. Their eyes met through the dust and the smoke and his face twisted into a snarl.

'I'LL – KILL – YOU!' His voice was a strangled snarl, twisted and distorted by the uncontrollable rage that seethed within him. 'YOU WON'T ESCAPE ME, YOU BITCH. I'M COMING FOR YOU!'

To India's horror, he placed the razor between his teeth and began to climb up the now vertical carriage, using the cell bars as a ladder. India searched around but could see no easy escape. Her legs dangled freely above the void and she could not reach the ladder. In a few moments, Romulus would be upon her and then...

She forced herself to stay calm. Behind her, the truck with the hostages groaned as it slipped inexorably towards the edge of the. If she was going to do something it had to be now.

And then she saw it. The lever which uncoupled the carriage was positioned to one side of her, almost within reach of her foot. Ignoring the ache building in her arms, she began to swing her weight back and forth. The carriage creaked alarmingly with each swing and, for a moment, she was afraid she might bring everything crashing down to the valley floor.

Her boot connected with the handle but then almost immediately slipped away. Romulus was at the top of the carriage now, reaching for the doorframe to pull himself out. She swung again and, this time, her foot landed firmly on the handle.

She quickly swung the other foot into place and stamped down hard. The handle did not move. She stamped again and this time the handle moved the coupling pin a fraction of an inch. Encouraged, she stamped down again, and again, each time moving the pin a fraction of an inch further out of its socket.

Romulus was nearly out of the prison van now. He looked up and saw what India was doing. With a furious yell, he snatched the razor from his mouth and slashed wildly at her legs. India cried out as the razor's edge sliced through her trousers and she felt the sting in the flesh of her calf. Using all her last remaining strength, she stamped again.

And the handle sprang open.

The metallic clunk cut through the background noise as the pin jerked free. Romulus's eyes widened and there was a moment of perfect stillness before the couplings released their hold.

India locked eyes with Romulus as the engine and the front carriages dropped soundlessly into the void. There was no fear in his face, just a stare that radiated cold hatred as he fell to his death.

The peace of the moment was shattered as the engine slammed into the valley floor. The boiler burst open in a violent explosion of pressurised steam and burning coals. The passenger carriage and the prison van hammered down on top of the engine an instant later with a boom that echoed off the hillsides as the wreckage disappeared in a rapidly expanding cloud of dust and fire.

A wash of heat and coal dust blasted upwards, engulfing India in its fury. She felt the carriages tremble and panic seized her at the thought that the rest of the train might still tumble over the edge into oblivion. She swung her body again and caught the ladder, then began to pull herself up on the rungs. By the time she hauled herself onto the roof of the carriage, her muscles burned with lactic acid and her fingers felt they had nearly been pulled from their sockets.

She was relieved to find Sniffer, still clinging to Sid's collar. The boy's eyes grew round when he saw her. 'You're alive?' he gasped. 'I was sure you'd gone over the edge with the rest of 'em.'

She fell back onto the carriage roof and screwed up her

eyes, grinding her teeth to quell the pain in her burning muscles. It was several seconds before she could muster the energy for a reply. 'Yeah, well, it takes more than a couple of giant babies to kill me,' she said. 'How's my bodyguard doing?'

She propped herself up on one elbow to see Sid, lying on his side but with his eyes open. 'I'm doing OK, tech-hunter,' he croaked. 'Looks like you managed to take care of things pretty well while I was out of it.'

She gave him a half smile. 'Yeah, I did, didn't I?' She winced as she felt a sting in her calf and looked down to find the end of her trousers soaked in blood where Romulus's razor had slashed her. 'Though I picked up a few more scars on the way.'

'Scars are just stories,' he said. 'You and me, we've got plenty of 'em.' He tried to sit up, assisted by Sniffer as his face twisted in pain. When he was upright, he took a moment to regain his breath.

'The guards in the arena did me over pretty well after you ran out on me,' he said. India began to protest but caught the wry smile on his face and stayed silent. 'I reckon I got a couple of busted ribs and a busted finger and I can't hear nothin' out of my left ear.' Then he shrugged. 'But it's nothin' that couldn't be sorted by a decent medic.' He slapped the roof with his undamaged hand. 'How about we open up this carriage and see if we can find one?'

20

AFTERMATH

It took nearly an hour to get all the prisoners out of the cattle truck. When India was able to stand, she discovered that, even without the weight of the front carriages, the truck was still teetering dangerously on the edge of the drop, creaking like an old schooner as it swayed in the wind.

She pulled open the trapdoor in the carriage roof. 'Bel, it's India. Can you hear me?'

Bella's pale and frightened face appeared in the square of light below her. 'I'm here,' she called. 'India, what's going on? Everyone's terrified. Have we crashed?'

'Not yet. But you've got to get everyone to the rear of the carriage, as quickly as you can. Don't ask questions, just do it.'

When Bella had moved everyone back as instructed, the carriage felt a little more stable. But she still couldn't risk opening the doors and letting everyone out until the carriage was safely pulled back from the edge.

'Calc, can you hear me?' The radio crackled like hot fat in a pan.

'I can hear you, India.' His voice sounded strangely faint, as though it was distanced by more than just a poor connection.

'I need you to move the train back at least twenty feet. Can you do it?'

There was a long pause before he replied. 'I will try,' he said. 'Though my capabilities are somewhat... *diminished*.'

She felt a stab of alarm at his words, but there was no time to ask questions. A minute later, the remains of the train gave a shuddering jolt along its length. As the carriages began to move, the damaged rails shrieked in protest and bent axles lurched, threatening to turn carriages on their sides. Gradually, the train rumbled backwards far enough to provide a safe margin between the front carriage and the edge of the precipice.

When India judged it was safe, she spoke into the radio again. 'OK, Calc. Stop it right there.' There was no answer from the other end, just a hiss of static. 'Calc? Are you OK?'

She jabbed the PTT button impatiently, but the radio seemed to be functioning perfectly well. The silence at the other end filled her with a sudden dread.

There was little time to investigate. Already the passengers in the truck were clamouring for release, the panic rising in their voices as they sensed their imminent rescue. India helped Sniffer to get Sid down the ladder and they stood beside the track, staring up at the sliding door in the side of the carriage. The door had been secured by a steel padlock the size of India's fist and doubtless the key was somewhere on the valley floor with the remains of Romulus Pinkerton.

As there were no tools to hand to pry it open, India pulled out one of Sid's pistols and aimed it at the lock.

'Bella, get everyone away from the door,' she shouted through the iron cladding.

The first shot sparked off the metal and sang away at high velocity over their heads, leaving the lock twisted but still intact. The second blasted away the rusted hasp from the door and the lock narrowly missed Sid's head as it sailed over the edge of the viaduct.

'Damn,' he croaked as he turned to watch it tumble away. 'Take it easy, will you. I wouldn't be the first sucker to get killed after the war had ended.'

India tore at the remaining bolts and, with Sniffer's help, hauled back the sliding door, releasing a stink of bodies from within. The men and women inside flinched and drew back as daylight filled the carriage, holding up their hands against the rising sun. India and Sniffer began to help people down onto the tracks, repeatedly assuring them that, yes, the Pinkertons were really gone, and no, the train wasn't going to fall off the bridge and no, they definitely weren't bandits.

Some people looked like they had been in the carriage for days. Pale and weak from hunger, they had to be lifted down by their friends and then stood drinking in the sunlight as though they could absorb its energy directly into their bones.

Tom's sister, Gilly, was among the children on the carriage. She shrieked with delight when she spotted India and threw her arms around her neck, laughing and sobbing in equal measure. 'India, you found me,' she sobbed as she hung on tightly. 'Bella said you'd come for us and she was right. How are Tom and Dad? Are they OK? Did anyone feed my chickens while I was gone?'

India laughed and assured the girl that her brother and father were fine and that chickens in Hampstead had a way of looking after themselves, whether or not anyone took the time to feed them.

The last person to get off the carriage after everyone else had left was Bella. She jumped to the ground and took in India's blood-soaked trouser leg and bloodied face with professional blue eyes.

'You look like shit.'

India grinned. 'Great to see you too, sis.'

Then Bella ran to her and buried her head in India's chest and hugged her so tightly that it sent spears of pain through India's cracked ribs. But India didn't mind; she held on to her sister and the two of them sobbed with the sheer joy of reunion.

Bella pulled back and looked up into her sister's face. 'You came for me,' she said in a hoarse voice. 'I thought I'd never see you or anyone I knew ever again but you saved me.'

India shrugged bashfully. 'It wasn't all down to me,' she said. 'I couldn't have done it without Sid and Calculus.'

Bella frowned. 'Calculus? Isn't that the name of the robot you used to hang out with? He's back?'

India smiled. 'Yes, he's back. I'll introduce you, but just don't call him a robot, OK? He doesn't like it.'

Bella returned the smile and nodded. Then her face clouded as the horrors of the last few hours crowded in on her again. 'Oh, India. Some of the stories the people in the carriage told about the Pinkertons... they were just... *horrible*.'

She buried her face in India's jacket again and sobbed. India stroked her hair. 'It's OK, Bel,' she said. 'They're gone now and I'm here. And I swear, I'm never going to go away and leave you again. I'm going to move back and live with you, here in London.'

Bella pushed away from her sister and gave a dry laugh. 'Don't make promises you can't keep, India Bentley,' she said.

'But I mean it.'

'I know you mean it now. At this moment you really believe you're going to move back here and live in a miserable, muddy village on the banks of Lake London. But give it six months and you'll be climbing the walls. You've got adventure in your soul, and you need to listen to it. I can't keep you here – no one can.' Then she smiled and it was like the sun coming out after the rain. 'Besides, now I know that if I ever get into serious trouble, you'll come back to get me.' She looked up at the wreckage of the train lying along the viaduct like the broken carcass of a slain beast. 'And heaven help anyone who gets in your way.'

With their arms around each other's shoulders, they joined the ragged line of passengers making their way back along the tracks towards the rear of the train. The air smelled sweet and fresh and the sun came out in its full glory, warming their skins and pushing away the horrors of the last few hours.

But as they approached the back of the train, some of India's dread returned. A crowd had gathered, wearing expressions that ranged from curiosity to sadness. Some of the children were crying openly.

As they drew closer, Sid peeled away from the crowd and came towards them. 'You better come, India,' he said. 'It's the robot.'

They found Calculus behind the end carriage, lying beside the track. When India saw him, she cried out and dropped to her knees in the clinker. 'Calc!'

Parts of the android's body looked like they had been chewed up by heavy machinery. His left arm was completely missing below the elbow, leaving a tangle of shredded muscle-fibres and conductive filaments. Elsewhere, there was a deep gash in his bodywork that oozed blue fluids, one of his legs was twisted at a strange angle and his visor was hazed by a web of cracks.

At the sound of her voice, he turned his head stiffly and his neck made a grating noise. 'India.' His voice sounded cracked, as though something broken lurked within it. 'I am sorry I was not able to help you earlier. As you can see, I am not operating at optimal efficiency right now.'

'Calc, what happened?' She looked up and down his broken body and felt the despair of the last few hours returning.

A shiver ran through the android's frame as he adjusted his position. 'After the bridge was blown up, I calculated that a train of this mass, travelling at sixty miles per hour, would require a braking force in excess of four hundred thousand Newtons. I further estimated that—'

'Just tell me what happened to you, Calc.'

The android made a noise that might have been a sigh. 'The only way to stop the train was to use my own body to apply additional braking force to the rear wheels.'

India gasped. 'You used your own body? But, just... *look* at you.' She felt a catch in her voice and her eyes stung. 'Calc, you're really badly hurt.'

'I do not feel pain, India,' he said. 'But you are correct, I have sustained serious damage.' He held up the stump of his missing arm and looked at it ruefully. 'For future reference, I do not advise trying to hold on to the wheels of a moving train.'

India looked down at the wrecked android and wiped her eyes as she tried to force herself to think straight. 'You have self-repair mechanisms,' she blurted eventually. 'You told me that your body can heal injuries. You can take care of this.'

The android was quiet for several seconds. 'Given enough time, perhaps,' he said. 'But my maintenance and repair systems work at the molecular level. They are meant to keep me operational until I can reach a properly equipped repair facility. Replacing a missing limb, if that's even possible, would take several months.'

'Then we'll wait.' India's voice was sharp. 'We'll make a camp and get you what you need and we'll wait however long it takes until you're better. I'll get some of the men to carry you to those trees over there.' She turned to beckon for help but the android laid his good hand on her arm.

'You know that is not possible, India,' he said. 'These people are relying on you to get them home to their families. If you wait here, then the bandit gangs will find you and I won't be able to help you. You have to get away. Leave me behind and I'll take my chances here.'

'No!' India was weeping openly now; her warms tears splashed on the android's body armour and mingled with the blue fluids leaking from his chest. 'I'm not going to leave you behind. I did that once before and I'm not going to do it again.'

'Well, we can't wait here,' said a woman in the crowd. 'The android's right: this is bandit country. If we hang around we'll just get taken prisoner by someone else. We've got to go now!'

An angry murmur ran through the adults in the group. 'She's right,' said someone else. 'I say let's go and leave the android behind. It's just a machine; it's no use to us now.'

'We are *not* leaving anyone behind.' India turned to see Bella pushing her way to the front of the group, wearing a furious expression. She shoved aside two men twice her size and turned to face them. 'You lot have all got short memories,' she said. 'Less than an hour ago you were locked in a slave train bound for who-knows-where and with no chance of ever seeing your families again. Have you forgotten that already?'

She examined the faces of the crowd but none of them would meet her eyes. She pointed at Calculus lying on the ground. 'This *machine* has got a mind of its own. He could have jumped off that train and left us all to go to our deaths on the valley floor, but he didn't. Instead, he stayed here and nearly died trying to save you. And in my book that makes him one of us. So I say we're going to take care of him like one of our own. Does anyone want to argue?'

No one replied.

She turned to Calculus. 'Android, how much time would your repair systems need to do the essential stuff? The bare minimum to get you moving.'

Calculus looked down at his injuries and then at Bella. 'If I confined the repairs to fixing the systems most critical for mobility, I estimate I could be functional in around twenty-two hours. But I would need to completely shut down all non-essential systems during that period.'

'OK,' said Bella firmly. 'Start getting it done. The rest of you, dig in; we're going to camp here until tomorrow morning.' She pointed to two women at the back of the group. 'You two, go and investigate those woods and see if you can find a campsite we can defend. The rest of you, go through the train and find anything we can use, weapons, food, blankets and medical supplies.' She glanced at India and Sid. '*Particularly* medical supplies.'

There was some grumbling but most people seemed roused by Bella's words. Two women went to investigate a small woodland on a nearby hill while the remainder began to clamber over the train, looking for anything they could scavenge.

When everyone had been given a job, India smiled gratefully at her sister. 'Thanks, Bel. I never knew you could be so scary.'

Bella laughed. 'Yeah, well, you're not the only one that knows how to give orders. Sometimes you have to kick a few backsides to get anything done around here.'

The group spent the next few hours collecting useful supplies from the wreckage of the train and transporting them up the hill towards a group of trees where the women had located a good campsite, hidden from view, but affording a vantage point over the surrounding countryside. The train had yielded several weapons, which Bella divided up among the adults as she organised them into pairs for sentry duty.

In addition to the guns, there were blankets and some meat sausage from the guards' van as well as an unlimited supply of fresh flour. One of the women made a paste of flour and water, which she smeared onto hot stones to make flatbreads for the children. A little while later, two men returned triumphantly with a wild pig they had shot in the forest, to be roundly berated by Bella.

'You're not on the Northside now,' she barked at them. 'And this isn't some Sunday hunting trip. Gunfire will bring every bandit from ten miles around down on our heads.' She inspected the pig contemptuously. 'Clean it and bury the guts so we don't attract dogs,' she ordered. 'The two of you get an extra sentry shift for being so stupid.'

Instead of protesting their treatment, the two men nodded meekly and did as Bella instructed. India watched her sister with growing astonishment at the way she effortlessly organised sentry parties, cooking duties and sleeping arrangements, giving everyone a job so that no one had the time to question her authority.

India herself found that she had little energy for the proceedings. From the moment they had succeeded in releasing the prisoners, she had felt an overwhelming tiredness creep over her, as though her body had decided it had no more to contribute. Fighting the fatigue, she forced herself to take care of Calculus, ensuring he was placed comfortably on a bed of dry leaves, a little way from the fire so he could undertake his internal repairs.

She looked down at his missing limb and twisted leg and didn't think she had ever seen him looking so vulnerable before. He looked like a broken toy.

'I have done as much work as I can, for now,' he said, settling back on the bed of leaves. 'The more complex repairs will require me to shut down for the next fourteen hours. Once my repair mechanisms have been engaged, the process cannot be interrupted. Are you sure you want me to do this, India? This is not a safe area and I have detected several bandit gangs just a few miles to the south of here. If you are attacked whilst I am in shutdown, I will not be much use to you.'

I hate to break it to you, Calc, but you're not much use to anyone in your current state either. Don't worry about us; Bella's got everything under control here and we have plenty of weapons if we need them. We'll be fine.' She hoped he could not hear the uncertainty in her voice.

The android looked at her for a few moments and then nodded. 'Very well, I am engaging the shutdown procedure now. Good luck, India.'

She watched as he lay back on the leaves and went still. Then, a moment later the faint blue glow behind his visor went out and there was a brief crackling as his limbs settled to immobility on the dry leaves.

India blinked and ran her hand through her hair. Every fibre in her body was screaming for rest but the adrenalin still surged around her body. She knew that trying to sleep would be hopeless. She looked down at the android's still frame and smiled.

'Sometimes, Calc, I envy you,' she said.

AS THE DAY WORE ON, the camp settled into a sort of domestic normality. By nightfall, the pig had been spit-roasted over the fire and the children had all been fed, wrapped in blankets and laid down to sleep on beds of leaves and bracken. The adults talked in low voices around the fire or patrolled the perimeter of the camp in pairs or just sat alone and stared into the flames, reliving the horrors of the previous few days.

Bella set up a makeshift hospital at one end of the camp, using a satchel of meagre medical supplies they had discovered on the train. There was not much for her to work with, but she managed to administer first aid to the cuts, abrasions and bruises that all of the prisoners seemed to have acquired.

She examined India's facial injuries and cleaned the deep gash in her leg from Remus's razor, then sewed it up with a length of fishing line from the med kit, trimming the stitches cleanly with a small scalpel. 'The cut's clean enough,' she said as she worked. 'It should heal up in a few days. But there's not much I can do about the cracked ribs and it looks like your nose is broken. You can either live with it crooked or I can straighten it out for you.'

India thought about what it might mean to go through

life with a crooked nose, looking like one of the fighters she saw in the bare-knuckle fights in the markets. It might bring some advantages if it made people more wary of her, she thought, but on balance she decided she liked her nose better the way it had been. She gave Bella a nod.

Bella's movement was quick and decisive; she laid her fingers along each side of India's nose and then jerked it sharply to the right. There was a loud, gristly snap and a wave of intense pain shot up India's nose. Her eyes streamed and her nose gushed blood for a full minute before Bella was able to staunch the bleeding.

'Shit, Bella,' gasped India as she held her head back. 'You might have given me a bit of warning.'

'Warning people never makes them feel any better, trust me,' said her sister drily as she stuffed more gauze up India's nose.

Bella was most concerned about Sid. He seemed cheerful enough as the girl bound his ribs, cleaned out the claw marks the bear had given him and strapped his broken fingers to a piece of wood. But even India noticed how badly he flinched when Bella examined the deep bruising on his body.

Bella frowned. 'They worked you over pretty good. These look like boot marks.'

Sid shrugged. 'They were just amateurs. I've had worse.'

'I don't doubt it,' said Bella. 'But I'm worried you might have internal injuries.'

'What I can't see can't kill me.'

'Actually, it can,' said Bella. 'You could be bleeding inside and never know it. Not much I can do about it, though. If you don't die in the next few days then I guess you're all right.'

Sid pushed back his hat and grinned at Bella, and India

caught the twinkle in his eye. 'You mean, I might have only hours to live? Maybe you'd better stay here and keep a close watch over me in case I have a relapse?'

Bella laughed and flipped off his hat playfully. 'I tell you what,' she said. 'If you die before sunrise, I'll knock ten per cent off my bill. Can't say fairer than that. Now stay here and get some rest; I've got other people to see.'

India studied Sid carefully as he watched Bella get up and walk away, his eyes never leaving her as she crossed the camp. A short while later, he got up and shambled awkwardly into the trees. India got up and followed.

She caught up with him a hundred feet into the forest. When he heard her approach, he spun around in alarm, his hand instinctively reaching to his belt and finding it empty. 'Shit, didn't anyone ever tell you never to sneak up on a person like that? And can't a guy take a piss in private?'

India bit her lip. 'I came to see if you were OK,' she said.

Sid tipped back his head to look down his nose at her and then smiled. 'Yeah, I'm OK, thanks to that sister of yours. She's quite a woman, ain't she? She'll make someone a good wife.'

India could not keep the frown off her face. 'Provided it's the right person.'

Sid's eyebrows went up in realisation and his mouth opened in a silent 'ahhhh'. 'I get it. You think I want to—'

'I saw the way you looked at her, Sid. She's not for you.'

'You jealous?'

'Jealous? What? No!' India felt her face flush and cursed herself for it. 'You can do what you want. I just don't want Bella sucked into this life too. She deserves better than that.'

Sid's eyes flashed. 'Better than me, you mean?' He snorted. 'D'you think I don't know what I am, India? I live off the dregs of the old world. When you really get down to it, I ain't much different from the Pinkertons. But Bella...' He looked back through the trees. 'I know she's not for me. When she talks, people listen.'

India smiled. 'Yeah, I noticed that about her. My little sister grew up while I wasn't looking.' She gave Sid a sideways look. 'I've been thinking about maybe staying in London when this is all over.'

Sid looked up sharply. 'You? Staying in one place?'

India smiled. 'Sure, why not? Bella is the sort of leader these people need, and she'll need all the help she can get. I think the two of us could make a good team. What do you think?'

Sid frowned. 'That don't sound like the India Bentley I know. I reckon you'd be climbing the walls inside a month.'

India laughed. 'Yeah, Bella said something similar but I'm serious about this. It's time I thought about putting down some roots. What about you – don't you ever have any thoughts about settling down?'

Sid shrugged his shoulders. 'Staying in one place was never really my thing. Besides, the sort of life I lead would put off most women. 'Cept for you, maybe.'

'Me?'

'Sure. You and me have been through the same stuff. We understand each other.'

India looked at him for several seconds to see if she could find the mockery in his face but she couldn't detect it. Then she laughed. 'Your charm doesn't work on me, Sid,' she said. 'Particularly when I've got a broken nose.'

Sid gave a sly grin. 'I guess it was worth a try,' he joked. 'So, was there anything else you wanted, or can I take that piss now?'

India smiled. 'I thought it was time I gave you these

back.' She reached behind her back and pulled Sid's two pistols from her own belt. 'Here.'

He took the guns and turned them over in his hand, inspecting them, like recovered treasure. 'Thanks,' he said. 'I was wondering what had happened to them.'

He tucked one of the guns into his belt but turned the other over in his hand carefully, as though he was considering an important question. 'Here,' he said suddenly, holding out the gun towards India. 'I reckon you deserve to have this. You did well today.'

'Me?' India looked at the gun and then stared at Sid in amazement. In all the years she had known Sid, he had cared for his guns more carefully than anything or anyone else in the world. It was almost inconceivable that he would give one away.

He shrugged bashfully. 'It don't mean we're engaged or nothin'.'

She took the gun and felt the weight of it in her hand before sliding it into position in her belt where she could reach it quickly. Then she smiled. 'Thanks. You once told me I couldn't be trusted with a gun. You said I wasn't a "gun person".'

He shrugged. 'People change. I guess you're a gun person now.'

India wondered if it was a good thing to be a gun person or not. The silence hung heavily between them for a moment, then she said, 'What were you going to say, Sid?'

He frowned. 'What was I going to say when?'

'When we were in the pit, with the ice-bear,' she said. 'When we thought we were going to die. You said there was something you'd always wanted to tell me but you didn't get time to say it. What was it?'

Sid swallowed. He looked at her and then quickly

looked away again. 'I...' He frowned and chewed his lip. 'It was just...' He looked up and there was a new earnestness in his face she had not seen before. 'What I was going to say was—' Then he broke off and looked away through the trees. 'Did you hear that?'

India sighed. 'Don't change the subject; I—' She stopped mid-sentence and listened. 'The camp's gone quiet,' she said.

And at that that moment, the screaming began.

21

IT RUNS IN THE FAMILY

uns drawn, they tore back through the trees and
burst into the clearing. The camp looked like the
aftermath of a small war. Two men lay dead on
the ground, their heads twisted at unnatural angles, one lay
across the fire, filling the air with the smell of charred flesh.
A dozen people cowered in the trees, eyes darting like frightened rabbits as children wailed inconsolably.

India scanned the area. Bella's medical supplies lay
strewn across the ground and the remains of the roasted pig
lay ten feet away. Calculus was still inert on his bier of dead
leaves, as silent and cold as a corpse. If they were under
attack, there was no sign of an attacker.

'What happened here?' she demanded.

'It's Benno and Dill,' stammered a man, pointing to the
two bodies on the ground. 'They went out to investigate a
noise and two minutes later somebody threw their bodies
back into the camp.'

'Threw them? Did you see who it was?'

'W-we didn't see nothing, miss,' said a timid-looking
young woman. 'They just come flying through the trees and

landed right there. Whoever threw 'em must have been unnatural strong.'

India looked at the bodies lying at least fifteen feet from the nearest trees. It seemed inconceivable that anyone could have thrown them so far. 'India! Look at this.' Sid crouched down and turned over the bodies to reveal a raw and bloody slash across each of their throats. She recognised them as the two men that had shot the pig earlier.

'Looks like they got taken from behind,' said Sid. 'Probably both had their windpipes cut before they could shout out.'

'Who could have done this?'

Sid shrugged. 'Bandits scouts most likely. Which means there'll be more on the way.' He jumped up. 'We've got to move everyone out of here, right now.'

'It weren't no bandits,' said a man at the back. 'It was them Pinkerton brothers. This is their doing. They've come to take us all back with 'em.'

A ripple of fear ran through the group at his words. Somebody screamed and several children began crying. One man pulled out a knife and slashed the air around him wildly. 'I won't go back,' he shrieked. 'They can't make me go with them. I'll kill myself first.'

'Will you shut up,' snarled India. 'The Pinkertons are both dead; they can't hurt you anymore. But someone's out there and that means we have to get out of here, now! Grab what you can carry and let's move! Where's Bella?' Nobody answered. India looked around the group for her sister but couldn't see her. She couldn't believe she hadn't noticed before now.

'Please, miss,' said the young woman. 'Bella went down to the stream to get water for the kids. About ten minutes ago.'

India felt her guts fill with ice water. 'Didn't anyone go with her?'

'I don't think so, miss. She went by herself.'

She turned on the group furiously. 'You let her go out there on her own? Without a guard? What were you all thinking?'

None of the men would catch her eye. Some of them looked down at the ground and kicked their shoes in the dust. India turned away in disgust. 'Sid, Bella's out there on her own. We've got to find her before those bandits do.'

'I think it's a bit late for that.' Said Sid, softly. He looked towards the far side of the clearing, where a pale form was emerging slowly from the shadows.

'Bella!' India started forwards, then stopped in her tracks. On the other side of the clearing, Bella stood deathly still, her blue eyes filled with fear. One meaty hand was clamped across her mouth and another held the steel point of a surgical scalpel to her throat.

Bella moved forward slowly into the campfire light and a collective wail went up from the group. Standing behind Bella, his mouth held close to her ear, was a familiar grinning baby face.

'Romulus!' gasped India. 'That's impossible. I saw you fall from the bridge. There was an explosion... you—'

'Not Romulus,' hissed the hideous apparition. 'I've seen your handiwork, India Bentley. Romulus rests in peace at the bottom of the valley.'

India studied the brother more closely. He looked like he had been in a fight. His clothes were torn and dusty, the leg of his trousers was dark with blood and there was a jagged cut along his forehead. Then realisation dawned on her. 'Remus!' she gasped.

The grin widened. 'At your service,' he hissed. 'I expect

you thought you'd seen the last of me after you threw me off the train. It did take me quite a while to get here with a broken leg.' He glanced down at the limb, which was twisted at an unusual angle. A piece of white bone projected from just above the ankle.

'But do you know what kept me going?' he continued. 'Hatred. If there is enough pain and hatred inside you, you can endure anything.'

'Let her go, Remus,' said India. 'If you hurt my sister, I'll kill you where you stand.'

'Probably,' said Remus. 'But you'll still have a dead sister and I *really* don't think you want that. Now be a good girl and put the gun down, you and the boyfriend, please.'

India swallowed and then laid the pistol in the grass, nodding to Sid to do the same. Sid frowned but followed suit.

'All right, Remus, the guns are down. Now, let her go. It's me you want. I'm the one who killed Romulus.'

'Romulus. My dear brother Romulus,' said Remus. 'He was my lifelong friend and partner in crime, ever since we killed and ate our first cat together. I knew the moment he died, did you know that? It was as though part of my soul had been ripped away. That's what it's like to lose a twin.'

He glanced at Bella, still frozen like a statue in his grip, and smiled. 'But at least I can take away something just as precious from you.' He took a step backwards pulling Bella with him. 'I'm going to leave now and I'm going to take your sister with me, do you understand?'

'India, do as he says.' Bella's voice was strangled as she tried to pull away from the scalpel's razor-thin edge. 'I'll go with him. Just promise me you'll get the others home safely.'

'No!' India's fists formed into tight, bloodless knots as

she bared her teeth. 'I won't let him just walk out of here with you. I won't let him turn my sister into a slave.'

Remus chuckled and pulled Bella's head back to expose her white neck. 'A slave? Who said anything about making her a slave? I have something far more important in mind for Bella. Your sister has a big part to play in the world's future; she is about to become food for a *god!*'

'I've met some batshit crazy sons of bitches in my time,' muttered Sid. 'But this guy takes the gold medal.'

'Damn you, Pinkerton, let her go!' India started forwards but Remus pressed the scalpel closer to Bella's throat so that a bead of blood appeared at its point.

'Ah, ah, ahh,' said Remus. 'Please don't do anything rash. I'm going now and if I see anyone following me, even a distant speck on the horizon, then I'll gut your sister and leave her entrails for the wild dogs.'

He took another awkward step back on his broken ankle. Every fibre in India's body wanted to tear Bella free of the big man's grasp but the blade against her neck made that impossible. Remus Pinkerton was going to leave and there was nothing she could do or say.

For all of India's anguish, Bella herself seemed quite calm. A strange peacefulness seemed to have settled over her and her eyes were serene. She allowed herself to be led from the clearing but when they reached the trees, she spoke in a gentle voice.

'I hear your brother died screaming like a child, Remus,' she said softly. 'You should take care that the same doesn't happen to you.'

Remus took his eyes off India and blinked. 'What did you say?' His knuckles tightened on the scalpel.

'Bella, don't,' cried India. 'He'll kill you. He'll—'

'He wouldn't hurt me, would you, Remus?' said Bella.

'For he knows he cannot hurt me while the wind is at my back.'

Remus frowned. He looked angry and confused. 'What?' he said again. 'What was that?' He licked his lips and removed the scalpel long enough to wipe the sweat from his eyes. Then he pressed it against Bella's neck again. 'That's enough talking,' he said.

But Bella had not finished. 'I can't stop now, Remus,' she murmured, 'because I have earth beneath my feet with mountains are made from the earth. And I have water in my blood, enough to drown a man.'

India gasped as she recognised the words of the spell she had once learned from a shaman in a distant Siberian forest. Remus's jaw had gone slack and his eyes stared as if some horror was being played in front his eyes that no one else could see. The arm holding the scalpel dropped to his side and Bella stepped free of his embrace.

India immediately snatched up her pistol. 'Bella, get away from him. Get behind me.'

But Bella did not move away. She turned to face Remus and looked deep into his eyes. The big man gasped and let out a choking sob as he felt the heat of the woman's stare and, for the first time, he noticed that her eyes were different colours, one was blue and the other, brown.

Bella leaned closer and spoke. Her voice was barely a whisper but was clearly heard by everyone in the camp. 'And know that I have fire in my heart, Remus,' she said. 'Enough fire to make a man like you burn.'

And Remus saw in her eyes something older than the mountains and far darker than his own soul. Something *alive*.

Remus screamed.

Those who heard it would later say that it was the worst

sound they had ever heard a man make, like the death shriek of a creature being burned alive. His screaming continued as he sank to his knees with his eyes screwed shut and a dark stain spreading across his crotch. 'Make it stop!' he sobbed, pressing the heels of his hands against his eyes. 'I don't want to see it anymore. Please make it stop!'

No one moved to help him. Then the scalpel was in his hand and he was slashing at his eyes, gouging his fingers deep into the sockets and tearing out gobbets of jelly until there was nothing left but two raw and bloody sockets and his howling became more and more inhuman.

And finally the scalpel found his throat. He slashed hard and deep, slicing his windpipe so that his head lolled backwards. His throat yawned like an obscene second mouth and arterial blood fountained into the air. And then the screaming ceased, the fountain of blood weakened and Remus's bloody carcass slumped onto the forest floor.

The shocked silence that followed was as thick as treacle. No one breathed and the only sound was the last of Remus's blood spattering faintly across the dry leaves. Then a child began to cry and the spell was broken.

'Holy crap,' said Sid. 'That was... messed up.'

India started towards her sister but stopped just short of her. Bella stood over the body, pale and unmoving, her eyes looking at some indeterminate point in the distance. Her face was streaked with drops of Remus's blood but she didn't seem to notice. India touched her gently on the arm.

'Bella?' she said softly. 'Are you alright?'

Bella blinked, then turned and smiled at India. 'Yes, thank you, India. I'm fine,' she said in a distant voice. 'Everything is fine now. Remus Pinkerton won't bother us anymore.'

India looked down at the ragged remains of Remus and

shuddered. 'What did you do to him?' she said, though in her heart she knew the answer.

'I showed him,' said Bella. 'I showed him what hell looks like.'

IT WAS some time before they could restore order to the camp. Panic had broken out among several of the group. At least six people had collected their belongings and run away into the forest and now refused to return. Of the ones who were left, Sid managed to threaten and cajole them sufficiently to start clearing up the camp.

He organised four of the group to carry the bodies of Remus and the other two men into the trees and bury them beneath some leaves. Some of the others rebuilt the fire and retrieved the burned remains of the pig. In less than an hour, the camp looked relatively normal except that everyone in it was wide-eyed and terrified and no one spoke out loud.

While Sid was organising the camp, India led Bella down to the stream at the bottom of the hill, using a burning brand from the fire to light the way. Bella did not resist and allowed herself to be led through the trees, her face expressionless, her eyes staring and distant.

India sat her sister down on a rock and took a piece of dry cloth from Bella's satchel, which she dipped in the cool waters of the stream. 'Just going to clean you up a bit,' she said softly. She dabbed lightly at Bella's face to remove Remus's blood, all the time studying her sister for any flicker of expression. She waited for Bella to show fear or anger or tears or anything that would indicate her mind was working to cope with the shock. But there was nothing.

When she had finished, India put away the cloth and

took Bella's hands. 'It was Cromerty, wasn't it?' she said softly.

Bella's eyes flickered and she blinked. She looked at India with the confusion of someone who has just woken from a deep sleep. 'What?'

'Cromerty showed you the weirding ways. She taught you the spells to reach into a man's soul, didn't she?'

Bella licked her lips. Then she nodded. 'It was about five years ago,' she began. 'After you left, Cromerty came to see me. She said I had a gift; she said all the women in our family had it.'

India nodded. 'I know about that. When I first went to Siberia, I met an old woman, a shaman called Nentu. She told me the same thing. She called it being a "soul voyager".'

Bella nodded rapidly as she clenched and unclenched her fists. 'That's it. I remember now. That's what Cromerty called it too. I wasn't sure about it at first. Everyone said Cromerty was just a mad old woman. But the more time I spent with her, the more I realised that she *knew* things, India. She knew about stuff that was going to happen, just by listening to the wind and feeling the rain. It sounds crazy but it was true. I saw her do it.'

Now she had started talking, Bella's words came thick and fast, falling over each other as she hurried to get her thoughts out. 'She taught me how to read the skies and how to use my voice so that people would listen to me and to persuade them to do things they didn't want to do. It's how I managed to survive after Dad had gone.'

India thought about Bella's ability to command attention from the group and the way people followed her instructions without question. It made sense that this was something the old woman had taught her. 'But she taught you something else, didn't she?' said India. 'She showed you how you could use that gift to kill a man.'

Bella nodded and looked down. 'S-she said I should only use it as a last resort.' She looked up and her eyes looked wide and frightened. 'And I never used it before today. But when I looked into Remus Pinkerton's soul, it was a terrible, seething thing... I saw all of his wickedness and cruelty. It was... *terrible*.' She fell silent and looked down at her feet.

It was a long time before India spoke. 'I know what that's like,' she said. 'When Nentu first showed me how to use that power, I was horrified. I swore it was something I'd never use.' She bit her lip. 'But I did use it. Two days ago, I used my powers to make a man tell me where you were being held and the shock of it killed him. I swear, I'll never use it again, Bella. It's evil.'

Bella looked up at her older sister and shook her head. 'You're wrong, India.'

'What?'

'The gift that you and I have been given. It's powerful. It gives us a weapon to fight people like the Pinkertons.' Her eyes narrowed. 'It makes us strong. Cromerty and Nentu both knew this.'

There was a hardness in Bella's voice that had not been there before. India looked at her quizzically. 'What you just did to Remus Pinkerton...' she said. 'Are you saying you'd do that again?'

'Of course! I'd do it in a heartbeat.' Bella's eyes seemed to glitter in a way that made the hairs on India's neck stand alert. 'And I'd do more besides. I'll do it to anyone who preys on us; I'll show them the horrors of hell and I'll make them tear themselves apart with their own hands. I'll do it a thousand times over until they leave us alone and I won't miss a moment's sleep over it.'

India felt the blood drain from her face. 'But, Bella...' she began.

Bella cut her off with a smile. 'I'm glad you came back,' she said. 'Now that we're together again, we can fight anyone who tries to prey on the Northside. Don't you see, with our combined powers you and I can rule London. We can make it into a place where only decent people are allowed live, and the rest can choose to either leave or die.'

India stared at her sister's shining face and saw the unwavering belief in her eyes. 'And who gets to decide who the "decent" people are? Who gets to decide who lives and who dies? You?'

Bella laughed. 'Really, India. Are you telling me the Pinkertons didn't deserve everything they had coming to them?'

'Maybe. But what about all those other people in Glass Town? The ones who only did bad things because they were trying to survive. Are you going to kill all of them too?'

Bella scowled and India saw the cold fire glitter within her eyes again. 'You're not going weak on me, are you?' she said. 'You and I can make London into a better place. We know perfectly well who deserves to die and who doesn't. We'll make the tough decisions that others are afraid to. Together we'll bring peace to London and the people will love us for it.'

India stood up and backed away from the shining, smiling young woman. 'You're wrong, Bella,' she said. 'Sure, there are bad people out there but there are also good people who have been forced to do bad things. It's not up to you to decide who's right and who's wrong.'

Bella's smile did not falter. She cocked her head sympathetically. 'I feel sorry for you, India. You're passing up on a great opportunity. We were chosen by Nentu and Cromerty to lead these people. Join me and together we will be all-powerful.'

India looked at her sister and gave a gasp of surprise. She opened her mouth to reply but nothing came. The woman who sat before her looked like her sister, but her eyes had changed. One was the colour of the clearest blue sky and the other had turned to the colour of coal.

India turned and fled through the woods, followed by Bella's laughter. She ran, blinded by tears, stumbling over roots and fallen branches until she arrived back at the camp, hot and breathless. Before she entered, she straightened her clothes and wiped her eyes, then strode stern-faced into the clearing.

The camp had returned to some sort of normality. Most of the children had been laid down to sleep again and the adults were gathered close to the fire, eating the last of the pig and talking in low voices among themselves. Several of them threw suspicious glances in her direction.

Sid crossed the clearing towards her. 'I reckon things are as calm as they're going to be,' he said, glancing at the people around the fire. 'But the men are as twitchy as hell, and twitchy and guns don't mix. We should move out of here at first light, just as soon as the robot's awake. The sooner we can get these people back home and off our hands, the better, as far as I'm concerned.'

'Yeah.' India bit her lip. 'If I never see this part of the world again it'll be too soon.'

Sid regarded her curiously. 'What happened to "putting down some roots"? Aren't you still planning to stay in the village with your sister?'

India sniffed and shook her head. 'No. Bella doesn't need me. She can do just fine on her own.'

22

ON LONDON SHORES

I t took them the best part of two weeks to make it back to Hampstead, scavenging and stealing what they could to survive and to feed the children.

After the incident with Remus, several Southsiders in the group refused to go anywhere with Bella, and had struck out alone. The remainder, mostly Northsiders, began the slow and weary walk across country, constantly constrained by the pace of the weakest.

There was one death along the way, an old woman who had caught pneumonia in the cattle truck and who died in her sleep. They left in her in a ditch, roughly covered with leaves and branches. Everyone bowed their heads for a few moments but no one could think of anything to say.

After a week of walking, Sid left camp one evening and returned at first light with two horses and a haycart. No one asked where he had got them; they were just grateful that they no longer had to walk. On good days, the spring sunshine came out and squirrels and small birds chased each other through the branches as they rumbled through forgotten lanes. On days like these, India was able to close her eyes and lie back in the cart and remember long childhood days spent by the lakeside.

Twice they had to fight off attacks from bandits who imagined they might be easy pickings. But both times the attackers backed off as soon as they caught sight of Calculus. After the android had woken from his shutdown period, he assured India that he had taken care of his most urgent repairs although he would not return to peak efficiency for some time. Looking down at the tangle of raw muscle fibres hanging from his damaged arm, India imagined she saw the first hints of order and healing among the sticky mass, but it was obvious that the repairs were likely to take several months.

India's own injuries healed much quicker. The skin around her eyes had gone from dark purple to yellow and finally green, and the swelling around her nose had eventually gone down, leaving only a small lump on one side of her nose. The stiches in her leg had done their job and had started to pull tight as the skin knitted together. Eventually she used her hunting knife to remove them so she would not have to ask Bella.

In all their time on the road, Bella and India had exchanged barely two dozen words. They avoided each other whenever possible, busying themselves with tasks that did not bring them into direct contact. When they did speak it was with a frigid politeness that only served to emphasise the distance between them.

India watched Bella move effortlessly around the camp in the evenings, stroking the hair of a crying child, pausing to reassure a worried mother or confidently giving orders to the men. The horror of what she had done to Remus seemed to have been forgotten now. The men and women in the group sought her counsel on every decision, they thanked her profusely for her help and they looked after her with wonder in their eyes as if she were some sort of holy visitation.

Bella herself seemed to take such adoration in her stride, smiling graciously as she walked among the group. She was beautiful and strong and it was clear that the Northsiders adored her. But each time India looked at her, all she could see was the strange glittering in Bella's mismatched eyes that had never left her since that night in the forest. After a while, India couldn't bear to look at her sister at all.

It was the first day of May when the old hay cart, led by Calculus, crested the hill overlooking the village of Hampstead. Sid pulled up alongside them, riding the back of an old plough horse with no saddle. As the android pulled the reins to bring them to a halt, the passengers stood up in the cart to get a better view.

Laughter and smiles broke out among the little group as soon as they saw the stone cottages and the charcoal-grey lines of smoke from the tyre furnaces. One man wept openly while others slapped each other on the back and children squealed with delight and begged to be allowed down.

At the bottom of the hill, a small crowd had begun to gather outside the village gates, staring and pointing in their direction. Excited shouts went up as more villagers came running from their houses or sprinting along the shoreline where they had been tending to the boats.

The passengers climbed happily out of the cart and stretched their limbs. The children, no longer able to contain their excitement, had to be restrained from running straight down the grassy slopes towards the village. 'Perhaps,' said Bella as she surveyed the scene, 'we should all walk down together, hand in hand. So that everyone can see that we've returned safe and well.' No one argued.

India stayed in the cart, watching as each of the adults took turns to hug Bella and thank her for returning them home safely, as if she had been solely responsible. None of them spoke to India or Sid and they studiously avoided any contact with Calculus. It seemed to India as if the group had picked up on the distance between her and Bella and had sided with her sister. Bella, for her part, accepted their thanks graciously, smiling benignly.

Sid manoeuvred his horse alongside India. 'People sure have short memories about who brought 'em home,' he muttered.

'I think we remind them of things they'd rather forget,' replied India.

They were interrupted by Sniffer and Gilly. The two children had become inseparable friends on the journey home and now stood hand in hand, looking up at India.

'Thanks for bringing us home, India,' said Gilly shyly. 'And you too, Sid, and especially you, Calc.' She beamed at the android.

Sid tipped his hat at the girl and Calculus bowed in her direction. 'It's nice to see that someone remembers us,' said India, smiling as Gilly hopped up on the cart to plant a kiss on her cheek.

'Hey, India,' said Sniffer with his best small-boy bravado. 'Miss Bella says you probably ain't coming back to the village with us.'

India raised an eyebrow. 'Did she now?'

Sniffer wiped his nose on his sleeve. 'Yeah, she did. So, I was wondering where you were headed to next 'cause I might consider coming with you, if the money was right, that was.'

India suppressed a grin. 'That's a generous offer, Sniffer,' she said. 'But I thought you were going to stay here in Hampstead? I'd feel a whole lot better if I knew you were keeping an eye on things while I was gone.'

Sniffer weighed this up before squinting at her shrewdly. 'Reckon I could do that,' he said airily. 'It'll cost you an ounce of gold, though.'

India nodded thoughtfully, then rummaged in her satchel before pulling out a silver-wrapped slab. 'All I've got is a bar of chocolate,' she said. 'Picked it up in Borneo, last year. It's the real deal.'

Sniffer's eyes focused on the bar and he licked his lips. 'Reckon that'll do,' he said. She tossed him the bar and he sniffed at it suspiciously, like a coin dealer inspecting a suspect doubloon. Then a broad smile spread across his face. 'It's the real deal, all right. Thanks, India. I'll keep an eye on things good and proper, you'll see.' He extended a grubby hand up towards the cart, which India shook solemnly.

Bella left the group of adults and approached the children, laying a hand on each of their shoulders. 'Now then, Sniffer,' she said. 'Why don't you let Gilly take you down to the village to meet the other children? I'm sure they'd all love to share some of that chocolate.' Sniffer started to protest but Bella held up a warning finger to silence him. 'None of that, please. If you're going to stay with us, you're going to have to learn to live by our rules.'

Sniffer's face fell as he saw his newly acquired fortune evaporating before his eyes, but he dipped his head obediently and said, 'Yes, Miss Bella,' before walking away hand in hand with Gilly.

Bella turned her attention to India and smiled serenely, clasping her hands in front of her like a Sunday school teacher. 'I wanted to thank you on behalf of all of us, India,' she said. 'For bringing us this far.'

India looked into Bella's coal-black eye, so dark that there was no difference between pupil and iris, and she suppressed a shiver. Then she glanced at the adults, standing at a respectful distance and watching them with shiny, happy faces.

'I guess we're not invited to the party, huh?' she said.

The smile faded from Bella's face and a small frown wrinkled her forehead. 'We've been over this,' she said. 'There's nothing I'd like better than to have you with me while we rebuild the community, and you too, Sid, if you want to stay. But you have to understand that things are going to be different from now on. Since I learned what it really is to be a soul voyager, I've realised I have a mission to bring peace to the Northside.'

Bella glanced down the hill towards the village. 'The violence of the old ways is behind us now.' She nodded towards the gun in India's belt. 'You'd have to surrender your weapons, of course. There'll be new rules for everyone to follow and there'll be no place for anyone who won't comply.'

India felt Sid bristle at the suggestion of surrendering his pistol. 'I see,' she said. 'But the village already has leaders. How do you think Vincent and Maggie are going to take the news about your "mission"?'

The smile returned and the coal-black eye glittered. 'They'll see things my way, I'm sure. People tend to see my point when I explain it to them. It's one of my "gifts".'

'And what would my job be in this brave new world if I stayed?'

The serene smile returned. 'We'd be equals, of course,' said Bella at once. 'Our combined powers would be feared and respected. I'd be the village leader, as I think I have the best rapport with the people here. But I'd consult with you about everything.'

India looked into Bella's eyes but saw nothing of the tough, outspoken woman her sister had been only two weeks previously. Something had shifted within her, some-thing dark that lurked behind those mismatched eyes and made India's blood run cold. Just for an instant, a vision of the bloodied remains of Remus Pinkerton flashed before her eyes and this time she was unable to suppress the shiver.

'Thanks for the offer, Bel,' she said, managing a tight smile. 'But I think my "mission" is elsewhere.'

'As you wish,' said Bella. 'Perhaps it's for the best. Good luck, India. Do come and see us... if you're in the neighbour-hood, that is.' Bella stepped onto the side of the cart and gave India the briefest kiss on the cheek. The touch of her flesh was as cold as snow.

Bella stepped down from the cart and joined the other adults. Then they all walked down the hill towards the village, holding hands and singing an old hymn that India remembered from her childhood. Not one of them looked back.

'I don't like to say this about someone's kin,' murmured Sid. 'But your sister turned out to be one cold-hearted bitch.'

India watched her sister leave and wondered what sort of community Bella might build under her leadership. She had no doubt that once the other villagers were exposed to her bright passion that they too would fall under her spell. But for India, this was not the Bella she knew. After the inci-dent in the forest, something dark had taken hold of her, something related to the 'gift' Cromerty had bestowed on her, the same gift that lurked within her.

She felt cold, despite the bright sunshine, and pulled her jacket tighter. 'Bella has her own ideas of how things should be,' she said. 'And who are we to say they're wrong? I just...' She reached for the words. 'I just want no part of it.'

There was a long silence between them. India reached into her bag once more and retrieved a small leather purse that clinked faintly and sat heavy in her hand. She tossed it to Sid. 'Here. There's a bit more than we agreed in there. But I reckon you earned it.'

Sid caught the purse with one hand and hefted it a few times before slipping it into the pocket of his long overcoat. 'Reckon I did too,' he said. 'So, what are you aiming to do next?'

India shrugged. 'I might see if I can pick up a job out East,' she said. 'I heard they found some rich new tech mines to the north of Sing City. They say a decent tech-hunter can make a fortune out there.'

'Yeah, well, *they* say a lot of things that ain't necessarily true.'

India smiled. 'We could find out together if you want to come with me?'

Sid shook his head. 'Nah. I got to head back to Siberia. The mining cartels have put a price on my head and if the Pinkerton brothers knew about it then you can bet there's others who do too. I need to go to Angel Town and clear up a few... *misunderstandings* before I do anything else.'

India frowned. 'Is that going to be safe?'

Sid laughed. 'Hell no! But I'll be OK. I was the best enforcer the cartels ever had. I'm sure we'll be able to reach some sort of agreement.'

India nodded. 'Will I see you again?'

'I would think so. Tech-hunting's a small business. We'll run into each other somewhere.' He grinned. 'Can't guarantee whose side I'll be on, though, so watch your step.' He nodded and tipped his hat. 'See you around, India. You too, robot.'

He slapped the reins and dug his heels into the horse's flanks and the old nag shambled away. India watched him head along one of the paths leading north. 'Hey, Sid,' she called out. 'You never did tell me what you were about to say when you thought we were going to die.'

'I never did, did I?' called out Sid without turning around. 'How about that.' India laughed softly and watched as the old cart horse plodded down the lane until it disappeared from view behind a copse of trees.

'I have noticed,' said Calculus, suddenly breaking his silence, 'that your relationship with Sid is frequently hostile and nearly always disrespectful. At times, you behave as though you dislike each other intensely and yet...' He paused. 'When I analyse your speech patterns and body language, I am drawn to the conclusion that in reality, you and Sid are really—'

'It's complicated,' she said without looking away from the path. 'Me and Sid have a long history and not all of it is good.' She shrugged. 'But who knows. One day, maybe...'

The android made a noise that sounded very much like a disapproving sniff. 'I fear I will never fully understand the algorithm governing human emotions,' he said. 'It seems to be one of the primary things holding you back as a species.'

India sighed. 'Yeah, well, it works for me.' She looked down at the android. 'So, what about you, Calc? Do you fancy a trip to Sing City?'

The android studied her for a long time before replying.

'A curious choice of destination,' he said. 'What made you decide to go there?'

India shrugged. 'It's like I said to Sid, I heard there's good pickings in the tech mines.'

'The stress patterns in your voice indicate that is untrue, India,' said the android. 'Perhaps you have forgotten that you cannot lie to me.'

India met the android's gaze for a full ten seconds, then rolled her eyes. 'All right, perhaps it's not the only reason,' she said.

'So why do you want to go?'

She studied him carefully. 'Just before Cromerty died, she said something about a "god of rain" who was coming from the East. She said he was going to kill us all.'

'From what I understand, India, that was typical of many things the old woman said. She was a little... *eccentric*.'

'That's what I thought at first. I just put it down to the ramblings of an old woman. But then, when we were on the train, Remus said something that made me think. He said he was taking the prisoners on a "pilgrimage to the East". He said they were going to be "food for a god".'

'And you think the two things are connected?' The android sounded sceptical.

India shrugged. 'I'm not sure. I know it sounds far-fetched, but I couldn't stop thinking about what Cromerty had said. If this escapade has taught me anything, it's that I should never underestimate that old woman. I'm convinced she was trying to warn me about something and it's connected to what the Pinkertons were doing. I can't explain it any better than that, Calc, but something is pulling me East. I thought I'd go to Sing City and make a few discreet investigations into this "god of rain". So, what do think? You want to come with me?'

The android was thoughtful. 'It is a remarkably far-fetched story, India. But my voice stress indicators suggest you believe what you are saying.' He paused to look around before turning back to her. 'And I suppose there is nothing else pressing on me at the moment so... why not.'

She grinned. 'Thanks, Calc. I can't pretend it won't be useful to have a war droid around in case things go pear-shaped. That's provided you haven't taken any more vows of non-violence, that is.'

'I have been thinking about that.' The android took the halter and led the horse around in a tight circle until the cart was facing the other way. 'In looking through my memory archives, I came across several historic references to the tradition of warrior monks.'

India picked up the reins as Calculus climbed into the cart alongside her. 'Warrior monks?'

'Warrior monks combine the ascetic lifestyle of a religious devotee with the martial skills of a warrior trained in violent conflict. It would provide me with ample opportunity to explore my spiritual development whilst still allowing me to participate fully in a combat situation. Provided such situations are morally justified, of course.'

'Oh yeah, of course.' She raised an eyebrow. 'If you ask me, that all sounds a bit wacky.'

'Not at all. There is a long tradition of spiritual warriors throughout human history, for example the Sōhei warriors of feudal Japan or the Knights Templar of old Jerusalem or even the monks of the Shaolin monastery.'

India laughed. 'It sounds fascinating,' she said. 'You can tell me all about it on the way. We've got a long journey ahead of us.'

Calculus looked back over his shoulder. 'Do you think you'll ever come back here?'

India turned and took a long look at the village, at the shoreline of Lake London and at the old towers sticking up from the lake like broken teeth. 'I don't know, Calc. Maybe not for a long time. After all, you know what they say.' She slapped the reins and the cart jerked forwards. 'Homecomings are dangerous affairs.'

India Bentley will return in RAIN GOD

DID YOU ENJOY TECH HUNTER?

Thank you for joining me on the latest India Bentley adventure. If you enjoyed the book and have a moment to spare, I would really appreciate a short review on the Amazon review page to let others know what you thought. Reviews are lifeblood to a writer and your assistance makes a huge difference helping me to find new readers.

And, if you'd like to join my mailing list, you'll receive a FREE copy of the first book in the series, IRONHEART as well as getting early notification of new releases and give-aways and receive behind-the-scenes updates on my work in progress.

For full details, go to www.allanboroughs.com

Thank you!

Allan

RAIN GOD…COMING SOON

If you're still hooked on the Legend of Ironheart series, then there is more in store for you - India Bentley will be back with a brand new adventure, RAIN GOD – coming in January 2024!

RAIN GOD
'Let sleeping gods lie'

A rare technology find takes India Bentley to Sing City, to sell her wares to Two-Buck Tim, the seediest tech trader in the East. But buyers with ready cash are in short supply and India and her companions are forced to venture into the jungle to find a blind prophet and his followers, said to be obsessed with old tech. Dogged by freak weather and beset by danger, the further they travel upriver he more the questions pile up. What is the source of the strange disturbances coming from deep within the jungle? Who are the mysterious tribe that seem so keen to keep them away and just what is the truth about the powerful god of rain, worshipped by the prophet?
As India journeys deeper into the heart of darkness, the answers

*she finds are stranger and more far-reaching than she could possibly have imagined. And when she finally comes face to face with the mythical god of rain, she realises an awful truth – **what lurks in the jungle may spell the beginning of the end for the human race.***

MORE INDIA BENTLEY
ADVENTURES…

If you've enjoyed the adventures of India Bentley then there's plenty more for you to enjoy

THE LEGEND OF IRONHEART

A century after the Great Rains drowned the world's cities, dark secrets stir beneath the ground. Now India Bentley must travel to the ends of the world to solve an ancient mystery – if she fails it will cost her the earth.

Book 1: Ironheart
Book 2: Bloodstone
Book 3: Tech Hunter
Book 4: Rain God

Books can be read in any order.

ABOUT THE AUTHOR

Allan Boroughs is a writer, a traveller an adventurer and a drummer with a passion for classic adventure stories 'in which lots of stuff happens'. His novels are inspired by his adventures in Siberia, Mongolia, China, Antarctica and Venezuela.

Allan's multiple past lives include working as a professional musician, a door to door salesman, a karate instructor and a partner in an international consulting firm.

When not working on the adventures of India Bentley, Allan finds time to write the 'After School Detective Club' series for children, which he co-authors with Mark Dawson.

Allan splits his time between London (head) and Cornwall (heart) and lives with his wife and two adult children.

He loves to hear from readers and you can find him online at www.allanboroughs.com . You can also reach him on email, allan@allanboroughs.com or at Twitter @allanboroughs .

A Faster-Than-Light book.

FASTER
THAN
LIGHT